Stalking Horse

By the same author

Stalking Horse

Collin Wilcox

Random House: New York

Library of Congress Cataloging in Publication Data
Wilcox, Collin.
    Stalking horse.
    I. Title.
PS3573.I395S8   813'.54   81-40231
ISBN 0-394-51173-5   AACR2

Manufactured in the United States of America
9 8 7 6 5 4 3 2
First Edition

This book is
dedicated to
Barbé Hammer,
editor extraordinary

Stalking Horse

One

"After all these years," Friedman said, unwrapping his first cigar of the day and dropping the balled-up cellophane wrapper on the floor of my office, "I've finally figured out what it takes to be a good homicide detective. Excluding, that is, a fearless disposition and a natural indifference to the sight of blood and the smell of decomposing flesh mingled with the odor of human excrement." He bit off the end of the cigar, clamped the cigar in his teeth and began the ritual search for a match, grunting heavily as he shifted from one big ham to another, exploring his pockets.

"Is that supposed to be a poetic way of saying that you've learned to hold your nose from the inside?"

Finally finding a match, he lit the cigar, puffed energetically, then flipped the still-smoking match into my wastebasket. For almost two years Friedman and I had shared command of Homicide. Each morning Friedman came down the hallway, settled himself in my visitor's chair and smoked a cigar while we discussed our case load. And each morning I expected my wastebasket to go up in flames. At first, the prospect bothered me. Lately, I found myself secretly hoping the wastebasket would catch fire—if only to see Friedman's reaction. During all the years I'd known him, first as my superior officer and lately as my senior co-lieutenant, I'd never seen Friedman surprised. I'd seen him puzzled, and I'd seen him scared. But I'd never seen him surprised.

"That's pretty good, Frank," he said condescendingly. "That's a pretty good comeback." He nodded, blinking heavily lidded eyes. " 'Hold your nose from the inside.' Not bad."

"So what's your secret of success?" I asked, at the same time initialing an interrogation report. "I'm curious."

"It's simple intuition," he said. "That's all good detective work is—applied intuition."

"You're not the first one to figure that out."

"I realize that," he answered blandly. "But the point is, it's something I keep rediscovering. Like that, for example—" He pointed to the interrogation report. "That's the Southwick case. Right?"

"Right." I tossed the report into my "file" basket. Reading the report had been a waste of time; I already knew what the pages contained. But, protecting myself, I'd learned long ago never to initial anything I hadn't at least skimmed.

"And you and I know," Friedman continued, "that Robert—the kid—dunnit." Friedman paused, drawing on his cigar and blowing a slow, reflective plume of smoke gently across the desk toward me. This was Friedman's favorite role: the lazy-lidded, Buddha-faced sage of the squad room, sitting in his rumpled suit, belly bulging, cigar ashes powdering his vest.

"However—" He raised a professorial finger. "However, it's odds on that we'll never—*never*—be able to prove what happened. Not as long as we don't have a weapon, or a witness, or a confession, we'll never be able to prove it. We know what happened, just as surely as if we'd seen the crime committed. All we have to do is listen to Robert talk, and watch his eyes, and his hands, and his face. He's crazy. We know he's crazy. His teachers, his friends, they all know he's crazy. But unless he changes his story, or we find the gun,

4

or a witness turns up, there's no way in the world that he'll ever fall."

I leaned back in my chair and clasped my hands behind my neck. "I don't understand. Is this an argument for intuition, or against it?"

As his full lips twitched into a slow smile, he shrugged his beefy shoulders. "Take your choice. By the way, how's your head? Still getting headaches?"

"Once in a while."

"What'd the doctor say?"

"He says to take aspirin and come back next week."

"Hmm—" Pensively, he tipped an inch-long ash into the ashtray. His eyes were thoughtful, his lips pursed. I knew that expression. He was about to ask me a personal question, poking into my private life.

Typically, he began obliquely: "How long has it been since you got that knock on the head?"

"Six weeks," I answered shortly, at the same time pointedly picking up a copy of a lab report.

"I was—ah—" He cleared his throat. "I was glad that Ann took you in after you got out of the hospital. I mean—" Still avoiding my stare, he tapped his cigar on the edge of the ashtray. "I mean, I like Ann, as you know. I like her very much. And she's got plenty of room, even with her two sons. So—" He waved the cigar. "So it was a good solution, I thought. Compared to your going from the hospital to your place and staying alone."

I decided not to reply, but instead pretended to study the lab report while I waited for Friedman to come out with it.

"I—ah—" Tentatively, he raised his eyes to meet mine. "I never seem to get you at your apartment, lately."

Suddenly, surprising myself, I guffawed. "The only time I ever see you at a loss for words is when you're asking questions that aren't any of your damn business."

Friedman's answering smile was almost demure as he delicately lowered his eyes.

"The answer to the question," I said, "is that, yes, I'm still at Ann's. And, yes, it feels great living with someone again." I let a rueful beat pass before I admitted: "And, yes, there are problems. Not big problems, but problems."

"Are the problems getting bigger?" he asked quietly, "or smaller?"

"That's a good question. I wish I knew the answer."

"Is it her kids?" he asked.

I shook my head. "No, the kids are fine. I've always liked them. And they like me, too, I think."

"What's the problem, then?"

"The problem," I said, "is her goddamn ex-husband."

"Ah—" He nodded: a single slow, thoughtful inclination of his head. "Ah, yes. The ex-husband. A psychiatrist, isn't he?"

"That's right," I said shortly.

"A society psychiatrist, I think you once said," he prodded.

"Right."

"A real asshole."

"Right again."

"Well—" He waved the cigar, now almost a stub. "If I were you, I'd tell him to stuff it. I'd talk to Ann, and then I'd—"

My phone rang. Glad of the interruption, I lifted the receiver and spoke into it. "Lieutenant Hastings."

"This is William Richter, Lieutenant. How are you?"

"Fine, thank you." It was an intentionally laconic response. Richter had taken over the local FBI office about the time I'd made lieutenant. For whatever reason, his fault or mine, we didn't like each other.

"I've just been talking to Chief Dwyer," Richter said. "He'd like you to work with us on a problem that's come up."

"What kind of a problem?" I asked. Across the desk, Friedman's thick eyebrows were raised in a questioning arc. I covered the mouthpiece and said, "Richter." Friedman grimaced, mouthing a silent obscenity.

"I'd rather not discuss it on the phone, Lieutenant." Translation: I should have known better than to ask. "I was hoping you could come over here—about ten-thirty, say. I'm setting up a meeting to get the ball rolling."

I glanced at the clock, saying, "Ten-thirty. I'll be there. Shall I bring Lieutenant Friedman?"

"No," he answered, sniffing slightly as he spoke. "No, that won't be necessary."

To myself, I smiled. For me, Richter was a minor irritation. But for Friedman, Richter was the enemy: a pompous, puffed-up bureaucrat, the natural target for Friedman's scorn.

"Whatever you say," I answered. "I'll see you in about an hour."

"It'll be a little less than an hour, actually," he reminded me. "It's nine forty-five, you know."

"Yes," I said, "I know."

Two

Sitting in his accustomed place at the head of a long, polished walnut conference table, Richter beckoned me to a seat on his left. As I sat down, I looked around the table. Besides Richter, I saw two resident FBI agents and two strangers. Both strangers sat across the table from me.

"This is Lieutenant Frank Hastings. And this—" Richter gestured deferentially to the first stranger. "This is Clarence Blake, Lieutenant. Mr. Blake is with the Secret Service. He's just flown out here to work with us on this thing." He paused a moment, then solemnly added, "Mr. Blake is deputy director of the Service."

Blake was a small, intense-looking man with dark, snapping eyes and a fierce guardsman's mustache. Like the FBI men, he was dressed in a conservative suit, white shirt and understated tie—the approved uniform for government law enforcement officers on the way up. Blake was almost totally bald, but his dark hair was carefully arranged in a glistening coil that only partially concealed a large expanse of gleaming white skull.

Blake bobbed his head in a vigorous up-and-down nod that reminded me of a parrot pecking at his perch. "We're glad to have you aboard, Lieutenant. This thing's got to be a combined operation if it's going to succeed." Plainly pleased with the phrase, he repeated, "A combined operation. That's our best shot, no question." As he said it, he glanced expectantly at Richter, then at the two FBI agents sitting to my right. On cue, Richter murmured agreement. The two agents both said something sincere-sounding.

"And this," Richter said, gesturing to the second stranger, "is Duane Hickman. Mr. Hickman heads up Senator Ryan's local office."

Senator Ryan . . .

Donald A. Ryan . . .

Majority leader of the U.S. Senate. California's kingmaker. The man behind the man in the Oval Office. One of the richest, most powerful men in America, infinitely larger than life, more an institution than a man. On camera or off, Donald Ryan looked and acted like a living legend.

And Duane Hickman, sitting across the table, looked and acted exactly as a living legend's top staffer should look: slim and trim, incredibly urbane and confident in his beautifully tailored gray flannel suit. He was slightly built, but his pale face was incongruously round and puffy, with a small button nose and a pursed mouth. It was a soft, self-indulgent face: the face of a thirty-year-old man who'd been spoiled as a child and never tested as an adult.

But, behind conventional horn-rimmed glasses, his shrewd eyes were quick and calculating. Hickman was a watchful man. The looseness of his indolent, Ivy-League mannerisms was meant to disarm and deceive.

"I've heard about you, Lieutenant," he said. "In fact, it seems to me that I saw you being carried off on a stretcher a month or so ago on TV. Am I right?" As he asked the question, his petulant mouth stirred, faintly smiling. The memory of my misfortune seemed to amuse him.

"You could be right," I answered quietly.

"It was in connection with the Rebecca Carlton murder, if I remember correctly." He spoke slowly and softly, almost lazily. But his eyes never left mine. He was sizing me up, deciding about me.

"Yes."

He straightened in his chair, leaning toward me, elbows on the table, hands folded under his chin. "Everyone here is filled in, except you, Lieutenant. So—" He glanced at Richter, who answered the silent question with a nod. "So I'll give you the picture." He paused momentarily, staring thoughtfully at a point just above my head. Then, in precisely measured sentences, he said, "The problem—the reason for this meeting—is that, for the last three weeks, Senator Ryan has been receiving anonymous threatening letters, one a week." As he spoke, he pointed to a manila file folder lying on the table before him. "There're Xerox copies for you, along with FBI reports and field studies."

At the head of the table, Richter cleared his throat. "We've been working on the case from the outset, Lieutenant." As always, Richter spoke quietly, with an air of condescending smugness. Richter was a tall man, narrowly built, with the prim face and fussy manner of a turn-of-the-century schoolmaster. He'd come up through the "accounting" side of the FBI, not the "field" side. Richter's most prized possession was a pair of cufflinks presented to him by J. Edgar Hoover. In his office or in the field, I'd never seen him without the cufflinks.

I nodded to Richter, then turned silently to Hickman. As I waited for him to continue, I was thinking that again Richter and his bureaucratic friends were succeeding in their obvious attempt to make me feel ill at ease in this elegantly furnished conference room with its superb view of the Golden Gate Bridge.

"As you'll see, Lieutenant," Hickman was saying, once more pointing to the folder, "all the letters have San Francisco postmarks. Which, of course, is where you come into the picture."

I couldn't help smiling at the regret in his voice. Obviously, he would prefer to have me out of the picture.

10

"Whoever wrote these letters," he said, tapping the folder, "means business. That's not only my opinion. Both the FBI and the Secret Service have had experts—psychologists—examine the letters. And they all agree."

"Are they extortion letters?" I asked. "Or death threats?"

"Death threats," Hickman said. "Every one of them."

I turned to Richter. "Are there any suspects?"

Instead of answering the question, Richter said, "When you read the letters, Lieutenant, you'll see that there's a strong possibility that the writer, whoever he is, has some kind of a personal connection to Senator Ryan. Or at least he thinks he has some connection. And that's the problem."

"The problem?"

"Yes, that's the problem," he repeated, at the same time looking to Hickman, who took up the explanation.

"Before I tell you this, Lieutenant," Hickman said, staring at me intently, "I must have your promise—your guarantee—that what I'm about to tell you won't go any farther than this room."

I glanced around the table, from Hickman, to Clarence Blake, to Richter, to the two agents sitting on my side of the table, both of them craning their necks to meet my gaze. Each man's expression was identical: almost comically grave.

I nodded—and promised.

Hickman exchanged a final look with both Blake and Richter. Then: "Almost exactly five weeks ago," he said, "Senator Ryan had a heart attack."

Surprised, I said, "I didn't know that."

"Of course you didn't. That's precisely the point. Nobody knows it. And that's the way we intend to keep it."

"We don't have to tell you," Blake said, speaking in his improbably high, tight voice, "how important the senator is to this country. Not only is he the Senate majority leader, but he's one of the handful of men who actually run this country. Which means, obviously, that his heart attack was nothing short of a national emergency."

"Which is the reason," Richter said, "that we've got to keep the whole matter of the letters strictly between us. We can't afford a leak. Because, sure as hell, the word would get to Senator Ryan. Which is something that can't happen."

"What you're really saying," I said, "is that we can't question Senator Ryan about the letters because of his heart attack. We can't risk his health by worrying him. Is that right?"

Almost in unison, the five other men at the table nodded, each one of them looking at me, hard.

"What's his prognosis?" I asked Hickman.

"His prognosis is excellent," Hickman said, speaking now in a brisker voice. "The senator is only sixty-six. He's basically healthy, and he's kept himself in good shape. His doctors agree unanimously that his heart wasn't damaged. If he follows medical advice, which he's doing, he should make a complete recovery. In fact, there's every hope that by Labor Day, when the Senate reconvenes, he'll be able to resume his normal duties. The public will be none the wiser. Which, of course, is the purpose of this exercise."

"Well, then, what's the problem? Isn't it possible to keep him under wraps until we find this letter-writer?"

But when I looked around the circle, I realized that there was more.

"The problem," Blake said, "is that one week from today, on June the nineteenth, the new federal office building here in San Francisco is being dedicated."

"It's the Donald A. Ryan Building," Hickman added heavily. "And everyone will be here for the dedication. Including the Vice-President and the secretary of state."

"Is it safe for him to show up?" I asked. "Medically, I mean."

"Medically," Hickman said, "There's no problem. As long as the senator just makes a little speech, and smiles, and gets in his car, there's nothing to worry about. As long as he avoids stress, it will do him good, according to the doctors. In fact," Hickman said, "that's the goddamn problem. His doctors *want* him to go to the dedication, as a means of phasing him back into his normal routine. It's made to order, they say," he added bitterly. "And of course we can't tell them different. Not without tipping our hand. Plus, the senator would go to the ceremony anyhow, no matter what the doctors said. I don't have to tell you what the Ryans mean to San Francisco—and what San Francisco means to the Ryans. So there's no way—no way at all—that we can keep him away. Because, literally, that building is Donald Ryan's monument. It's his own personal pile of marble."

"But if someone should take a shot at him," I said quietly, "that would be the end. Even if the bullet misses, the shock would probably kill him."

The five men nodded in unison while Richter said, "That's your department, Lieutenant. You've got to make sure that shot is never fired. And you've got to do it secretly, without the senator ever knowing."

"But, Christ—" I waved an angry hand. "But that's impossible. That's absolutely impossible. You're asking me to put out a dragnet for someone I can't even identify. And besides, you're asking me to keep some significant facts from my own men."

"It's possible," Richter said, "that we'll have to tell Chief Dwyer the details, to get you the men you need. If so, then we'll do it. But don't forget, all we need from you is a name. We'll handle the rest. In fact, that's the only way we want it."

Looking Richter hard in the eye, I said, "I can't do it. Not alone, I can't do it. Not without at least one person who knows the whole story to work with me at the command level. I don't mean Chief Dwyer, either. I mean a field commander like me."

Richter's eyes narrowed. "One person? Who?"

"Lieutenant Friedman," I answered. "We work together. There's no way—no way at all—that I can work on anything without Friedman knowing."

"Friedman is a troublemaker," Richter snapped. "He's

good. I'll admit he's good. He's smart, and he knows the streets, there's no question about it. And, frankly, I thought about him first. But he's too—too—" Peevishly, he let it go unfinished.

"Too what?" Blake asked quietly, turning in his chair to face Richter fully.

"Too abrasive," Richter replied. But as he spoke he dropped his eyes before Blake's hard, flat stare. I saw the Secret Service man draw a long, measured breath. He waited for Richter to raise his eyes. Then, speaking very quietly, he said, "We've just been saying, Mr. Richter, that we've got what amounts to a national crisis here. It doesn't seem to be the time or the place for intramural bickering."

"But—"

"It's not the time," Blake repeated. He waited while Richter's indignation slowly faded, leaving the FBI man sitting slack in his chair, mouth loose, eyes impotent, hands making futile gestures on the gleaming walnut conference table.

"Of course," Blake continued softly, "strictly speaking, I'm only here as an observer. However—" He let it go unfinished, at the same time glancing meaningfully at his watch. Around the table, everyone looked discreetly away from Richter—everyone but me.

"All right," Richter said, suddenly pushing his chair back from the table as his hot, baleful eyes met mine. "All right. Get Friedman, then. But just keep him away from me, that's all."

Not replying, I reached across the table for the thick manila folder.

Three

Disgustedly, Friedman closed the file folder and slid it across my desk. "Richter strikes again," he muttered.

I decided not to answer.

"You know how it'll go, don't you?" Friedman grated.

"How'll it go?"

"How it'll go," he said, "is that, with luck, we'll find this guy and turn him over to Richter. Whereupon, surprise, it'll turn out that suddenly there's no further need for secrecy. So Richter calls in the reporters and carves another notch in his gold cufflinks."

"You make the whole thing sound like a publicity stunt."

"No," Friedman said slowly, staring thoughtfully at the folder. "No, I don't think it's a stunt. Whoever wrote those letters means business, I'd say. I think he really intends to try and kill Ryan."

"You think so?" As I spoke, I opened the folder and looked at the first letter, only a few typewritten lines:

Vengeance is mine, sayeth the Lord. For what you have done to us, you must pay. Can you guess who we are? Can you guess who I am? When you know, then you must die. But first, you must suffer, as you made us suffer. You must pay, as we paid. Then you must die.

"You don't think so?" Friedman asked. "You don't think he's got murder on his mind?"

I shrugged. "Talk is cheap. As I understand it, Ryan gets dozens of crank letters a year. Most of them don't mean a thing."

Friedman pointed to the folder. "The FBI's psychologists seem to agree with me."

"I know. Still—" I turned to the second letter, reading:

This is your second notice. Your second chance to make the winning guess, and save yourself. Whenever you're in a crowd, look around. At your dedication, look around. One of the faces will be mine. You know it very well. You will recognize me. Then you will die.

"To me," I said, "he sounds like a talker. And I learned, back in the schoolyard, that there're the talkers and the doers."

"To me," Friedman said, "he—or she—sounds like someone with a plan." He reached across the desk and flipped to the third letter.

You have only one chance to save yourself. You will be told only once. Prepare yourself.

He tapped the letter with a stubby forefinger. "He—or she —wants something. He's used the first two letters to soften Ryan up, or so he thought. Now he's getting down to business."

"Extortion, you mean."

He shrugged. "If I had to guess, I'd say, yes, extortion. Money. I've learned a few things too. Like, premeditated murder is mostly a matter of money."

I tapped the letters thoughtfully. "What d'you make of

16

this guessing game? 'Can you guess who I am?' he says. That implies that he's known to Ryan."

"I agree. So, obviously, we've got to find out what the senator knows. Except that according to the ground rules, we can't find out. At least, not from the senator." He settled back in his chair and produced a cigar. After the cigar was lit to Friedman's satisfaction and the smoking match had sailed unerringly into my wastebasket, he said, "What's our situation in all this, anyhow? How much authority do we have?"

"I talked to Dwyer as soon as I got back from the FBI, about noon. By that time, apparently, he'd gotten a call from Washington. And the answer to the question is, we've got everything we need, as long as we ask quietly."

"How much does Dwyer know? Does he know about the death threats?"

"No. All he knows is that the FBI needs local help for security at the dedication. We're on detached duty. *Secret* detached duty."

Friedman grinned. "I'll bet Dwyer's stewing."

"You're right, he's stewing. But he's behaving. Whoever called from Washington knew which buttons to push and how hard."

"I hate to admit it," Friedman said, "but Richter, for once, is being smart. With Dwyer's big mouth and his tiny brain, plus his thirst for publicity, the secret would be out in twenty minutes. It's happened before."

"I know."

"Well," Friedman said, "where do we start?"

I spread my hands, then pointed to the file folder. "So far, that's all we've—"

My phone rang.

"Lieutenant Hastings."

"This is Duane Hickman, Lieutenant. Can you talk?"

"Yes, I can talk. Except that this isn't a secure line. You understand that." As I spoke, I gestured for Friedman to pick up an extension phone.

"Yes, I understand."

"What can I do for you?"

"I wanted to update you on a few recent developments. I've just been on the phone to Washington."

"All right." I reached for a notepad. "Go ahead."

"First," Hickman said, "Jack Ferguson, the senator's chief of staff, is scheduled to arrive in San Francisco two days from now. On Friday, in other words. He'll probably want to see you, so you should hold yourself in readiness. He expects to arrive about one P.M. He'll come directly here to the senator's office." He paused, obviously expecting a reply. Deciding that I didn't like his tone, I didn't oblige. Across the desk, Friedman cast his eyes up to the ceiling, sighing deeply.

"*Do* you understand?" Hickman prompted impatiently.

"Yes," I answered wearily, "I understand."

"Good," he said fussily. "Then the following day, Saturday, the senator and his wife will arrive."

"Does Jack Ferguson know about the letters?" I asked.

"Yes, he does. My understanding is that in Washington only Jack and one other staffer know about them."

"Do you have an itinerary for the senator when he arrives in San Francisco?"

"Not yet. The senator's doctors are hoping to convince him that he should stay in the family home until the dedication, but I'm not sure whether they'll be successful."

"Where's the family home?"

"In San Francisco."

"Where in San Francisco?"

"In Pacific Heights," he answered. "On Broadway."

"Today or tomorrow," I said, "I'd like to get together with you. I need background. A lot of background. This material you've given me doesn't amount to much. All I've got, really, are the letters and the FBI lab reports saying that there aren't any fingerprints, and the paper came from the dime store, and a different typewriter was used each time. Except for a few interoffice memos and psychologists' evaluations, there really isn't much for us to go on."

"Lieutenant—" His tone was both harassed and faintly patronizing. "Today and tomorrow I'm going to be working sixteen hours a day on this dedication." He paused a moment, then irritatedly asked, "What kind of background is it you need, anyhow?"

"To begin with, I want a rundown on the senator's family."

"The family?" His voice betrayed sudden anxiety. "You're going to talk to the family?"

"I've got to start somewhere. I've got to have information. The family is the obvious place to start."

"But if you ask the family about this, it'll get back to the senator. Which is just what we're trying to avoid."

"You're also trying to avoid getting him killed." As I said it, Friedman nodded emphatic approval, circling his thumb and forefinger.

"Lieutenant—" Hickman paused, drawing a deep breath. "I appreciate the fact that you're trying to do your job. But you should understand that there are two separate threats here. The first threat, real or imagined, is the one that this —this letter-writer poses to the senator. That threat's hard to handicap. After all, this has happened before, many times. But the second threat, the threat that stress poses to his life, that's real. And, in my judgment, it's the more serious threat of the two."

"This letter-writer doesn't worry you, then."

"I didn't say that. Look—" He drew another breath. "You've got to understand the senator's importance. You've probably heard all the stories—that he dominates the party, that he handpicked the President and controls him. Well, Lieutenant, I can tell you that it's all true. And the effect of all this is that staff people handle a lot of the senator's low-level decisions, leaving him free to take on the big problems. That's my job. And it's a tough job. There're a lot of decisions that're hard to call. Like this one."

"The problem is, I've got a job too. And to do my job, I need information."

I heard an exasperated sigh. "Listen, Lieutenant, I'm not trying to stop you from doing your job."

"Then give me the information I need, Mr. Hickman. Or else give me a memo saying you refuse."

Still listening on the extension, Friedman was nodding vigorously, smiling as he saluted me with clenched fist.

"Oh, Jesus," Hickman groaned. Then, deeply reluctant, he said heavily, "All right, if you're going to play the memo game, then I don't have a choice. What is it that you want, anyhow?"

Careful not to let my voice reveal the satisfaction I felt, I said, "For starters, I want a rundown on his family. Then I want the names of anyone who has a grudge against Senator Ryan. Anyone at all."

"As to the last part," he said, "I really can't help you. There are, of course, hundreds of political enemies—and business enemies too. Lots of people think the Ryans ruined them, I suppose, going back to the senator's grandfather. As you know, the Ryan fortune is enormous—as big as the Rockefeller fortune, at least. That kind of money and power makes enemies. Lots of enemies."

"But aren't there any special enemies? Anyone that stands out?"

A moment of silence followed before he said, "I honestly can't think of any, Lieutenant. If I do, I'll call you."

"All right. Now, what about the family? Give me the family tree, why don't you? Briefly."

"Well," he said, "I guess you'd have to start with Patrick Ryan, the senator's father. Or maybe with James Ryan, his grandfather. James was born in 1850, and died in 1910. He was on the fringes of the great San Francisco fortunes—the Comstock Lode and the railroad czars. He was a stock speculator. He made and lost several fortunes, as the saying goes. But the crash of 1907 finished him for good, and he died broke, unfortunately. He still had the mansion and the diamond stickpins. But that was all.

"Patrick was James's only son. He was born in 1890, and died in 1960. Patrick had three sons, two of them older than Donald. His wife died in 1946. Her two older sons were killed in the war, and that certainly contributed to Mrs. Ryan's death." He paused for breath. Clearly, this was a ritualistic recitation, learned by heart and delivered in a slightly bored monotone. Listening to him, I wondered whether an intimate knowledge of the Ryan genealogy was a prerequisite for his job, in the same way that priests must learn the details of Christ's life. Opposite me, Friedman was projecting a similar reaction.

"From the first," Hickman was saying, "Patrick Ryan demonstrated incredible skill in business. He was only twenty years old when his father died, but within five years, by 1915, he was already a millionaire."

"How'd he make his money?" I asked.

"He started out in banking, as a clerk. But he was able to realize something from the sale of the family home, and he took the money and started speculating in stock, just like he'd seen his father do. But, as I'm sure you know, Patrick Ryan had an absolute genius for timing. Whatever he touched turned to gold. During the 'panics,' as recessions were called in those days, he was always out of the stock market and in a cash position. He'd take the opportunity to buy distressed businesses for a few cents on the dollar, so he had the resources to wait out the hard times, when he'd sell the businesses for enormous profits after he'd built them up.

"In 1929 it was the same story all over again, and the rest is history. He picked up bankrupt shipyards at bargain prices and merged them into huge conglomerates. By that time, in the early thirties, Donald was in the business. He was given his first 'command,' as his father called it, in 1935, when he was twenty-one."

He paused again. Across the desk, I saw Friedman's gaze

wander thoughtfully off across the office. Like me, he was interested in the Ryan story.

"In the middle thirties," Hickman continued, "aviation was just coming into its own. As you probably know, Patrick Ryan had acquired Jessup Aviation down in Los Angeles. Jessup was Donald's first command. He saw the war coming and he developed the P-50, one of the best fighters the war produced. He was ready for peace, too, and for the jet age. By 1950, Jessup Aviation was already what it is now—the biggest, most successful aerospace combine in the world. Of course, the term 'aerospace' hadn't even been coined then. But that's what it was. By the mid-fifties, Donald Ryan was married and had two children. He was already in politics. He was elected to the U.S. Senate in 1956, the first time he ran."

"He went into politics because his father wanted him to do it," I said. "Isn't that right?"

"Yes," Hickman answered, "that's right. It's no secret that Patrick Ryan was an ambitious man. Some, of course—" He coughed self-consciously, departing from his prepared speech. "Some call him other things, less complimentary. He was determined, absolutely determined, that his son should run the country. He was thinking of the presidency. What he got, of course, was almost as good. Some say better." He paused again, longer this time. Then, on a note of unmistakable finality, he asked, "Is there anything else, Lieutenant?"

To myself, I smiled. "Nothing except my original request."

"Which was?" It was a frosty question. Hickman obviously didn't appreciate liberties taken at his expense.

"Which was a rundown on his immediate family. Names, ages, occupations, places of residence." As I said it, I drew the notepad closer, pencil poised.

"The senator's wife," Hickman intoned, "is the former Belle Cardwell, daughter of Wilson Cardwell, the financier. She's, ah, in her fifties. James Ryan, the senator's son, is thirty years old and lives in Washington. He's the senator's legislative assistant. He's married and has two children.

22

Susan is the senator's daughter. She, ah, lives in San Francisco."

"Is she married?"

A pause. Then: "She's recently divorced, Lieutenant. She's, ah, living in seclusion, I guess you'd say."

"What was her married name?"

He sighed, answering reluctantly, "Robinson. But I don't think—"

"Does Mrs. Ryan live here in San Francisco?"

"Part of the time she lives here, part of the time in Washington with the senator. Naturally." He spoke curtly, defensively. I wondered why.

"She'll be arriving with the senator, then," I said. "And James will be coming, too, I imagine."

"Considering the importance of the occasion—the dedication of the complex—I'm sure they'll be here. Whether or not they come with the senator, I couldn't say."

"Will the three of them stay at the family home?"

"As I mentioned earlier, I hope they will. However, we've also reserved a floor at the Fairmont Hotel for the senator's staff and visiting dignitaries."

"A floor?"

"Yes, Lieutenant," he said briskly. As he spoke, I heard a telephone ringing in the background. "I'm sorry," he said, "but that's the senator's office in Washington again. I've got to go. I hope I've helped you."

"You have, Mr. Hickman. You've helped a lot. Thank you."

Not replying, he abruptly broke the connection.

Four

I pulled to a stop behind Ann's bright orange Datsun and switched off the engine. Dan's car was parked across the street. In front of Ann's building, Billy's ten-speed bike was chained to a small juniper tree. Everyone was home. Ann would be in the kitchen cooking dinner. At five-thirty on a June evening Dan, seventeen, was probably in his room talking to his girl friend on the phone. Unless Ann had been able to press him into service helping with dinner, Billy, twelve, would be sprawled in the living room watching TV.

Six weeks ago, lying in a hospital bed while the world around me slipped in and out of focus like some monstrous movie made by a mad cameraman, I'd turned my head to find Ann beside me. "When you get out of here," she'd whispered, "you're coming home with me. That's all the doctor will let me say—except that I love you." She'd kissed me, and gently stroked my forehead. Then, smiling tremulously, she'd turned toward the door.

Yet, only two days before I'd gotten injured, we'd wondered, separately, whether our love affair was strong enough to last. "Nothing stays the same," Ann had said. "We either go ahead, or we don't. We go backward."

We'd been together for a year and a half. If we didn't make a commitment to each other—didn't take a deep breath and say that, yes, we would get married—then we would probably drift apart.

At bottom, neither of us could make the commitment. If a spaced-out drug cultist hadn't clubbed me from behind, sending me to the hospital, we might have drifted further apart, not closer together.

When we'd met, she'd been divorced for about a year. Working as a grammar-school teacher and raising two sons, harassed by a sadistic ex-husband who would never forgive her for leaving him, she'd been painfully unsure of herself both as a parent and a lover. If the children were home, she would never stay all night with me. Until I'd gotten injured, she'd never let me stay with her, even in the spare bedroom.

But now the spare bedroom was my room.

And I was using my own key to open the front door. In my arms I carried a bagful of groceries, bought from a list that Ann had given me on the phone.

"Hi, Frank." Watching TV, Billy was wearing a fresh shirt and a navy blue blazer. His hair was combed, and his shoes were shined. He was sitting stiffly on the couch, plainly uncomfortable.

"Hi. Where're you going?"

"My dad's taking me out to dinner to Pier 39. Then we're going to a movie." As he spoke, he paid me the compliment of turning away from the TV.

Standing with the groceries in my arms, I asked, "Is Dan going too?"

"No. Dan's over at a friend's in Marin County. His friend's dad's got an airplane, and they're going flying. I wish I was going."

"Well," I said, "you're going out to dinner and a movie. It could be worse."

Always suspicious of adult platitudes, he looked at me silently for a moment.

"I'm going to get rid of these," I said, nodding to the bag

of groceries as Billy turned back to the TV. I walked down the hallway to the kitchen where Ann was standing in front of the stove. She was wearing a checked cotton shirt and blue jeans. The jeans were her favorite pair, old and blue-white, soft and supple enough to cling provocatively to her thighs, hips and buttocks. The blouse was tight at the waist, accenting the trim, exciting taper of her torso and the flare of her hips.

I put the groceries softly on the counter and stepped behind her, circling her waist with my arms. She leaned back against me, murmuring a greeting. She'd known I was in the room.

I drew her close, caressing her stomach as I kissed the nape of her neck through her long ash-blond hair. My genitals stirred as I felt her come closer, fitting her body subtly to mine, back to front.

If Dan was gone, and Billy would soon go . . .

At the thought, my caress became more specific, exploring the feel of her flesh beneath the gingham blouse.

I felt her giggle. She put aside her wooden stirring spoon and turned in my arms, smiling up into my eyes.

"What, exactly, are you getting at?" she asked. Her gray eyes danced mischievously. As she spoke, she circled my waist, drawing me intimately closer.

"I think," I whispered, "that I'm getting at the same thing you're getting at."

"I'm making potato soup," she said, kissing me on the tip of the nose. "And, besides, Billy's home."

"Not for long, he tells me."

As I said it, I sensed her body tightening. I knew that response; I'd felt it before, often. Whenever she thought of her ex-husband, she involuntarily stiffened. Drawing slightly back to look at me, she was about to answer when, suddenly, we heard a sputtering from the stove.

"Damn." She whirled, reaching for the burner knob. But the damage was done. The potato soup was boiling over. She turned off the gas, snatched up the spoon and began stirring.

26

"It's stuck on the bottom. All stuck. It—"

The doorbell sounded: two long, imperious buzzes.

"That," she said, her eyes on the clock, "would be Victor." Turning to the hallway, she called, "Answer the door, Billy." And to me she muttered, "Why can't he pull up outside and honk, like any normal divorced father?" She turned back to the potato soup, spitefully scraping the bottom of the pan with the wooden spoon. Our moment of tumescent intimacy was gone.

From the front of the house I heard voices: Billy's voice and Victor Haywood's. During all the time I'd known Ann, I'd only seen Haywood twice, face to face. Both times Haywood and I had argued; once politely, the second time bitterly. At the end of our second encounter, I realized that I was trembling with suppressed rage.

"Why don't you forget about the soup?" I said softly. "Let's go out to dinner. We can go to Freddy's. You won't have to change. Or we can—"

"Mom—" Billy was standing in the kitchen doorway.

"Yes?" As she turned to him, I caught a note of resignation in her voice. She knew what was coming.

"Dad wants to talk to you."

She looked at me with quick apology as she said, "All right."

"Here—" I reached for the spoon, saying, "I'll stir it."

Without answering, she turned away and followed Billy down the hallway. I turned the flame on low under the soup and began stirring dutifully. From the hallway, I could hear their voices: Haywood speaking with crisp, brusque authority, Ann answering in a low, cowed voice. He was bullying her. With his head-shrinker's tricks, he was mercilessly, methodically attacking her, speaking in a low, vicious voice. I'd seen him do it before—just once.

I switched off the stove and moved closer to the door, where I could hear Ann say, "Victor, this—this isn't the time to talk about it. Please. Can't we—?"

"That's what you said when I called you last week, Ann."

"But I was in the teachers' room. I couldn't—"

"Billy," he said sharply. "Here. Take the keys. Get in the car. It's around the corner, on Filbert."

In the silence that followed, I heard Ann making some stumbling, indistinct protest. Then the door opened—and clicked closed. Billy was gone.

"You might as well know, Ann," Haywood said, "that I've talked to my lawyer about this. When you didn't make any effort to get back to me after I called, I realized that I didn't have any choice."

"You had a choice, Victor. You could have called me here at home."

"Oh? Really? Do you think it was up to me to go following around after you, trying to get an explanation? Don't you think it was your place to contact me? After all, you're the one at fault here. You're the one who's doing damage to my sons."

"But that's not—"

"You've never been able to function as a mother, Ann. That's something you've never been able to face, have you? You're totally out of your depth. You're simply not up to the job. But at least until now you've always managed to keep up appearances. I always gave you that. You might not offer much intellectual stimulation or cultural guidance, but at least—"

"But he was *hurt,*" she protested. "He was badly injured. I *told* you that. From the first day, I told you that."

"That was six weeks ago, Ann. Six weeks. And I'm here, this evening, to tell you that I'm not going to—"

Stepping into the hallway, I realized that I still had the wooden stirring spoon clutched tightly in my hand. As I advanced down the hall, I put the spoon on a small marble-topped table.

Facing me, with his back to the front door, Haywood smiled: an unpleasant twisting of his small, tight mouth. He was a tall, slim man, elegantly dressed in casual clothing. Behind fashionable glasses, his eyes were bright and avid,

fixed on mine. Victor Haywood was looking for a fight: his
kind of fight, with words for weapons.

"Ah, Lieutenant. We were just talking about you."

"So I heard." I moved to stand beside Ann, who stood
with her back to the wall of the narrow hallway, partly facing
Haywood. "What's the problem?" I asked.

"The problem," he said, "briefly stated, is that Ann isn't
providing a fit and proper home for my two sons."

"Because I'm here, you mean."

He nodded. "That's exactly what I mean."

"Ann told you how I happened to be here—that I was
hurt."

"Whether you were hurt or not is no concern of mine,
Lieutenant. And for that matter, whatever you and Ann do
at your place, or in some motel, or wherever else you do it,
is no concern of mine either. But what you do here, while I'm
paying to maintain a proper home for my two sons, that's my
concern."

"It's Ann's home too."

"That's a matter of definition," he snapped. "As it happens, I pay the rent. And the rent is expensive. Very, very
expensive. And I have no intention of—"

"Why don't you let Ann and me talk about this?" I said
quietly. "Why don't you take Billy to dinner, and let us talk
about it?"

For a long, baleful moment he stared at me. "Don't you
tell me to leave my own house, Hastings."

"It's not your house. It's Ann's house. That's the law."

"Oh—" Venomously, he nodded, his eyes malevolently
bright. "So it's 'the law,' is it? Are you a lawyer, by any
chance?"

"No. But I—"

"But you know the law. Is that what you're going to say?
You scrape a few winos off the sidewalk, so you think you're
an authority."

Drawing a deep breath, I stepped around him and put my
hand on the doorknob. But, defiantly, he wouldn't move,

wouldn't step aside to let the door swing open.

"Excuse me," I said, turning the knob. We were standing close together, close enough for me to smell liquor on his breath. Staring hard into his eyes, I saw a gleam of manic hatred. If I touched him off, he would hit me. I could sense a surge of wild, false courage in him.

"You can't throw me out," he breathed furiously.

"I'm not throwing you out. But I'm telling you to leave. You're bothering this lady. And I'm telling you to stop it." I drew the door open until it touched his shoulder. Suddenly he struck the door with the flat of his hand, hard. I braced myself and pulled against him. The door hit his shoulder, throwing him off balance. I stepped aside, pivoting to face him as he staggered. He whirled to face me, eyes blazing, fists clenched.

"You son of a bitch," he hissed.

I backed against the wall, giving myself room. If he came for me, I'd hit him in the solar plexus, where no bruise would show. Crouching silently, ready, I watched his eyes—and saw the wild courage suddenly fade. He straightened slowly, squared his shoulders, tugged his expensive jacket into place and walked through the door without looking back. By the time he'd reached the iron gate at the end of the short brick sidewalk, he'd regained his composure. He closed the gate with an ominously controlled click.

We would hear from Victor Haywood again. Soon.

I closed the door and locked it. Ann came quickly into my arms, and I held her close for a long, intimate moment. Then, whispering into the soft flax of her hair, I said, "How could you have done it—stayed married to the bastard?"

She didn't answer, but only held me closer, pressing her face into the hollow of my shoulder. I could remember holding my daughter like this, feeling her sob against me. How long had it been? How many long, empty years separated me from my children?

Finally, still with her face tucked against my shoulder, she said, "What're we going to do, Frank?"

"We're going to go out to Freddy's and have dinner."

She drew away from me, snuffled, and wiped at her eyes with the back of her hand. It was another evocation of Claudia, my fair-haired daughter. Suddenly it seemed as if I loved both of them with the same part of myself.

She sniffed and tried to smile, timidly asking, "Did you turn off the soup?"

I smiled down at her. "Yes, I—"

At my belt, a buzzer sounded: my pager. "You get ready," I said, striding to the phone. "But don't bother to change. I'm hungry."

"All right."

As she went down the hallway to her room, I dialed Communications, identifying myself.

"You have a message to call Mr. Duane Hickman, Lieutenant. We were instructed to call you if we heard from him," the voice reminded me.

I sighed, took the number, broke the connection and dialed. The phone rang six, seven, eight times. I was about to hang up when Hickman's voice sounded sharply in my ear: "Yes?"

"This is Lieutenant Hastings. I have a message to call you."

"Oh, yes, Lieutenant. Sorry it rang so long. Everyone's gone home but me."

"What can I do for you?"

"I wanted to remind you that Jack Ferguson, the senator's chief of staff, will be arriving tomorrow. He's coming in earlier than expected, about eleven. He'll meet with Richter about noon. I told him you wanted to talk to him, and he's got you slotted for quarter to one. You'll have about a half hour, maybe a little less. So you should have all your questions prepared. Have them organized, hopefully with notes. That's the way Mr. Ferguson prefers it to go."

"All right. Fine. Quarter to one, at your office."

"Yes. Right. Tell me, have you made any progress?"

"Well," I answered, "we've pulled a lot of jackets yesterday and today—a lot of case histories. We've gone over them, and we've picked out twelve subjects with backgrounds that might be a match-up. We're having them screened."

"I hope you aren't mentioning Senator Ryan."

"No. We're doing what we call a switch, pretending that we're investigating another crime. A similar crime to the one we're really investigating."

"Good. But it doesn't sound like you'll have any progress to report to Mr. Ferguson." He sounded disappointed.

"Maybe Ferguson will have some information that'll help."

"That's, ah—" He coughed apologetically. "That's *Mister* Ferguson, Lieutenant."

"Of course. *Mister* Ferguson. Good night, *Mister* Hickman."

As I put down the phone, Ann came down the hallway toward me. She was smiling as she slipped an arm around my waist. Really smiling.

Five

The stylish woman behind the stylish desk caught my eye and smiled. "Mr. Ferguson will be with you in just a few more minutes, Lieutenant. Are you sure I can't get you some coffee?"

"No, thanks." I recrossed my legs and settled deeper into my chair. I was sitting in a small, elegantly furnished reception room, obviously reserved for special visitors. Outside, in a larger area, another stylish woman dealt smoothly and efficiently with the senator's off-the-street constituents.

I watched the receptionist as she got to her feet and stepped to a bank of file drawers that had been set into the wall behind her desk. She was about thirty and moved with the calm efficiency of a highly paid executive. Her figure was good, and her clothes expensive. Her shoulder-length hair was ash blond, like Ann's. Her figure, too, was like Ann's; she was about the same height, with small breasts and trim hips. Even their mannerisms were similar: thoughtful and, with strangers, remote.

As I watched the woman, I found myself remembering my first meeting with Ann. I'd met her the way I met hundreds of people: with my badge in my hand, ringing her doorbell in the middle of the night. Her older son, Dan, had been a witness to murder, and at first it seemed possible that he might have pulled the trigger. Ann had taken me into her living room and invited me to sit on the sofa. She'd listened to me quietly. Only her hands, clutched desperately together in her lap, betrayed the fear she felt.

Last night, in that same living room, we'd sat side by side on that same sofa. With the stereo playing softly, we'd talked about the future. Yet, really, we didn't talk about it. Because the future for us came down to one simple question: would we get married? Did we love each other enough? Like each other enough? Did we—

"Lieutenant Hastings."

Startled, I looked at the receptionist. She was smiling at me, nodding toward a tall walnut door.

"Mr. Ferguson will see you now."

"Oh. Thanks." I opened the door and found myself in a spacious office that offered a spectacular view of San Francisco Bay, with Alcatraz to the right, the Golden Gate Bridge to the left and the Marin headlands in the background. The bay was a bright, sparkling blue, scattered with tiny white sails and slow-moving merchant ships.

Standing behind his desk, Ferguson gestured me to a seat, smiled perfunctorily and sat down again in his big black leather swivel chair. He was about forty years old, a heavyset man with big shoulders, a squared-off face and dark hair carelessly combed. He was in his shirtsleeves, tie loosened, cuffs rolled up twice, exposing thick, hairy forearms. He looked about thirty pounds overweight; his belly bulged over his belt, and his face was pale and jowly. But, despite his flaccid appearance, he conveyed a remorseless sense of restless purpose: an executive's executive, a man who used power as deftly and skillfully as a surgeon used his scalpel—and just as impersonally, just as ruthlessly. His eyes, too, were impersonal. In a lineup, rumpled and unshaven, glowering at the lights, he would look dangerous: a murderer's murderer.

"I'm afraid I don't have much time, Lieutenant. But I

wanted to take a few minutes and talk to you, separate from Richter."

"Thank you."

"What d'you make of these letters?" he asked. "What kind of a threat do you think they represent to Senator Ryan?"

"I think that we'll know more when we get the next letter."

"Why do you say that?"

"Because I think it's possible that the writer is after something. He's building up to something that we don't know about yet."

He frowned. "Building up to what?"

"Money, maybe."

"Hmm." He stared at me briefly, dubiously thinking about it.

"I'd like to ask you some questions." As I said it, I thought about the list I'd prepared at Hickman's suggestion. I decided that since I wasn't interested in impressing Ferguson, I'd leave the list in my pocket.

"All right," he said, waving permission. "Ask."

"I understand that it's not uncommon for the senator to get threatening letters."

He frowned again, drawing his heavy eyebrows together. "He gets lots of hostile mail. But out-and-out death threats, that's something else."

"He *has* received death threats, though."

"Yes. Maybe one a year. No more."

"How are they handled?"

"They're turned over to the FBI, and also to the Secret Service. As these letters were."

"I gather that the FBI and the Secret Service are taking these letters more seriously than some others. Why?"

"You'll have to ask them, Lieutenant. Ask Richter."

"I've already done that," I said. "Now I'd like to question the members of the senator's family."

"You mean question them about the letters?"

"Yes."

Quickly, he shook his head. "That's impossible."

"Why?"

"Because word would get back to the senator." He shot me a hard, appraising look. "Haven't you been briefed on the senator's health?"

"Yes, I have. But I assumed that his family knows about his heart attack."

"Certainly they know." He spoke impatiently, looking at me with cold calculation. Clearly, he was deciding whether I was the right man for the job I'd been given.

"Well, then, assuming that they want to protect him from stress, doesn't it make sense that they'd keep news of the letters from him?"

He looked at me for another long, coldly calculating moment. Finally he drew a deep breath, at the same time hunching his shoulders and leaning across the desk, drawing closer. He'd made his decision.

"There are only three members of the senator's immediate family—his wife, Belle, his son, James, and his daughter, Susan. Now—" He lowered his voice to a note of solemn warning as he said, "Now, what I'm going to tell you is confidential, Lieutenant. *Very* confidential. Do you understand?"

Meeting his eyes, I spoke quietly. "I know lots of secrets, Mr. Ferguson. It goes with the territory."

"Yes. Well—" He drew another deep breath. Apparently Ferguson was in the habit of using deep, theatrical sighs to emphasize whatever he considered extremely important. "Well, the fact is—the truth is—that the senator's wife has a drinking problem. It's, ah, very common in Washington, as you may know. I mean, without being dramatic about it, politics for a man like Donald Ryan is an all-consuming thing. It's his whole life. And when that happens, the wife sometimes loses her way. It's sad, when it happens. And, of course—" His voice changed to a smoother, more unctuous note. "Of course, both the senator and Mrs. Ryan are fighting as hard as they can to lick this thing. But until they do lick it, the truth is that it's just not wise to confide in Mrs. Ryan."

"You're saying that she wouldn't keep the secret."

"Yes," he said, "that's correct. It's a simple matter of security." With the hardest part over, he spoke more briskly. "As for James, the senator's son, he works on the senator's staff as a legislative assistant. James is thirty, and he's only just gotten involved in politics after trying—" He hesitated. "After trying other things first. So although the senator hopes James will eventually be an important part of his organization, at the moment that just isn't the case." He paused, watching me for a reaction.

"What you're saying is that you don't trust him with important decisions."

A smile touched Ferguson's hard, humorless mouth. "Yes, Lieutenant," he said softly. "Yes, that's it. Exactly."

"So James doesn't know about the letters."

"No, he doesn't. However, at this point, I think I'll have to put him in the picture. After all, he's bound to realize that something's up. So I suppose there wouldn't be any objection to your talking to him."

"What about the daughter? Susan? What's her story?"

"Ever since she was a teenager," he said, "Susan has gone her own way. I suppose you'd call her a child of the sixties, a rebel without a cause. She married too young. In fact, she married twice. She's recently divorced for the second time. So you see, she's not exactly close to the senator, at least not during this part of her life. She's got her own problems."

"Susan isn't in the picture, then."

"No. She knows about her father's heart attack, naturally. But she doesn't know about the letters."

"And Susan lives in San Francisco."

He grimaced slightly. "When she's not traveling, she lives in San Francisco."

"Will Mrs. Ryan and Susan be present at the dedication?"

"Yes, they will. The senator and Mrs. Ryan will be arriving tomorrow, in fact. And Susan has promised to be in town."

"You've been in touch with Susan, then."

"I haven't, personally. But it's been taken care of."

I wondered whether the senator or his wife had taken care of it, but decided not to ask. Instead, I rose to my feet, saying, "I won't take up any more of your time, Mr. Ferguson. If I need anything, can I call you?"

"Either me or Duane Hickman. I'll alert the girls who handle incoming calls." Also on his feet, he said, "You understand, Lieutenant, that the most important consideration is to keep all this from the senator. It's essential that we don't subject him to—"

His phone rang. As I turned to go, he raised a detaining hand. He wasn't finished with me yet.

"Yes?" he said, speaking sharply into the phone. I saw him listen for a moment, then saw his eyes involuntarily widen with surprise. "Yes," he said again, his eyes now seeking mine. Plainly, the call concerned our business at hand. "Yes—" He sat down again, saying, "Put her on." Then: "Hello, Susan. I just arrived in town. I was going to call you. What's the problem?" Asking the question, his manner was smoother, more conciliatory. Obviously he was speaking to the boss's daughter. Another moment of silence followed as he sat with the phone to his ear. Now he turned away to glower at his spectacular view of the city. Finally: "I'm very sorry to hear that, Susan." He paused, listening. "Yes, we're aware that there's someone who's been threatening your father. And, in fact, I've got someone right here who's working on it. He's Lieutenant Hastings of the San Francisco Police Department. He—" Another pause, while his eyes once more sought mine, more speculatively now. "Yes," he said, "I understand. Listen, Susan, why don't I have Lieutenant Hastings come over and talk to you? Shall I?" A final pause. "All right, I'll send him right over. Then we'll talk again, before your parents arrive. Yes. Fine. Goodbye."

Thoughtfully, he cradled the phone as he swiveled in his chair to face me.

"That was the senator's daughter," he said slowly. "Someone just called her, she says—" He let it go unfinished as he rubbed his jaw with the back of his hand. He'd just had an unpleasant surprise.

"She says that the caller told her she might be able to save her father's life. She says he'll call again."

I took out my ball-point pen and flipped open my notebook. "What's her address?"

Six

She lived in a new townhouse, one of scores built in recent years across the top of Twin Peaks. The houses were small but expensive: concrete, redwood and glass, each one with a soaring view of the Bay Bridge and the Oakland hills beyond, with a sliver of the South Bay showing in the foreground, along with the huge skeletal cranes of the Hunter's Point shipyard. Because of its chronic wind and periodic fog, and because of the steep, rocky terrain that made building difficult, Twin Peaks was the last part of San Francisco to be turned into big money by the city's real estate developers.

As I turned away from the view, took out my badge and pressed the doorbell button, all in one long-practiced motion, I realized that I'd forgotten Susan Ryan's married name. I looked for a mailbox, but couldn't find a name.

The intricately carved oak door opened on a chain. "Yes?"

I held up the badge. "I'm Lieutenant Frank Hastings. I've just come from Mr. Ferguson's office."

"Just a minute." Her voice was low and husky. She closed the door, then opened it wide. "Come in." She was a tall, slim woman, dark-haired, wearing leather sandals, blue jeans and a khaki shirt over the jeans. Her hair was long, worn in a ponytail. Like her body, her face was long and lean, strongly sculpted, with a broad forehead and dark, flaring eyebrows. Her mouth was a little too large for the face, and her nose was a little too thin and too long. But the wide, strong line of her jaw was intriguing, and I could see a challenge in her clear blue eyes. It was a bold face, both willful and aristocratic, the face of an intelligent woman.

She gestured to a short flight of stairs and preceded me up to the living room, where she motioned me to a seat. Her body moved quickly and smoothly, suggesting a restless energy.

Still standing, she took a long, calm moment to look me over before she asked, "Would you like something to drink?"

"No, thanks."

"Coffee?"

"No. But you have something."

She shook her head and sat down in a high-backed vintage wooden chair with lion heads carved on the arms, and claws on the feet. As I took out my notebook and pen, I glanced around the room. The architecture was simple and modern, with one wall of glass facing the view. But the furnishings included a little of everything: modern, antique, European and Chinese. The walls were covered with a museum-class collection of paintings, most of them large and abstract.

"First of all," I said apologetically, "I have to ask what your name is. Your married name, I mean."

"It's Robinson. Susan Robinson." She crossed one long leg over the other and leaned back in her medieval chair. With her hands resting on the carved lion heads, chin raised, she looked calm and confident, in complete control. Her blue eyes gazed steadily into mine.

"Are you listed in the telephone book?" I asked.

She nodded. "It's listed as F.R. Robinson, which is—was —my husband's name."

"How long have you lived here, Mrs. Robinson?"

"We moved in about a year and a half ago. And my

husband moved out about six months ago." She spoke calmly, indifferently.

"When did you get the phone call?"

"About ten-thirty this morning."

"And you called Mr. Ferguson a little before two o'clock."

"Yes."

"Did you call anyone else? Your father or mother? Your brother?"

"No," she answered quietly, looking me squarely in the eye. "I didn't call anyone else."

I thought I could hear a faint note of regret in her voice, as if she were admitting to some shameful secret. Was it possible that, besides Ferguson, there was no one else she could call? What did a frightened woman do when her father was an institution, and her mother was a drunk, and her brother lived in Washington and her husband wasn't around? Whom could she turn to for aid and comfort?

"What did this caller say?" I asked, poising pen over paper.

"He said—" She cleared her throat, impersonally reciting, "He said, 'Is this Susan Ryan?' I said I was, and he said, 'Then I have a message for your father. Tell him that he only has a few more days to live.' "

"That was it? Everything?"

She shook her head. "No, that was the—the prepared text, you might say. I said, 'Who is this?' Or, more like it, 'Who the hell is this?' "

"What did he say to that?"

She frowned. "I can't remember exactly. I've tried to remember, but I can't. I should've written it down. It was something like, 'I'm a friend of the family.' Anyhow, the implication was that he was—" She hesitated, searching for the phrase. "He seemed to be implying that he was close to the family—close to me."

"Did you question the caller about what he said? Ask him to clarify it?"

"No, I didn't. I have to say that, initially, I didn't take it

42

very seriously. After all—" She raised one hand in a gesture of futility. "After all, my father's been in politics ever since I can remember. I've always known that he got crank calls, and crank mail. I've taken a few of the calls myself, in the past."

"What made you take the call seriously, then?"

"I don't know," she answered thoughtfully. "Maybe it was the—the menace I felt after I hung up and thought about what he'd said. The menace, and the purposefulness." She shook her head. "I don't know—I'm not sure."

"Did you make any response at all when he said he was close to you? Did you try to draw him out?"

"No. I'm afraid I wasn't very smart," she admitted ruefully. "I remember asking him again who he was. He didn't answer. He just repeated the first message, as if he were reading it. And at that point, I'm afraid that I got mad. I said—" Her wide, expressive mouth twitched in a half smile. "I said, 'Fuck off, asshole,' if I remember correctly." Repeating the phrase, she spoke with finishing-school precision. A hint of bawdy humor glinted in her eyes. "Then I hung up," she finished. "Hard."

Smiling in return, I asked, "How many phones do you have?"

"Two. One here—" She pointed. "And one in the bedroom."

"I'd like to put a tap on your phone line."

She shrugged. "All right, if it'll help."

"What was your impression of the caller?" I asked.

"What d'you mean?"

"I mean was he young or old, educated or uneducated? What kind of a voice did he have? How'd he strike you?"

"He struck me as being very purposeful, as I said. Very hard, very determined. As far as education goes—" She looked absently away, nibbling at her lower lip with small white teeth. "I'd say he was certainly literate. I mean, he spoke well enough. It wasn't Oxford English, but it wasn't gutter talk either."

"Did he talk like a crazy man, would you say? Did he rave?"

Decisively, she shook her head. "No. Just the opposite, in fact. He was very much in control. He knew exactly what he wanted to say, and he said it."

"Was he young? Old?"

"It's difficult to say."

"Make a guess."

She shrugged, then smiled faintly. "How about middle-aged? Forty, say."

I put my notebook aside, looked at her for a moment and then decided to ask, "Did he frighten you?"

"Not at the time," she answered. "Mostly I was angry at having my privacy invaded. But then I thought that I should tell someone about it. Which I did. Apparently Jack Ferguson takes it seriously. So do you."

"There's a reason for that," I said, and when she asked what I meant, I told her about the letters. To my surprise, her response was a grim smile.

"You don't seem worried," I said quietly.

"I'm afraid," she said, "that, emotionally, I'm pretty much a burnt-out case where my father is concerned."

"You don't feel very close to your father. Is that it?"

"Yes, Lieutenant," she answered regretfully. "I'm afraid that's exactly it."

"May I ask why?"

She let another long, deliberate moment pass, staring straight into my eyes. Then, calmly, she said, "I'm twenty-eight years old, Lieutenant, and I've just realized that I'm a pretty typical poor little rich girl. All my life I've been surrounded by so much money, and so much power, and so much pure establishment bullshit, that I've never had a chance to form even the faintest idea of who I really am. My brother has the same problem, only worse. Because he's quit fighting and settled in under my father's shadow. He'll die there, trying to do his impression of his father, and his grandfather, and his great-great-grandfather."

"But you're trying to break away."

"Yes," she replied. "Yes, I'm trying to break away, so far without much success. I've had two marriages, and two disastrous divorces. Both times I picked exactly the kind of man that my father couldn't tolerate. Between marriages I did a little traveling and a little partying and a lot of screwing around. All of it was carefully calculated to hurt my father and to demonstrate to my mother how wrong she was when she married him." She broke off and dropped her eyes for the first time. Then, softly, she added, "Of course, in the end, the only person I hurt was myself. That's part of the pattern, you see. If you don't like your father, and he gives you a toy, you try to hurt him by breaking it. If he gives you a car, you smash it up—along with yourself, of course."

"Have you smashed up many cars?"

"Yes," she answered, still staring down at the floor. "Yes," I've smashed up several cars. I even smashed up an airplane once. Whereupon, surprise, my analyst decided that instead of hating my father, I was really sexually attracted to him, and that I was trying to punish myself for the guilt I felt." She spoke in a soft voice, sadly ironic. "Of course, I fired him. He was my first and last shrink."

I let a few seconds go by before I said, "If you were me, Mrs. Robinson, how would you go about finding this caller?"

With an effort, she raised her eyes, meeting mine. Now, for the first time, I caught a clear glimpse of her loneliness and her misery.

"Can you give me some idea?" I prompted. "Some starting place?"

She drew a long, deep breath before she said, "You'll find, Lieutenant, that my father's life is pretty much under the control of two people, Jack Ferguson and Katherine Bayliss. Between them, they get my father to the right place at the right time, dressed in the right suit, with the right speech in his pocket. He takes it from there."

"Who's Katherine Bayliss?" I asked, writing the name in my notebook.

"I guess you'd call Katherine Dad's personal manager. Jack is his political manager. Katherine takes care of him when he's off camera."

"How old is Katherine Bayliss?"

"I don't know. About fifty, I'd say."

"And how old is your father?"

"He's sixty-six."

"Is your father really as sick as they say he is?"

"I don't know," she answered coolly. "I haven't seen him since his heart attack. I've talked to him, and to James and Mother. But I haven't seen them for months. Any of them."

"Will you see them while they're here?"

"Oh, sure—" She said it casually, bitterly offhanded. "Oh, sure, I'll show up at the Fairmont for the photographers. There'll be a family dinner, too, at the family mansion on Sunday, with the photographers in before and after dinner. That's the normal routine. Which, naturally, Dad will adhere to, sick or not. Then, of course, there'll be the dedication. I'll be there, too, smiling for the cameras."

I watched her for a moment, sitting in her big baronial chair with its carved lion heads and claws. She was staring down at her hands, clasped forlornly in her lap.

Now, finally, she looked the part of the character she'd cast herself as: the poor little rich girl.

Seven

"What we've got here," Friedman said, gesturing to a list of possible suspects supplied by Records, "is very, very little. So far, all we've done is waste a lot of man-hours going around in large, widening circles. And this is Saturday, I don't have to remind you."

"I know it's Saturday," I said sourly. This afternoon, Ann and I had intended to visit Betty and Jim Lamb, old friends of Ann's. Two years ago, with an inheritance, Betty and Jim had bought a small winery in the Napa Valley. They'd invited us for dinner tonight, and for Sunday breakfast, too. But with Senator and Mrs. Ryan scheduled to arrive before noon today, I'd told Ann that I couldn't leave town. She'd decided to go alone, announcing that I could mind the boys. Then she'd changed her mind, reluctantly.

"You're looking a little preoccupied," Friedman observed.

I sighed, absently fingering the useless list of possible suspects. "I guess I am," I admitted.

"Does it, ah, have anything to do with Ann? Or her ex-husband?"

I looked at him for a moment: a lumpy, swarthy, owl-eyed man wearing a wrinkled suit and a not-quite-clean shirt.

Years ago, after he'd gotten out of the Air Force, Friedman had wanted to act. He'd spent a year in Hollywood, making the rounds of the studios with a sheaf of eight-by-ten glossies. He'd finally gotten a bit part in a "B" movie. But he hadn't liked actors, and he'd hated Los Angeles. So, broke, he'd come back to San Francisco and taken the civil service exam.

Friedman didn't belong here, sitting across the desk, lolling belly-up in my visitor's chair.

I didn't belong here either. Both of us were misfits. That fact, more than any other, had probably made us friends. In all the world, besides Ann, Friedman was my closest confidant.

So I answered, "Yes, it's about Ann. Her husband paid us a visit. He says we're corrupting the morals of his children."

"It sounds," Friedman observed, "like you've got two choices. Either move out, or else marry the lady."

Morosely, I nodded. "I know."

"Well," he demanded, "which'll it be?"

"If I knew," I said, "I probably wouldn't tell you. At least not until I'd told Ann."

Instead of smiling, he looked at me steadily for a moment before he said, "It's your choice. You know that, don't you? Not Ann's. Yours."

"Yes," I answered heavily, "I—"

My phone rang.

"Lieutenant Hastings," I answered.

"This is Duane Hickman, Lieutenant. Mr. Ferguson wanted me to pass on a few things to you."

"Yes. All right." Reluctantly, I reached for a notepad. Having been prodded by Friedman, I wished that I could have had a chance to talk with him about Ann.

"Senator and Mrs. Ryan will be arriving at the airport in about two hours. They'll be traveling by private jet, just the senator and Mrs. Ryan, along with a man from the FBI and Lloyd Eason."

"Who's Lloyd Eason?" I asked, scribbling the name on the notepad.

Hickman sounded surprised at the question as he answered, "Lloyd Eason is Senator Ryan's personal bodyguard. They've been together for years. Weren't you told about him?"

"No."

"Well," Hickman said crisply, "that was an oversight. Because you'll certainly be working closely with Eason, I'm sure." In the short silence that followed, I could imagine Hickman calculating how best to blame Ferguson for the oversight—before Ferguson fixed the blame on him. "Anyhow," he continued, "they'll be arriving entirely without prior notice to the press. That's partly for security reasons, and partly so the senator won't have to exert himself answering questions at the airport after a long trip. They'll go right to the Fairmont."

"Why not to his home?"

"When he's in town the senator usually headquarters at the Fairmont, because of all the commitments he has and all the people he sees. And, actually, that could be a plus, securitywise. It should be easier to protect him at the Fairmont than at home. Don't you agree?" Once more, I could imagine him exploiting a difference of opinion to his own advantage.

"I don't know," I answered shortly. "I haven't seen the Ryan mansion."

"Mr. Richter says that the hotel environment makes it easier to post guards who won't be recognized. Anyhow, that's the decision."

I didn't reply.

"I understand," he said, "that Susan Ryan has become involved in this thing." He spoke slowly and tentatively, obviously probing for information.

"That's right."

"Have you talked to her?"

"Yes. Yesterday."

"What were your conclusions?"

"I thought that whoever is after the senator is getting

49

serious about it. Which is another reason that I need more cooperation."

"Well, Lieutenant," he answered, "it happens that Mr. Ferguson agrees with you. He talked to Susan after you did, and he agreed that we've got to change course on this thing." He made it sound stiff and pompous, like a major policy pronouncement.

"Oh. Good." I hoped he caught the ironic note in my reply.

"So," he said, "Mr. Ferguson has set up an appointment for you with Mrs. Bayliss. She's at the Fairmont in Suite 1140. If it's convenient, she'd like to see you as soon as possible."

"Mrs. Bayliss is the senator's personal secretary?"

"Well," he answered stiffly, "she's more like his personal assistant, I'd say. She—" He hesitated. "She's definitely a part of the senator's inner circle."

I let a moment of silence pass while I thought about his comments. If I was picking up the right signal from him about Mrs. Bayliss's influence with the senator, Hickman was presenting me with an unexpected prize.

"I'll be glad to see Mrs. Bayliss," I said. "I'll leave for the Fairmont immediately. By the way, where's the senator's son?"

"He's here," Hickman answered. "He arrived last night with Mrs. Bayliss."

"Isn't he part of the inner circle?" I asked, probing.

"Yes, of course he is," came the quick, annoyed reply. "But James Ryan is—busy. He's busy with the dedication arrangements."

"Still, I'd like to see him if possible. Is he staying at the Fairmont?"

"Lieutenant—" I heard him heave a deep, long-suffering sigh. "Let's just take it one step at a time, shall we? We're doing everything we can to cooperate with you. But you've got to realize how big this dedication is—how important. Even the Vice-President will be here, along with several cabinet members. And James, as a member of the family, is sorting out the protocol. He's busy. *Very* busy."

But the statement had a false sound, protesting too much.

I promised that I would arrive at the Fairmont within a half hour and called for my car.

Eight

As Canelli waited for a red light, he pointed to the radio. "You want it on, Lieutenant?"

"No, never mind."

"You couldn't answer a call, I guess," he ventured. Canelli was fishing, trying to discover the reason for the assignments he'd been getting and for the secrecy that surrounded them. Canelli had been my driver for almost two years. At age twenty-seven, Canelli weighed almost two hundred forty pounds, most of it fat. His face was round and guileless, exactly suiting his disposition. Canelli didn't look like a cop or act like a cop or think like a cop. As a result, he was seldom "made." Which meant that Canelli enjoyed a continued streak of incredible good luck. On stakeout, despite his size, he sometimes seemed invisible. During a hot pursuit, I'd actually seen suspects run in Canelli's direction, thinking he was a civilian.

"That's right," I agreed. "I couldn't answer a call."

"Who're we going to see at the Fairmont?"

To myself, I smiled. "You're just dropping me off, Canelli. Then you can go back to the Hall. I'll get a black-and-white when I'm finished."

"You don't want me to come in, huh?" His sidelong look was wistfully eloquent. Canelli was the only cop I'd ever known who could get his feelings hurt.

"No. Sorry. This is part of the FBI thing I'm working on."

"The one where we're pulling the jackets on assassination threats and psychos?"

I nodded. "That's right."

"It's just you and Lieutenant Friedman on the inside, huh?" His soft brown eyes reproached me.

"For now, yes." I pointed ahead. "Just pull in behind that cab. I'll walk the rest of the way."

"Yessir." Heaving a deep, self-pitying sigh, Canelli turned the cruiser to the curb and stopped.

As I stepped out of the elevator, a tall, athletic-looking young man dressed in a dark blue suit moved forward to intercept me.

"This is the eleventh floor," he said. "It's closed. Sorry." Smiling, he spoke pleasantly. But his eyes were alert as he looked me quickly up and down.

"I'm looking for Suite 1140. Katherine Bayliss." I produced my badge and ID card. "I'm Lieutenant Frank Hastings."

"Oh—yes." He nodded, drew a paper from his inside pocket and consulted it. "Yes. SFPD."

"You're FBI."

He looked at me with quick, alert eyes. "How'd you know?"

"I guessed."

He was silent while he decided what my remark really meant. Finally, speaking in a neutral voice, he said, "I came in from Washington. Last night."

I pocketed my shield case and watched him while he replaced the paper inside his jacket. From another pocket he withdrew a small lapel button.

"That's for identification," he explained.

"I know." I fastened the button in place and looked up and

down the hushed corridor, thickly carpeted and furnished with expensive antiques. Suddenly I wished I'd worn a better suit.

"Mrs. Bayliss is down there," he said, pointing. "Just to the left, around the corner."

"Thanks." As I walked to the corner and turned left, I saw two more agents posted at either end of the intersecting corridor. I nodded to one of them, straightened my tie and pressed the bell-button for the door marked 1140. Almost immediately, the door swung open, revealing a young woman dressed in a beige travel suit. Her severely styled hair, no-nonsense horn-rimmed glasses and the cool efficiency glittering in her eyes behind the glasses labeled her a fast-rising executive, feminine gender.

"I'm Lieutenant Frank Hastings. I have an appointment with Mrs. Bayliss."

"Yes, Lieutenant." She stepped back, motioning me into a beautifully furnished sitting room. She didn't smile. "If you'll have a seat, I'll tell Mrs. Bayliss you're here. If you'd like something—" She gestured to a portable bar, stocked with a dozen different bottles and rows of sparkling glasses.

"No, thanks." I sat in a comfortable armchair that commanded a view of downtown San Francisco. Skyscrapers gleamed in the afternoon sunshine. Beyond them, across the bright blue bay, I could see the Berkeley hills, scattered with tiny houses and accented by the spire of the Campanile, the University of California's landmark bell tower.

The young woman knocked discreetly at one of the suite's inner doors and immediately entered the next room. Before the door closed, I heard a woman's voice, probably talking on the phone. I'd once read that the telephone is to the modern leader what the lance and sword had been to the ancient knights and noblemen: their instruments of power, and badges of rank. As the executive climbs the ladder, his —or her—private communication console becomes more and more sophisticated, commanding ever-widening circles of influence. Until, at the apex of power, the President sits in his Oval Office—with one button that, if pressed, could cancel out the world.

I adjusted my tie again, finger-combed my hair and withdrew my notebook and pen, putting them on an end table beside my chair. For the first time I noticed that large, elaborately arranged bouquets of flowers had been placed on every available surface.

I heard a door open and rose to my feet, turning to face Katherine Bayliss. She was a strikingly handsome woman. Her dark hair, styled close to her head, was gray-streaked. Her face was small, but its features were perfectly balanced: dark, steady eyes, a firm mouth, a decisive jaw. She was dressed in a simply cut suit and a white silk blouse that revealed an exciting torso. She was a small, compactly made woman, but she carried herself with the assurance of someone accustomed to center stage. She moved with the graceful, sensual economy of a trained model on her high heels: shoulders squared, head up, hips rhythmically swinging.

She gestured me to my seat and sat on a small brocade loveseat facing me. From the other room, through the closed door, I heard the faint sound of voices.

"What can I do for you, Lieutenant Hastings?" Her voice was low-pitched and husky, a little like Susan Ryan's. Her eyes remained on my face, steady and calm.

"I guess the question is, what can I do for you?"

Her eyes narrowed slightly; her dark brows contracted as she studied me for a moment. Then she said, "I just talked to Duane Hickman. I called Susan, too. Both of them seem to feel that this letter-writer might be more than just a harmless crank. Do you agree?"

I nodded. "Yes, I do."

"Do you think he lives here? In San Francisco?"

"My feeling is that he probably does live here," I answered. "But I'm not sure." I paused for emphasis, then said, "And that's the problem, Mrs. Bayliss. I'm not getting the information I need. I've got to break through this—this security ring that you've got around the senator. I've got four men doing nothing but checking out kooks in San Francisco who have a history of threatening dignitaries, especially politicians. They might get lucky. Anything is possible. But my instincts tell me that the person we're looking for isn't in our files. My instincts also tell me that the person we're looking for has some connection to Senator Ryan—some close connection."

She sat silently for a moment, staring me straight in the eye. Then she rose suddenly to her feet and strode to the large view window. She stood for a moment with her back to me. It was a vaguely theatrical turn, calculated for effect.

But what effect?

Finally she pivoted to face me. Backlit by bright light from the window, her expression was unreadable as she said, "Frankly, Lieutenant, I don't get the feeling that you're approaching this matter very professionally."

"Why do you say that?"

"All you talk about—your only tools—seem to be your so-called instincts. Somehow I'd expected more." She spoke in a low, tight voice, as if she were suppressing sudden anger.

"The fact is, Mrs. Bayliss," I answered quietly, "that most police work, at least at my level, is a matter of playing the hunches. You might not like to hear that, but it happens to be the truth."

Standing rigidly, with her hands clasped at her waist, she looked at me for a moment of final appraisal before she returned to the loveseat.

"There's no point in fencing," she said. "I'm told you're the best the city has to offer, and I assume you are. I'm here to help you any way I can. I've made time to help you." She gestured gracefully, giving me permission to continue with my questions.

I smiled, trying to disarm her. She didn't return the smile. So, at random, I asked, "How long have you known the senator?"

She looked at me steadily for a moment, her dark eyes

expressionless. Then, speaking in a slow, measured voice, she said, "I've known him since the early fifties, when he first began in TV."

"TV?"

She nodded. "Senator Ryan was one of the pioneers in commercial television, down in Los Angeles. A lot of people don't realize it, but his TV interests, over the years, have been just as important to him and just as lucrative as his aerospace interests."

"And that, I understand, is very lucrative."

Now she displayed a small, formal smile, followed by a small, formal nod. She could have been a highly styled mother superior, talking about Jesus Christ. "Yes," she answered, still slightly smiling. "Yes, very lucrative."

"You were in television, then, when you went to work for him."

She hesitated, then said, "In a manner of speaking, I was in TV. I was an actress. But I was never very good. And, besides, acting is degrading, especially for a woman. The more I knew about it, the more I hated it. So when Mr. Ryan offered me a job, I took it."

"As his assistant?"

"As his secretary."

"Were you married before you went to work for the senator? Or afterward?"

Instantly, caution froze her face. "What's that got to do with this?"

"Nothing," I answered. "Just background." I ventured another smile. "Police work is like politics. Nothing is private."

Unsmiling, sitting stiffly, knees together, hands folded in her lap, she looked at me coldly. Then, formally, she said, "I was married when I was nineteen. It was a mistake. I was divorced a year later. When I was twenty-three, I went to work for Don—for Senator Ryan."

I nodded soberly over the statement, then said, "In that

case, I imagine you're about as close to the senator as anyone, except for his family."

She studied me intently. "Yes, Lieutenant, that's probably right." There was a grim, purposeful undertone to her reply, warning me not to go any further in pressing my luck.

"Then you should be able to point me in the right direction," I said. "Let's assume that the writer of these letters has some close connection to the senator. Can you—"

Beside her on the table, a phone buzzed.

"Excuse me." Turning slightly away, she spoke into the phone: "Yes?" She listened briefly, then said, "Who at the White House?" A pause. Then: "Well, find out, please. If it's Stewart, I don't want to talk to him until I have a chance to talk with the senator first. That should be in about an hour. His airplane is just about to land. If it's Pottinger, find out what it's about, and tell him I'll call him in fifteen minutes." She listened again, then nodded. "That's right." She hung up the phone and turned to me. "Sorry."

"I was asking you for help," I said. "If I'm right, and the suspect has some close connection to the senator, then you should be able to give me some names."

"That depends on the connection," she answered.

"A family connection, maybe. Outside the immediate family."

Impatiently, she shook her head, at the same time glancing pointedly at her watch. "That's impossible. There're no aunts or uncles, no nieces or nephews. Nothing."

"What about business connections, then? Personal connections?" I was about to add "lovers," but thought better of it. Instead I said, "He must have enemies. He's obviously got at least one enemy. Who do you think it is?"

"Lieutenant—" She waved a graceful, regretful hand. "I'm sorry. I'm afraid I can't even make a guess."

"Mrs. Bayliss—" I hesitated, for emphasis. "I already know that the senator's wife isn't much help to him. And I know that Susan and her father don't keep in touch. My impression is that James isn't exactly close to his father." I paused again, watching for a reaction. Her face remained impassive. "That leaves you and Jack Ferguson," I said. "I've already talked to Mr. Ferguson. Frankly, he wasn't much help. So—" I spread my hands. "So that leaves you."

"Well, Lieutenant," she said, speaking in a slow, deliberate voice, "I'm sorry to disappoint you, but I can't help you either. I've thought about it, but—"

From the hallway door I heard the sound of a knock. She frowned, rose to her feet and walked quickly to the door. Once again I admired the way she moved, so economically, so gracefully assured. She opened the door to greet a tall man in his late twenties or early thirties. He was dressed in a white shirt, dark slacks and what looked like an old school tie, loosened at the collar. The man glanced at me, frowned, then spoke to Katherine Bayliss:

"Is this Lieutenant Hastings?"

"Yes."

"Well," the stranger said, "we could have a problem. There're reporters downstairs. Someone from the hotel probably called a friend and gave him a tip. That part's manageable. But one of the reporters is a guy named Kanter. Dan Kanter, from the *Sentinel.* And he's asking about an assassination plot." The stranger shot me a hostile glance, as if to accuse me of the leak. Involuntarily, I rose to my feet, facing them. When they turned toward me, their eyes were cold. At the same time the phone rang again: a single long buzz, discreetly insistent.

"I've got something to do," Katherine Bayliss said, moving toward the phone. "Why don't the two of you talk about it, and get back to me in about forty-five minutes?"

"Where'll you be?" the stranger asked. He spoke peevishly, in a tense, high-pitched voice. Once more he shot me a resentful look.

"I'll be here," she answered, at the same time turning to me. "This is James Ryan, Lieutenant. James, this is Lieutenant Hastings." And to me, deftly dismissing both of us, she said, "You can talk in James's room."

Without acknowledging the introduction, James Ryan had stepped back into the hallway. Before I'd reached the door, Katherine Bayliss was already on the phone, talking to someone at the White House.

Nine

"I suppose you know," James said, "that we're doing everything we can to keep this whole letter thing from my father.
And I also suppose you know that if this thing gets in the
papers, it all hits the fan." Sitting with one long leg slung
over the arm of his chair, he stared at me with sulky eyes.
Like his sister, James was tall and slim. But, unlike Susan's,
his body was awkwardly made. His head was too small and
his neck was too long. His dark hair was thinning fast, balding on top. His arms and legs moved at cross-purposes,
uncoordinated. His features, too, resembled his sister's: generous mouth, long nose, large eyes under flaring brows. But,
like his body, James's face hadn't come together in any organized whole.

In three generations, the Ryan blood had thinned to pro-
duce this petulant, ineffectual man. When he'd first entered
his room, he'd gone immediately to the portable bar and
poured a strong Scotch on the rocks. Without inviting me to
be seated, without offering me a drink, he slouched to a chair,
drank off half the drink and stared at me with accusing eyes.

"Do you know this Dan Kanter?" he demanded.

"Yes."

"Then you'd better talk to him," he ordered. "Meanwhile, Jack Ferguson is going to call the *Sentinel*'s publisher. So maybe it'll be all right. I certainly hope so."

"I'll talk to Kanter, but I don't know how much good it'll do. And I'm not sure how much good it'll do to call the publisher. I've seen pressure tried before with the *Sentinel.* And it didn't work."

"But we could be talking about a man's life, for God's sake. A very important man's life."

I looked at him without speaking. Then I decided to say, "For several days now, I've been hearing about what would happen if this news got through to your father. But then I hear that crank letters are almost routine. So what's so special about these letters that your father shouldn't know about them? Why wouldn't it have been simpler to just mention the letters to him casually? You'd have saved yourself a lot of trouble, I think."

He finished the drink, set the glass aside and stared at me ruefully for a moment before he said, "In this business, Lieutenant—in this shop, as they call it in the trade—there's a chain of command. My father, of course, is the head man. He works out the grand design. But Jack Ferguson is the chief of staff. What Ferguson says goes. And Ferguson decided that we shouldn't tell my father. So—" He shrugged. "So we won't. It's as simple as that."

"What you're telling me is that Ferguson tells you what you can say to your own father."

He shrugged again, conveying a sense of both resignation and futility. "You have to understand that politicians of Donald Ryan's stature are larger than life. That might sound a little strange coming from me. But it's what happens. A lot of people have a lot invested in my father. Not just money, but other things. Like jobs, and plans, and dreams of glory. So he's an institution, like it or not."

"I don't think your sister feels that way."

"Wrong, Lieutenant," he said wearily. "She does feel that way. The only difference is that she's burning herself out, rebelling. Me, I've joined the team." His lips twisted in a wry imitation of a smile. As he talked, his eyes had become slightly unfocused. At three in the afternoon, he was a little drunk.

"I'd like to go back to my question," I said. "Who decided that your father shouldn't know about the letters? And why?"

"I've already *told* you," he said plaintively. "It was Ferguson. He talked to—" He broke off, frowning as he sat up a little straighter. "He talked to Lloyd. And then he decided that we had a problem."

"Lloyd Eason? Your father's bodyguard?"

"Yes." He spoke absently now, staring off across the room. "Yes."

"I didn't even know Lloyd Eason was in the chain of command."

"He's not, really," he said, still staring off at nothing. "Lloyd doesn't make policy. But, on the other hand, there's no one closer to my father than Lloyd. They go way back, my father and Lloyd. *Way* back."

"Where's Eason now?"

"He's with my father. He's always with my father." He checked the time. "Right now, they're probably on their way here from the airport."

"Did Eason actually see the letters, do you know?"

"I'm not sure," he answered slowly. "But I don't think so. He was told about them in a general way. But he didn't actually see them."

"Yet you said that Ferguson didn't take the letters seriously until he'd talked to Eason."

He gestured irritably. "I'm just giving you my impressions, Lieutenant. It's up to you to fit the pieces together. All I'm telling you is that, all along, Jack Ferguson and Katherine have been the only ones on the inside—the only ones to decide who knows what and when." Then, as an afterthought, he said bitterly, "I was included late in the game. Yesterday, to be exact. Obviously Jack told me so that I wouldn't hear it from someone else. You, for instance."

Across the room, a phone rang. He got to his feet and moved a little unsteadily to answer it. He listened a moment, nodded, mumbled something in reply, then beckoned to me. "It's for you, Lieutenant. Jack Ferguson."

I took the receiver and heard Ferguson order, "Come to Suite 1160, Lieutenant. The man in the corridor will show you the way. Then give me James." His voice was tight: the commander, coping with an emergency.

"Right." I handed over the phone and turned to the door.

Wearing an inconspicuous suit and tie, Ferguson was waiting at the closed door of his suite. Gesturing for the FBI man to return to his post at the intersection of two corridors, Ferguson glanced up and down the hallway before he slipped a plain white envelope from his inside pocket. "This just came from the front desk," he said, speaking in a low, urgent voice. "Read it."

The envelope had been neatly slit at the top. The address was simply SENATOR DONALD RYAN, typed in capital letters. The word URGENT, in red capitals, had been typed in the lower left-hand corner.

Carefully touching only the corners, I unfolded a sheet of plain white paper. The size and quality were the same as the other letters, and it was folded the same way. Like the others, this message was very short, typed in the center of the page:

If you see me face to face, the moment of your death will be at hand. Vengeance will be mine.

But this letter was different from the others. It was signed with a typewritten "F."

Beneath the signature was typed:

You know me now. But do you know how to save yourself?

I reread the letter, then looked at Jack Ferguson. But before I could speak, he gripped my forearm hard, drawing me closer. Speaking urgently, eyes boring into mine, he said, "You're going to have to handle this, Lieutenant. Do you understand?" His fingers tightened on my arm. "This is your baby. All yours. The senator and Mrs. Ryan will be arriving downstairs within minutes. No one knows about this but the two of us. Got it?" With his hand and his eyes, he held me for one fierce final moment before he turned on his heel and strode toward the elevators. He walked with the grim, headlong purpose of a general advancing to inspect his troops. I fell into step beside him, saying:

"What's 'F' mean? Who's 'F'?"

The elevator was being held for him. Inside, I saw half a dozen dignified-looking men and women, all impeccably dressed, all looking at Ferguson with a kind of pious expectation. James Ryan stood in the front rank, along with Katherine Bayliss. This was the senator's welcoming committee, the lords and ladies of his court, waiting for Ferguson to lead them downstairs. Ferguson stepped into the elevator, turned to me, and spoke quietly:

"Handle it, Lieutenant. It's all yours." He signaled, and the elevator doors slid shut.

Ten

I dialed 9, waited for the tone, then dialed Police Communications. Recognizing the voice on the line, I said, "This is Lieutenant Hastings, Allingham."

"Yessir."

"Were you able to locate Lieutenant Friedman?"

"Yessir. He's on his way to the Fairmont. He should be there in just a few minutes. Did Inspector Canelli get there?"

"Yes, he's here." I glanced across the room at Canelli, lounging at his ease on a green velvet sofa. Having finally been briefed on the Ryan case, Canelli was contented. "What about Culligan?" I asked Farley. "Did you find him?"

"No, sir. I haven't been able to—oh, oh. Wait." The line clicked momentarily dead. Then I heard Culligan's thin, dry voice.

"Where are you?" I asked.

"At home," Culligan answered sourly.

"How'd you like some overtime?"

"Well—" I heard him sigh. "All right."

"I want you to get two other men and get down to the Hall. Go through all the jackets we pulled and see if there's anyone whose name has the initial 'F.' First or last name, it doesn't matter. Just 'F.' Got it?"

"Yessir." He sighed again, this time more deeply.

"If you find anything, contact me at the Fairmont, Room 1016."

"1016. Right."

"Also, I want you to locate a woman named Susan Robinson on Carnelian Way. She's in the book. When you get her, tell her to call here too."

"Right. Got it."

"Keep in touch with Communications. I've been working with Allingham."

"Allingham. Right."

"It's quarter after four. I'd plan on working until ten P.M., at least. Okay?"

"Yes," Culligan answered heavily. "Okay."

As I hung up, I heard a knock at the door. A moment later Friedman strode into the room, whistling appreciatively as he sailed his hat onto the satin-covered bed.

"This," he said, "is class." He stretched out on the bed, adjusting the pillows as he announced, "I'm ready. Let's have it."

I tossed a photocopy of the letter and the envelope on the mound of his stomach and made an impatient circuit of the room while he studied them. Finally he looked up, saying, " 'F.' It's not much, but it's something. How was it delivered?"

"It came to the front desk about twelve-thirty. The desk clerk doesn't know who brought it. He just looked down at the counter, and there it was. He gave it to the mail clerk, who wrote the room number on the envelope in pencil. It was put in Jack Ferguson's box about one P.M."

"Not Ryan's box?"

I shook my head. "Everything for Ryan goes through Ferguson. *Everything.*"

"All right. What happened next?"

"The letter got to Ferguson's secretary about one o'clock. She had orders to pass any mail addressed to Ryan directly through to Ferguson. As soon as Ferguson read the letter, he called me. That was about two-fifteen. I decided that, first, I should call Richter, which I did." As I said it, I mentally braced myself for Friedman's predictable response:

"Richter." Exasperated, he shook his head. "You never learn."

Ignoring the remark, I said, "I've got two men down in the lobby interviewing possible witnesses. Richter must have half a dozen. So far, no one's been able to find anyone who saw the letter put on the counter."

"With all that ruckus," he observed, "it'll be a miracle if they're able to keep the press from suspecting that something's up."

I shrugged. "We have to take the chance. I told our men to watch themselves and stay out of sight as much as possible. Richter did the same. That's all we can do."

"Was the counter staked out at twelve-thirty?"

"No."

"What about 'F'?" Friedman asked, shifting to a more comfortable position on the bed. "Doesn't anyone close to Ryan have an idea who 'F' might be?"

"So far," I admitted, "except for Ferguson, I haven't been able to talk to anyone who might know. The senator just arrived, and everyone's busy."

"Do you get the feeling they're holding something back?"

"Yes," I answered slowly, "I guess I do. I don't get the feeling of a conspiracy, but I get the feeling they know more than they're telling. Not a lot more. But a little more."

"A little here and a little there," Friedman said. "It all adds up."

A knock sounded. As I nodded to Canelli, Friedman swung his legs off the bed and levered himself to a sitting position facing the door. A big man with close-cropped gray hair and the square, stolid face of a middle-aged prizefighter stood in the doorway. He wore a dark suit and quiet tie, the uniform of Ryan's entourage. With his huge shoulders squared and his clenched hands held rigidly at his sides, he seemed to be standing at attention as he spoke to Canelli.

"Lieutenant Hastings?"

Amiably, Canelli shook his head, pointing to me. "That's Lieutenant Hastings, there."

The big man came into the room and stopped before me. Without offering his hand, he said, "I'm Lloyd Eason." His voice, like his face, revealed nothing. Staring into mine, his eyes were as expressionless as agates, sunk deep beneath his heavy brows.

Introducing him to Friedman, I said, "Mr. Eason is Donald Ryan's bodyguard." And to Eason I said, "You've worked for him several years, I understand." As I said it, I motioned him to a chair. He sat as he'd stood: solidly, shoulders squared, feet flat on the floor, hands clenched one on either knee—at attention, awaiting orders.

"Since 1952," he said, looking from me to Friedman, then back to me. He spoke slowly and carefully in a deep, rough voice. Like his slab-sided face and his thick, muscular body, Eason's voice was heavy and ponderous. He was a Neanderthal man incongruously dressed in a carefully buttoned business suit.

"Did Mr. Ferguson tell you to see me?" I asked.

He shook his massive head. "No. James said I should see you."

"How's the senator feeling?" I asked. "How'd he stand the trip?"

"He's feeling fine." Still staring at me with his impassive eyes, he spoke quietly, without inflection.

"How's Mr. Ryan's health?" Friedman asked. "We understand that he had a heart attack, and that he's recuperating from it. Do you think he's making good progress?"

"Yes," Eason answered, "I think he's making good progress."

"But it's still necessary for him to be protected from stress. Is that correct?"

Gravely, Eason nodded. "That's right. Absolutely right."

Remembering James Ryan's statement that Ferguson hadn't decided to call in the FBI until he'd talked to Eason, I said, "Do you know about the letters that Senator Ryan has been getting—the threatening letters?"

"Yes."

"How did you find out about them?"

"Mr. Ferguson told me about them."

"Did he show them to you?"

"Yes. Just now. Today. About an hour ago."

"When were you first told about the letters?" I asked.

He frowned, then said, "Two or three weeks ago, I think."

"Were you aware that others besides you and Mr. Ferguson knew about the letters?"

"No."

"Did you ask around?" Friedman said.

Eason studied Friedman a moment. The question obviously puzzled him. Finally he said, "No, I didn't ask around."

"Weren't you curious?" Friedman pressed.

"I'm not sure what you mean." He looked at me, as if for help. Looking at him in return, I wondered how this serious, slow-witted man fitted into the high-powered, high-styled group that surrounded Senator Ryan.

I glanced at Friedman, then passed the copies of the letter and the envelope to Eason. "This came about one o'clock," I said. "It was delivered here, to the hotel."

Eason took the letter, looked at it, then handed it back. His face was still utterly expressionless. His eyes were calm. Dead calm.

"None of the other letters were signed," Friedman said. He paused a moment, waiting for Eason to look at him. Then he said, "The fact that it's signed and the fact that the writer probably delivered it in person suggests that he's getting bolder, more threatening. Wouldn't you agree?"

"Yes," Eason said. "I agree." He paused. Then, heavily thoughtful, he said, "It's getting worse. More dangerous."

"Susan Ryan received a threatening phone call, too," I said. "The caller threatened her father."

Now Eason's eyes hardened. His big fists clenched as he said, "He called Susan? Here? In San Francisco?"

"That's right," I said. "He called her yesterday."

He didn't reply, but instead sat staring down at the floor. Along the side of his thick, heavy jaw, I saw muscles knotting.

"Do you have any idea who's writing these letters, Mr. Eason?" I asked quietly.

"No," he answered. "I wish I did." As he said it, his hands unclenched, then clenched again. Subconsciously, he was grappling with an unseen antagonist.

"What about the letter 'F'?" Friedman asked. "Does that mean anything to you?"

Slowly, he shook his head. "No. Nothing."

"Are you sure? Can you think of anyone—anyone at all —with a first or last name beginning with 'F' who has ever threatened Mr. Ryan?"

Once more, he shook his head.

"You've worked for Mr. Ryan since 1952," I said. "That's a long time. I don't see how you can answer so quickly."

He studied me for a moment before he said, "You're right. I'll think about it." He dropped his eyes again to the floor. A curtain had fallen.

"What's the nature of your work, Mr. Eason?" Friedman asked.

Eason frowned, transferring his attention to Friedman as he said, "I'm Mr. Ryan's bodyguard. I already told you that."

"I know you did," Friedman said amiably. "But I'd like to know a little more about how you work. Do you have a staff?"

"No. There's just me."

"So you go everywhere with Mr. Ryan."

"Yes," he said with one more slow, grave nod of his grizzled gladiator's head.

"Do you live with him? In the same house?"

"Yes."

"If you've been with him since 1952," I said, "you were with him before he got into politics."

"Mr. Ryan was making airplanes when I first knew him, airplanes and movies down in Los Angeles."

I frowned. "Movies?"

"Mr. Ryan made two movies before he went into the TV business." He said it with a kind of quiet satisfaction, as if he were describing the successes of some favored member of his family.

"Why did he think he needed a bodyguard when he was making movies and airplanes?" Friedman asked. "That seems strange."

Eason examined Friedman for a moment before he said, "Mr. Ryan—Mr. Donald Ryan—didn't hire me. His father hired me."

"But why?" Friedman pressed.

"Mr. Ryan's father had enemies," Eason answered.

"That was Patrick Ryan," Friedman said. "The tycoon's tycoon."

Obviously disapproving of Friedman's jocular tone, Eason didn't reply, but simply sat silently, impassively observing Friedman.

"After all those years," I said, "you must know everything there is to know about the Ryan family. If anyone outside of the family could steer us to this 'F,' it should be you."

"But I can't," he answered. "I don't know anyone with that initial." He hesitated, then said, "Mr. Ryan doesn't tell me everything, you know. All his business affairs, and his work in Washington, he never tells me about those things."

"But if he had an enemy," Friedman said, "one particular enemy, you'd know about it."

"Yes."

"And has he ever had an enemy? Has anyone tried to harm him?"

Eason shook his head. "No. No one's tried."

"But I understand," I said, "that he's received threatening letters before."

"That's only since he got into politics," he said. "Especially the past few years."

Impatiently, I nodded. "I understand that. But—"

At the door, someone was knocking. At a signal from me, Canelli swung the door open. Dan Kanter, the *Sentinel*'s crime reporter, stood on the threshold. Without being invited, he strode into the room. Eason, meanwhile, rose to his feet, saying, "I'd better be getting back."

I handed him my card. "If you think of anyone," I said, "or if you need any help, call me. If I'm not in, leave a message."

Eason stepped closer to me, asking quietly, "Do you think there's really danger? Really something to worry about?"

Glancing over his shoulder at Kanter, who was frankly trying to listen, I said, "I don't know, Mr. Eason. I'm just not sure." I shook hands with him. For a big man, Eason's grip was gentle. Not soft, but gentle.

When the door closed, Kanter looked at both Friedman and me in turn, his eyes lively. Kanter was a small, wiry man, almost totally bald. His ruddy face was as seamed as a seafarer's. His bushy mustache and matching eyebrows bristled aggressively, coarse and spiky, salt-and-pepper gray. He talked quickly, moved quickly and thought quickly. In his earlier years he'd been a jockey. When he retired at forty, he'd gone to the *Sentinel* as a sports writer. But he'd always been fascinated by crime, and he quickly changed to the police beat. At sixty years of age, Kanter was a thorough professional: energetic, resourceful and fair. He professed to be unsentimental, a total cynic. Yet, occasionally, his stories betrayed a strong sense of outrage, especially aimed at wanton crime and the senseless toll it took.

"Well," Kanter said, sitting down—still uninvited. "*Is* there danger?"

I looked at Friedman. Because he was a fast thinker and good talker, Kanter was one of Friedman's favorite sparring partners.

"Danger of what?" Friedman asked blandly.

"Danger to Donald Ryan," Kanter said. "You know, the most powerful man in America, according to his publicity staff."

"Politics is a risky business," Friedman said, elaborately yawning as he resumed his position on the bed.

"Come on, Pete. Something's up. The lobby is crawling with cops, yours and the feds both."

"Like you said," Friedman countered, "Donald Ryan is a very powerful man. When he's in town, we've got to be careful."

"I happen to know," Kanter said, "that you guys have been working for about three days on some threat to Senator Ryan's life. Naturally, I didn't want to break the story without talking to you." He looked quizzically at both of us in turn. Speaking to me, he said, "You've got that stubborn look on your face, Frank. As long as I've known you, that means only one thing. It means you're sitting on a story that could get me that Pulitzer."

I smiled. "You've been talking about that Pulitzer ever since—"

The phone rang. Canelli questioned me with thick eyebrows upraised, but I shook my head and took the call.

"This is Susan Ryan, Lieutenant. Inspector Culligan says you wanted to talk to me."

"Oh—yes. Where are you?"

"I just got home. Is anything wrong?"

"No, nothing's wrong. But I want to talk to you. I'll call you in fifteen minutes. You'll be there?"

"Yes. I'll wait for your call. But I've got to leave in about an hour."

"I'll call before then. Thanks."

As I hung up the phone Kanter asked, "What was that all about?" His bright, lively eyes danced from me to Friedman.

With his bald head fringed with gray hair, his imp's face and his adolescent body with its small, improbable paunch, Kanter always reminded me of one of the dwarfs in *Snow White*.

"You may as well tell me," Kanter said cheerfully. "I'm going to print something. It might as well be the truth."

I exchanged another look with Friedman, who shrugged his beefy shoulders. His message: the rules of the game required that we give Kanter something. Since the case was my responsibility, it was I who must decide how much to give him.

"It's no big deal," I said. "The senator got a crank letter about a week ago, in Washington. Since he was scheduled to come here to dedicate the new federal building, we got the job of trying to find the letter-writer."

"The letter came from San Francisco," Kanter said.

I nodded.

"Was it just one letter?" Kanter asked, fixing me with his shrewd, speculative stare.

"There may have been more. We started with one. Originally, it was an FBI case. It still is, really. We're just handling the local investigation."

"One nasty letter gets you this?" Kanter asked, waving his hand around the room. "You expect my city editor to believe that?"

"We got this," I said, "when someone dropped a threatening letter at the desk downstairs. That's the reason for all the troops."

"So now there're two letters."

"That's right."

"Were both letters written by the same guy?"

"Personally, I don't think so," I lied. "I think two crazies are involved, neither one of whom is very serious. Still, we've got to do what we can. But there's one problem—a big problem."

"What problem?"

"Senator Ryan hasn't been feeling well. It's nothing that

he won't get over, but his doctors put him on a reduced schedule until Labor Day, when Congress convenes."

"So he doesn't know about the threats."

I nodded again.

"And he's not going to know, if you can help it," Kanter said.

"It's not my idea to keep it from him. Personally, I don't see the harm in telling him. He's gotten threats before. But I'm following orders."

"And the orders come from the top," Kanter said, eyeing me narrowly.

"That's right," Friedman put in meaningfully. "All the way from the top, from the people who bust detectives to patrolmen and turn big-shot reporters into copy boys."

Blandly ignoring the threat, Kanter mused, "Why shouldn't Ryan welcome the idea of a story about a threat to his life? Handled properly, the publicity would be a plus." As he said it, Kanter stared at me with narrowed eyes, thoughtfully speculative. "Unless, of course," he said slowly, "the senator is really sick. And if that's true—" Looking away, he was chewing busily at his mustache. He was sorting out the bits and pieces, calculating how he could parlay his speculations into an angle that might bring him closer to his Pulitzer.

As if to confirm my thoughts, Kanter said, "We could be on the trail of something big here. That's the feeling I get, that we're looking at the tip of what might be a very big, very promising iceberg."

"By 'we,'" Friedman said, "are you including Frank and me?" He smiled a knowing, horsetrading smile. "Because if you are, I don't see why we can't all turn a profit on this thing."

"Oh, Jesus—" Kanter threw me a broad look of mock distress. "Whenever I see that grin on Pete's face, I automatically feel for where my wallet should be."

For a moment we all sat silently, considering the possibilities. Then Friedman said, "I suppose you're the only one who's on to this thing." He spoke casually, as if Kanter's answering nod had been taken for granted.

"Well, then," Friedman said, once more smiling, "I don't see that we've got a problem. You just sit on the story for a few more days while Frank and I see if we can get someone in handcuffs. If we make the collar, then you get the first phone call."

Kanter's expression didn't change as he stared stonily at Friedman. Finally he said, "You know as well as I do, Pete, that once you collar someone, every crime reporter in town will know about it."

"That may be," Friedman countered smoothly. "But they wouldn't know the background. And they wouldn't get it from us, either. Not until we'd told you. And with a story like this, background's everything."

Suddenly Kanter released a breezy, what-the-hell smile. He got to his feet and nodded genially. "Okay," he said, "it's a deal. Just don't forget my number." He waited for Canelli to open the door, waved jauntily, and was gone.

I turned to the phone, dialing Susan Ryan's number.

"Yes, Lieutenant," she said, "what is it?" Her voice sounded tense, anxious.

I read her the note, including the signature, and described how it had been delivered. Immediately she realized the note's significance. "It's the first time he's signed himself," she mused. "Is that it?"

"That's it."

"He's closing in," she said softly. "That's what my phone call meant. That's the significance of his delivering the letter in person. And the signature, too. It's all part of a plan."

"I agree." I let her have a minute to think about it. Then: "Does 'F' mean anything to you, Mrs. Robinson?"

"No," she answered slowly. "No, it doesn't. Nothing at all." She hesitated, then said, "Have you talked to Jack Ferguson—asked him?"

"Yes. He couldn't think of anyone."

"Who else did you ask?"

"I asked Lloyd Eason. Same thing."

"If anyone would know," she said, "Lloyd would. He didn't have any ideas?"

"No. None."

After a moment of silence she said, "What about Katherine Bayliss?"

"I haven't had a chance to ask her about it yet."

"You should."

"I will."

"This—this whole thing is frightening," she said. "The more I think about that phone call—" She let it go unfinished.

"Have you talked to your parents since they arrived?"

"No," she answered. Then, in a heavily ironic voice, she added, "Katherine called, though, just before you did. There'll be a family dinner tomorrow."

"Will it be at the Fairmont, or at your home?"

"It'll be at home."

"It seems that I'm not allowed to see your father," I said. "So if you can find out anything, I'd appreciate knowing about it."

"Yes," she answered absently. "Yes, I'll tell you."

I thanked her, asked her to keep in touch and broke the connection.

Eleven

I knocked once, softly, then twisted the knob and entered the darkened bedroom. I closed the door, locked it and turned toward the bed. Sheets and blankets rustled as Ann moved to her side, making room. It was an exciting, intimate sound, a special secret we'd shared during the past two months.

For the trip down the hallway, I'd worn pajamas. Ann, too, wore pajamas. Without ever having said it, we'd come to agree that the ritual of lovemaking was more erotic, more fulfilling, when it began slowly, with our pajama-clad bodies first touching, then exploring, finally demanding the naked touch of flesh on flesh.

I drew back the light blanket and slipped in beside her.

"Hi—" In the darkness, I found her face, lightly stroking her hair, her cheek, the base of her throat. For more than an hour, lying in my own bed, I'd been thinking of her, wanting her. So that now my genitals were already tightening, straining to touch her with desire.

"Hi—" I felt her move toward me. But only tentatively. Not urgently. Not erotically. First, Ann wanted to talk.

All evening, sitting beside her on the sofa while we watched a movie on TV, I'd sensed that something was troubling her. But the three-hour movie had been one that both Billy and Dan had wanted to see, so I hadn't had a chance to talk to her privately.

I moved my hand down to the curve of her hip, gently caressing. Once more she responded, but only tentatively.

We must talk, then.

With my hand still resting on her hip, but more lightly now, I said, "Did you talk to Victor today?"

I heard her sigh, felt her body shift slightly under my hand as if she'd experienced a twitch of pain.

"How'd you know?" She sighed again.

"Policemen are very intuitive. I keep telling you that."

"I know you're very intuitive, Frank," she whispered. "*I* keep telling *you*. Remember?"

"What'd Victor say?"

A long moment of dispirited silence followed. Then: "He says that he talked to his lawyer yesterday."

"Do you think he really did?"

"Yes," she answered slowly. "Yes, I think he really did. Victor doesn't bluff."

I took my hand from her hip, slipped my other arm under her head and turned on my back. At the thought of Victor Haywood's badgering Ann, my desire had faded.

"So what happens now?" I asked.

"I suppose I'll hear from his lawyer."

"What'll the lawyer say?"

"He'll threaten to cut off my child support, I suppose. Or maybe even threaten to sue for custody of the children."

"Christ."

For a moment we lay silently side by side. Finally I said, "I wish we could move somewhere out of the city. He could take his goddamn child support and stuff it. As long as you're getting it, you're dancing to his tune." But, even as I said it, I knew we couldn't move. Ann was a schoolteacher, forty years old. I was a middle-aged cop. Both of us, like it or not, were civil servants. We were both too old to start over again somewhere else at the bottom of the civil service advancement roster. The system simply wouldn't hire us for entry-level jobs.

"No, we couldn't move," she said, echoing my thoughts. "Not really. Not unless I wanted to wait tables and you wanted to pump gas. And, besides that, I *wouldn't* move. This is home for the boys. All their friends are here. They might think they'd like to go live in another town, but they wouldn't. Not really. At school I see too many kids who've been uprooted. It's hard on them. It's *very* hard on them."

"Christ."

Once more, we lay silently side by side, staring up at the ceiling. We both knew that we hadn't talked about the only workable solution—marriage. We both knew it, and we both knew the other knew it. Separately, we were thinking identical thoughts.

Was this the time? Should I turn toward her and tell her that—?

Beside the bed, her phone rang.

As I quickly lifted the receiver, I glanced at the bedside clock. The time was almost midnight.

"Lieutenant Hastings?" It was Canelli's voice. Only Canelli and Culligan and Friedman had Ann's number.

"What is it, Canelli?" I spoke softly, hoping that the boys wouldn't hear me talking from behind Ann's bedroom door.

As usual, even at midnight, Canelli began with a rambling, bumbling preamble: "Jeeze, I'm really sorry to bother you, Lieutenant. But the more I thought about it, the more I figured that you might be madder if I didn't than if I did. Bother you, I mean."

"Canelli. Please. What's it all about?"

"Well, it's Katherine Bayliss, Lieutenant. You know, Senator Ryan's assistant, or whatever she is. She wants you to call her. She wouldn't tell me what it's about. All she'd say is that Senator Ryan told her to get hold of you."

"Are you sure that's what she said, that Senator Ryan told her to call?"

"That's what she said, Lieutenant. See, that's the reason

I figured I should see if I could get you. I mean, if she hadn't said that, then I probably wouldn't't've. Phoned you, I mean."

"Where are you?"

"At the Hall."

"When'd she call?"

"Just about fifteen minutes ago. Communications got it for you and gave it to me, naturally, because I'm catching this week. So I figured that—"

"Did she leave a number?"

"Yes." He gave me the number. I hung up and told Ann that I would make the call from the living room.

Minutes later, I heard Katherine Bayliss's calm, precise voice on the phone. "Something's happened," she said. "If you can—if you possibly can—we'd like you to come down here, to the Fairmont."

"Who'll I be seeing?" I asked. "Senator Ryan?"

I heard her draw a deep breath. "Yes," she answered, plainly reluctant. "Yes, you'll be seeing Senator Ryan. Come to the eleventh floor. They'll take you to me. And I'll take you to the senator."

"I'll be there in about a half hour."

"Yes. As fast as you can. Please."

Twelve

Katherine Bayliss met me at the door of her suite and stepped out into the hallway, closing the door. Her hair was loose around her shoulders. She was casually dressed in slacks and a simple shirtwaist blouse. On her feet she wore big, woolly slippers. The slippers touched a tiny chord far back in my memory. For as long as I could remember, my mother had worn woolly slippers.

At quarter to one in the morning, with her makeup neglected, Katherine Bayliss looked worn and worried. Yet I was aware of sexual electricity as I walked beside her down the deserted hotel hallway. I was conscious of her loose hair, her breasts beneath the blouse, and her bare feet thrust into the woolly slippers, so unexpectedly evocative.

Or was I remembering Ann, warm and tousled in her bed?

"What happened?" I asked quietly.

Still walking beside me, she said, "I'm not sure."

"You're not sure?" I let her hear the late-night irritation in my voice. "You're not sure?"

"I was already asleep," she said. "Lloyd knocked on my door and said that the senator wanted to see you." As she said it, we turned a corner. Ahead, at the end of the corridor,

I saw a large, ornate double door. This, certainly, was the entrance to the senator's master suite, guarded by an FBI agent.

"That's all Eason said?" I asked.

"That's all. But obviously the senator has heard about the letters. That's all it could be."

"But why would he want to see me? How would he know about me?"

"I don't know, unless Lloyd told him about you."

At the door of the suite, the guard smiled at Katherine, glanced at my lapel ID button and pressed the door buzzer. A moment later, Lloyd Eason stood in the open doorway. I waited for Katherine to precede me, but she hesitated, questioning Eason with a quick glance.

"He just wants to see the lieutenant," Eason said. His inflection was apologetic.

Impassively, she nodded, gesturing me inside.

Dressed in pajamas and a bathrobe, Senator Donald Ryan was half reclining on a sofa. A blanket covered his legs. His face was so familiar that recognition came almost as a shock: the reincarnation of thousands of front-page pictures and television images, with its dramatic white hair, its high-bridged nose, its forceful mouth and jaw, its dark, compelling eyes and its aura of overwhelming command. As I advanced toward him, I felt as if the scene was being recorded for history by dozens of invisible cameramen.

But when I came closer to the couch, I realized that flesh and blood were pale imitations of all the thousands of bold, brave pictures. Deeply lined, the skin of his face was sickly, parched and flaccid. Beneath the powerful arch of their brows, the dark eyes were vague and wandering. The mouth was clenched, but the effect in closeup was more desperate than decisive.

Ferguson, Bayliss and Company hadn't been lying. Senator Donald Ryan was a sick man.

Stopping in front of the sofa, I realized that, unconsciously, I was standing at attention before him.

"Senator Ryan."

He motioned to a nearby chair. Then he looked at Lloyd Eason and inclined his head toward an inner door. Eason was being dismissed. Surprised, I glanced around the elegantly furnished living room, confirming that, yes, I was alone with Senator Donald Ryan. Once more, irrationally, I felt as if I were on the stage of history in the making. I realized that I was sitting stiffly in my chair, still posing for the invisible cameramen.

Without changing his position on the sofa, Ryan studied me for a moment before he said, "I'm sorry to get you out of bed, Lieutenant. But I've had to make some decisions, and when the process was complete, your name came out on top." He spoke in a low, uninflected monotone: a white-haired, gray-faced man struggling to save his strength. His eyes moved uncertainly, almost furtively, revealing a kind of fretful, exhausted fear. I recognized that look; I'd seen it many times in the line of duty. He'd seen the shadow of death stalking him. He was afraid.

"My name?" As I said it, I realized how silly and ineffectual I must sound.

He nodded, at the same time reaching into the pocket of his dressing gown for an envelope.

I could see the words SENATOR DONALD RYAN typed in the exact center of the envelope, like the letter left at the desk earlier in the day.

"I see you know what this is," he said, gesturing with the envelope.

"Yes."

"I went to bed about eleven," he said. "I found this under my pillow."

"Under your—" Incredulous, I couldn't finish it.

Under his pillow . . .

Watching me closely, he leaned forward, offering the letter. I got hastily to my feet, took it and returned to my chair. Automatically handling the letter by its corners, even though I knew the precaution was useless, I read:

At this moment, you could be dead. If you want to save yourself, the price will be one million dollars. Instructions will follow.

F

Everything was the same: the paper, the neat, square-block typing, the writing style, the signature. Everything.

Under his pillow . . .

"Who else knows about this?" I asked.

"Lloyd Eason and Jack Ferguson," he answered.

Not Katherine Bayliss. Not his wife, nor his son.

I looked at my watch. The time was exactly one o'clock. Two hours had elapsed since the letter had been found. Automatically, I looked for a phone. There were calls to make, orders to give, witnesses to interrogate—and questions to ask: When had the bed been made? Who had made it? Who had been in the bedroom since the bed had been made? When? For how long?

"As you know," Ryan was saying, "all of this had been kept secret from me for reasons that you know about. The result, of course—" The ghost of a smile touched his mouth. "The result was that when I finally learned about it tonight, the shock was probably more profound than it might otherwise have been. However—" Once more a pale smile briefly touched the wasted face. "However, the worst didn't happen, as you can see."

"I'm very glad it didn't, sir." Once more, the reply sounded inadequate, faintly silly.

"You're wondering why I sent for you," he said. Even though his voice was weak, the statement had an authoritative ring of flat-sounding finality. When Donald Ryan made a pronouncement, he didn't expect a reply.

"I sent for you," he said, "for two reasons. First, both Jack Ferguson and Lloyd Eason were favorably impressed with you. And, secondly, I've got something that needs to be handled by a local policeman—a *discreet* local policeman who knows his job." For a moment he looked at me steadily, making his final assessment. "Do you understand what I mean, Lieutenant?"

"I think so," I answered. "You want me to conduct an investigation, and you want it kept secret."

He was plainly pleased with my reply. "That's correct."

"Who do I report to?"

"You'll report directly to me." The tired eyes sharpened, looking into mine. "Do you have any objections to that?"

"I don't have an objection, exactly. But—" I hesitated. "But I work for the City and County of San Francisco."

He nodded, wearily impatient. "I understand that, Lieutenant. Which is, obviously, why I need you. I have other options, of course. Private investigators, for instance. However, for the moment, all I need is information—and discretion. For that, one man is desirable—one man who's plugged into local law enforcement."

"What's the information you need, Senator?"

He hesitated one final moment, making his decision. Then, with obvious reluctance, he said, "There's a man named Frederick Tharp. He's a resident of San Francisco. He's twenty-six years old, and he's lived here for about ten years."

Frederick Tharp—F.T.

I tried to keep excitement out of my voice as I said, "Do you have an address?"

"No, I don't have an address. At least, not a current address. However, it's probably moot. Because, as far as I know, Frederick Tharp is in prison."

"Do I understand that you think Frederick Tharp is the one who's been sending these letters?"

He didn't reply, but only stared at me with inscrutable, implacable eyes. Finally: "Let's take it one step at a time, Lieutenant. Let's see whether he's still in jail. Then we'll talk further."

"Was he jailed on a federal charge or a state of California charge?"

"I have no idea." As he spoke, he allowed his eyes to close

as he leaned his head back against the sofa. My audience was ending.

Should I try for more information? Or should I bide my time? Should I leave quietly, or should I wait to be dismissed? I looked at the door where Eason had disappeared. Logically, I should—

"I understand," Ryan was saying, "that you've talked to my daughter." He spoke softly. His eyes were still closed. His face looked even more drawn, paler, more deeply lined.

"That's right, I have." Surprised, I settled uneasily back in my chair. Did he want to talk? Or did he want information? Or both?

"What did you think of her?" he asked.

"I—ah—I thought she was a very unusual person. Very—very strong. Very determined."

"Well, Lieutenant, I'm afraid you aren't correct. I'm afraid Susan's confused. Badly confused."

I didn't reply.

Why was he asking me about his daughter? The time was almost one-thirty. He was a sick man, and he'd just had a scare. Why wasn't he in bed? Why had he sent for me, instead of the FBI? Why hadn't he assigned Ferguson the job of briefing me?

Thinking about it, I realized that there could be only one answer: Ferguson didn't know of Frederick Tharp's existence. And Donald Ryan intended to keep it that way.

"You're wondering why I'm asking you about Susan," he said, still speaking with his eyes closed.

"Yes," I admitted, "I am."

"I suppose it's got something to do with my heart attack," he said. Now he opened his eyes, looking at me squarely. "Have you ever been sick, Lieutenant? Dangerously sick?"

"No. At least, I've never been sick with a disease."

"But you've faced death. You could have died, I was told, a few months ago."

"Yes," I answered, "that's true."

"There've probably been other times too," he said.

"Other times?"

"That you faced death."

"Yes," I answered, "there have been other times. Not many. But a few."

"Then you know what I'm talking about. You know how you change—how everything changes—when you open your eyes and see death staring back at you."

"Yes," I said quietly. "Yes, I know."

He gestured to the letter that I still held in my hand. "A year ago, these letters wouldn't've been a problem. They would've been a minor irritation, nothing more. They would've been handled. But suddenly, one morning about ten o'clock, I got a pain in my chest. And, instantly, the whole world changed. One moment I was in control. The next moment I was helpless. And I was frightened, too— terribly frightened, and terribly alone. And then I realized that the people around me were frightened too. Not frightened for me, but for themselves. So they decided to conceal the fact that I can't wield the power that keeps *them* in power. They made a—a mannequin of me, and propped it up in the window where it can been seen but not heard.

"But what they didn't know, what they can't know, is that I've changed. I'm not the same person I was before that pain started in my chest. I'm a different person, a totally different person. But they don't know that, because they don't know me. They know the image I've created—the private image, or the public image, depending on the situation. But that's all they see, so that's all they know. And so—" He smiled at me. "And so you see, it's all illusory, this power game. It's not real power, it's the appearance of power that counts."

"You make it all sound pretty grim. Pretty worthless, really."

He nodded. "It is worthless. That's the whole point. The more power you get, the more you want. The more you need. And, in the process, you realize that you've become an—an anachronism. You aren't really a person, you're a symbol. You aren't a son, or a husband, or a father. Not really.

Because you've constantly got to pretend that you're *more* than a son, or a husband, or a father, or a friend. The result being you're none of them. You don't experience normal emotions, because you've debased them all in the process of projecting them for the public—for votes. You don't really love anyone, and nobody really loves you, or even likes you. They fear you, but they don't like you, no matter how loudly they may protest to the contrary. Which is the reason—" He looked me squarely in the eye, sadly smiling. "Which is the reason I'm telling a stranger all this. Do you see?"

For a moment I held his gaze before I finally shook my head. "No, I don't think I do see. Not really."

"I can understand how you wouldn't, Lieutenant." He sighed: a ragged, regretful exhalation, full of pain and mystery. "Maybe it'll simplify it for you if I just say that I'm sixty-six years old, and I'm sick, and I'm scared. But mostly—" He shook his head, saying almost inaudibly, "Mostly, I'm lonely. Suddenly I'm very, very lonely."

Thirteen

At nine o'clock the next morning, Sunday, I was in the Police Records office, leaning against a counter and yawning as I scanned the computer printout on Frederick Tharp.

Caucasian male, twenty-six, born Santa Barbara, California. Mother: Juanita Tharp, fifty-two, 8754 Dolores Street, San Francisco (also subject's residence at time of last arrest). No known father. Juvenile record—Charge: breaking and entering, age fourteen. Probation, City and County of Los Angeles. Charge: grand theft auto, age sixteen. Sentence: five years; served six months at juvenile hall, Los Angeles; paroled to San Francisco Youth Authority. Adult Record—Charge: aggravated assault, age eighteen. Acquitted. Charge: burglary, age nineteen. Acquitted. Charge: assault with intent to commit murder, age nineteen. Sentence: seven years to life; served thirty-six months. Charge: attempted rape, age twenty-three. Sentence: habitual offender, seven years to life; served thirty-six months.

Paroled on May 17, this year.

The first letter to Donald Ryan was written on May 24, postmarked San Francisco.

Dropping down the page, I noted his physical characteris-

91

tics: seventy inches tall, weight 160. Musculature, average. Hair, dark brown. Eyes, brown. Scars: three-inch scar, right hand, base of thumb; six-inch scar, lower back; two-inch scar above left eyebrow.

Under "General," I read: "Subject's features are regular. He normally dresses well, hair medium long, usually carefully combed. Appearance, average to above average. Speech and manner, above average."

The psychological evaluation came next, written and signed by C. Estes, Staff, San Quentin: "Subject has an IQ of 135. He is intelligent and well-spoken. He is sociopathic, with strong schizoid tendencies. He has pronounced delusions of grandeur, and considers himself superior to his fellow inmates. Strong feelings of suppressed sexual anxieties, probably resulting from suppressed inadequacies. Sexually ambivalent. Subject's solutions to common problems are transient and ineffective, exhibiting strong antisocial (criminal) bias. Although he is institutionally cooperative, this inmate's prognosis for accommodation to society is rated poor. Conclusion: Sociopathic behavior profile, latent habitual criminal type."

The next section contained brief evaluations by a series of arresting officers:

"Subject is extremely smart and dangerous."

"Subject is habitual criminal type, doesn't know right from wrong, doesn't care."

"Subject has strange ideas, doesn't fit normal criminal category. Not strong-arm, not con man. Some of both."

"Subject is a pervert, abuses either women or men, also young boys."

"Subject is unable to control his temper once he's incited. A very strange type: a pretty boy, angel-faced criminal, the most dangerous kind."

"Subject seems to live in a fantasy world. Always talking about get-rich-quick schemes. Doesn't work. Doesn't react normally. Has a definite superiority complex, delusions of grandeur."

The final entry was signed "Gerald Olsen, Parole Officer," and dated May 17. "Frederick Tharp is paroled to the custody of Byron Tharp, 4174 26th Street, San Francisco, California. Reporting day, Tuesday, 10:30 A.M. Employer: Trader John's, 5782 The Embarcadero, San Francisco."

I folded the long printout sheet, slipped it into my pocket and took the elevator up to Homicide on the third floor. Canelli sat at the reception desk reading the Sunday paper. At his own desk, with his chair in a reclining position, Culligan was dozing.

"Oh, jeeze—" Guiltily, Canelli slapped the comic section down on his desk. Startled, Culligan came upright in his chair, blinking and yawning.

"I want the two of you to come with me," I ordered. "And get a backup team from another division. Make sure they have a shotgun. You'll have to get someone to cover for you at the desk, Canelli. I'll meet you in the garage, at my car." I turned to the door, then turned back to face Canelli. "You might as well bring the newspaper," I said. "I didn't get a chance to read it either."

4174 26th Street was a large apartment building that had been newly built on the steep, rocky slope of the Army Street hill, part of the foggy Twin Peaks arc of hills that overlooked the eastern half of the city. The building was typical of its kind: cheaply but cleverly built, giving a false impression of luxury. Yet, when the fog lifted, the views from 4174 26th Street would be spectacular.

But the month was June, and as we drew up across the street from 4174, the fog was blowing in from the ocean, thick and cold. Backed up against the hill, the building faced east toward the bay. The tenants entered through a small front lobby. Fire escapes offered the only exit from the back.

"Jeeze," Canelli said, "I wouldn't live here for anything, with this goddamn fog and everything." When neither Culligan nor I responded, Canelli pointed out the window of our car toward a nearby mini-park, newly scratched out of one of the few flat sites on the hill. "I can remember when I was a kid," Canelli said, "there used to be goats over there."

"Goats?" Culligan said, sourly disbelieving.

"Goats," Canelli answered firmly. "I swear to God. There was a crazy old woman they called the Goat Lady. She lived in a shack up here, and she had goats. She was famous."

"I think you're putting me on," Culligan said, staring at the terraced tiers of the new low-rise buildings that covered most of the Twin Peaks slopes.

"No, he's right," I said. "I can even remember a horse— an old sway-backed horse that someone kept as a pet."

"Did you grow up in San Francisco, Lieutenant?" Culligan asked.

"Yes. I lived out in the Sunset when it was mostly sand dunes. On Saturdays we used to ride our bikes up here and explore."

"Huh—" Shaking his head, Culligan stared again at the surrounding hills. Looking at his face, I knew that he didn't quite believe me. Culligan was a confirmed skeptic.

"This should be easy," I said, nodding to the comfortable middle-class neighborhood, peaceful on a Sunday morning. "We'll go in the front, and let Haskell and Fowler cover the back." I ducked my head and switched on the tiny surveillance microphone.

"Tach two," I said, "how do you read?"

"Loud and clear, Lieutenant," a voice answered.

"You two take the back. Don't bother with shotguns, it's not that kind of a neighborhood. We'll use walkie-talkie channel nine. Clear?"

"Yes, sir. Channel nine."

"You've got his description in mind?"

"Yes, sir."

"Let's check the radios." I picked up my walkie-talkie, switched to channel nine and said a few words.

"Loud and clear, Lieutenant."

"You are, too. All right, let's do it." I handed the walkie-talkie to Canelli, and got out of the car.

*　　*　　*

The third-floor corridor was narrow, but the building's designer had hung cheap prints on the walls and used plastic plants and artificial rocks to make a fake rock garden at one end of the corridor, complete with a recirculating waterfall lit by multicolored lights.

"There it is," I said softly, pointing. "Apartment five." I walked to the door, gesturing Canelli to my left and Culligan to my right. I unbuttoned my corduroy sports jacket, loosened my revolver in its spring holster and pressed the button set into the door frame over a plastic plate inscribed "Byron Tharp."

On the third ring, I heard footsteps on the other side of the door and saw something reflected in the door's peephole. I nodded to Canelli and moved back a step, slipping my right hand inside my jacket.

The door opened on a chain. Through the narrow opening I saw the face of a middle-aged man: dark-eyed, balding, with dark hair, a dark mustache and a small black beard, neatly trimmed. The black hair that matted his chest curled in the "V" of his bathrobe.

"Mr. Tharp? Byron Tharp?" As I spoke, I used my left hand to reach into my hip pocket for my shield case.

"That's right. Who're you?" His voice was heavy and coarse, annoyed. He was frowning angrily.

"I'm Lieutenant Frank Hastings, police department. I'd like to come in and talk to you."

"About what?"

"About your nephew, Frederick Tharp. Is he here?"

"No," he answered curtly, "he isn't here. The no-good little bastard."

Relaxing, I stepped closer. "Let us in, Mr. Tharp. We can't talk like this."

He stared at me, muttered something unintelligible, and closed the door. I heard the chain rattle, and a moment later the door swung grudgingly open.

"Three of you, eh?" Tharp said. He nodded, as if our

presence outside his door confirmed something he'd already suspected. "What's he done now, the asshole?" With his fists propped on his hips, legs braced, chin lifted aggressively, he looked ready for a barroom fight.

"Let's go inside, Mr. Tharp."

"Listen—" He glanced back over his shoulder. "Listen, I've got company. This isn't exactly a good time."

"I'm sorry, sir," I said. I tried a man-to-man smile. "In our business, we can't phone ahead."

His frown only deepened. He was a short, stocky, bandy-legged man with hard eyes and a small, suspicious mouth. His face was swarthy and thickening, like his body. It was a closed, truculent face.

"This is important, Mr. Tharp," I said quietly, at the same time slipping an envelope from my pocket. "We've got a warrant to search your premises for Frederick Tharp. And that's what we're going to do, the hard way or the easy way. It's up to you." I unfolded the warrant and handed it to him. He glanced at it, threw one last resentful look at us, then turned away, stalking on his short, hairy legs, barefoot, into a Pullman-style kitchen.

"We can talk in here," he announced.

"All right. Fine." And to Canelli I said, "Take a look, then dismiss the backup."

"Yessir." Canelli and Culligan moved down the hallway to a small living room.

"Where're they going?" Tharp demanded.

"They're going to search the premises. As I told you."

"*Shit.*" He sat down at a small Formica breakfast table. His short bathrobe was skimpily cut, and parted across his thick knees and upper thighs. He plucked angrily at the bathrobe, trying futilely to cover his knees as he said, "He's not here. He hasn't been around for a week. I already told you that."

"We've got to look."

"There's a friend in the bedroom. A lady."

"I'm sorry. We don't have a choice, Mr. Tharp. I get the

impression that you know your nephew has problems with the law. So you should know that we didn't come here just to turn around and go home."

"My word isn't good enough for you," he said bitterly, challenging me with his angry eyes. "I'm a businessman in this city, you know. And a taxpayer, too. A big taxpayer. But still you won't take my word."

Rather than argue with him, I tried to simply stare him down. When I finally succeeded, I said, "When's the last time you saw your nephew, Mr. Tharp?"

"Today's Sunday," he said. "I haven't seen him since last Saturday."

"Eight days ago."

He nodded.

"Where'd he go, do you know?"

"I don't have the slightest idea."

"He's on parole. He isn't supposed to change addresses without notifying his parole officer."

He didn't reply. Giving up on the bathrobe, he began drumming irritably on the tabletop with his thick, strong fingers. Sitting across from him, I put my notebook and ball-point pen on the table between us. From the rear of the apartment, I heard the sound of a woman's voice, swearing querulously. Moments later, Canelli and Culligan entered the kitchen.

"It's okay, Lieutenant," Canelli said. "All clear." As he spoke, he glanced down at Tharp's exposed knees, smiling.

Scowling at Canelli, Tharp sighed explosively. "I told you he wasn't here, for crissake. Now, if it's not asking too much, I wish you'd leave. Please." The last word was laden with sarcasm.

I turned to Canelli and Culligan. "Wait for me outside. Call off the backup." I waited until they'd left, then turned again to Tharp. "I need some information from you, Mr. Tharp. And I need it now. Right now. I'm sorry that we've screwed up your morning. But I simply don't have a choice. Your nephew is suspected of committing a very serious crime. Believe me, I wouldn't be here on a Sunday morning with four men if it wasn't serious."

"Four men?"

"Two in back."

"Oh." For the first time his hard, resentful eyes left mine, wandering thoughtfully away. Byron Tharp was apparently a man who was impressed by numbers.

"Where can I find your nephew, Mr. Tharp?" Looking him hard in the eye, I spoke quietly, confidentially.

"I haven't the slightest idea. I've already told you. He left last Saturday. Or, at least, I guess it was Saturday. I was out of town for a couple of days. When I got back on Sunday, I saw the crap piling up that he was supposed to take care of. So I knocked on his door. And he was gone. His room was cleaned out. He'd taken all his things and split."

"What d'you mean by 'crap piling up'?"

"I own this building. Part of our parole deal was, he was supposed to do some work around here. Keep things picked up, keep the hallways clean, things like that. He got a free room, for God's sake. It was a good deal."

"A free room. You mean—" Involuntarily, I looked around. "You mean he doesn't live here?"

"No. Christ, that's what I've been trying to tell you. There's a room and bath off the garage. That's where he lived. Until last Saturday, that is. Then he—"

I heard the sharp staccato of high heels pounding down the hallway. A woman appeared in the kitchen doorway, then disappeared without a glance at us. A moment later, the outside door slammed.

"So much for that," Tharp grated. *"Shit."*

"I'm sorry," I said again. "But I don't have—"

"Oh, Jesus, never mind." Resigned, he shook his head. "Let's just get it over with, all right?"

"If you want to get dressed—"

"No, no—" He gestured impatiently. "It's all right. Christ, I should've known something like this would happen." Once more, he shook his head. "I should've known. I

98

did know, in fact. But I didn't have a choice."

"You didn't have a choice?"

"No. Juanita—his mother—she's out of it. Completely out of it."

"What d'you mean?"

"I mean that she's flipped out. She's crazy. She's at a goddamn sanitarium."

"She's your sister. Is that right?"

"Yes."

"Did you put her in the sanitarium?"

"I couldn't do anything else. She was running around the streets naked, for God's sake. For years I tried to take care of her. But you can't fix something like that, like running around naked. So I committed her."

"How long has she been in the sanitarium?"

"Just about a year."

"So you had to take Frederick, when he came up for parole."

"Believe me," he said vehemently, "I wouldn't've done it if there was any other way."

"Do you happen to know whether he's been reporting for work this last week?"

"At the club, you mean?"

"Yes. He works at Trader John's."

"Hell, no, he hasn't been to work. He didn't come in Friday night, and he hasn't been back since. I didn't find that out until Monday, though, when I went in."

"Went in?"

"To the club. Trader John's. That's my club. I thought you knew."

"No, I didn't." I studied him for a moment, then said, "You do pretty well, Mr. Tharp—an apartment building, a club."

He shrugged. "I do all right."

"Did you support your sister?"

"For the last five years or so, I did. Before that, she used to work for me. I've got another place, a neighborhood bar, out in the Mission. She used to work there, hit or miss. But then—" He shook his head. "She started screwing up so bad, I had to tell her to just stay home."

"You're not married, I gather."

"No. I'm divorced. I've been married. Twice. That's enough."

"Did your sister ever marry?"

"No. Never." As he said it, he shot me a sidelong look.

"What's her story?"

"Her story?"

"How'd she—" I hesitated, groping. "How'd she become what she—became?"

"Crazy, you mean."

"I mean, what's her history? I gather that she lived down south for a while—Santa Barbara and Los Angeles."

"She never really lived in Santa Barbara," he said. "She mostly lived in Los Angeles." As he said it, he looked carefully at me, assessing my reaction.

"Her son was born in Santa Barbara."

"Yeah. Well—you know. I guess she wanted to get out of town. You know. In those days, things weren't as free and easy as they are now." He shifted uncomfortably and tugged again at his bathrobe. With the mention of his sister, his aggressive, truculent assurance seemed to have deserted him. For most of his life, apparently, she'd been his cross to bear.

"How long has she lived in San Francisco?"

"About ten years."

"Did she grow up in Los Angeles?"

"No. Both of us grew up in Dayton, Ohio. The family moved out to Los Angeles during the war to work in defense. You know, Lockheed. I came up to San Francisco when I was twenty-five, twenty-six years old, but Juanita stayed down there. She always wanted to get into the movies."

"Did she?"

He snorted: a harsh, flatulent sound. "You might say she did. She had lots of walk-ons, and a few times she even had a few lines. But that was it. She had the looks, at least in the beginning. But she didn't have anything else. No brains, no talent. Nothing. If she'd been half smart, with her looks, she could've done something for herself, got someplace. But—" Shaking his head, he let it go unfinished.

"How old was she when she had Frederick?"

"She was—let's see. She's fifty-two now, and he's twenty-six, so she was twenty-six years old. She had Fred and then she started to drink. And that was it. Between the booze and that kid of hers, it was the beginning of the end." With a shrug and another flatulent snort, he dismissed the rest of his sister's life.

It was the kind of life that appears regularly on police blotters: a short, sad chronicle of futility and despair, gathering momentum as it rushes downhill toward oblivion. Her parents had migrated from the Midwest, looking for better pay. Because she'd been good-looking, she'd wandered into the skin trade. She'd gotten in over her head. Next came the drinking, or the drugs, or both. Now, at age fifty-two, she was living on borrowed time, waiting for a death that only her brother had managed to postpone.

"Her son was always a problem, then," I said, probing.

Vehemently, he nodded. "From the start, that kid was a pain in the ass. From the first day he was born."

"So she eventually came to San Francisco to be near you. Is that it?"

"I suppose you could say that," he said. Disgustedly, he shook his head.

"Where is your sister? Which sanitarium?"

"Brentwood. It's down near Daly City."

"Is it a private sanitarium?"

"Yeah."

"So you're paying her bills. Still."

He shrugged. "Do I have a choice?"

"You could put her in a state hospital."

"Not with my assets, I couldn't. I checked."

"I guess you're right," I answered. Except that he wasn't right. Only a spouse's income was considered, qualifying a patient for state aid.

"Did you have her declared legally insane?" I asked.

"Yes. I already told you."

I sat silently for a moment, studying him. He owned a well-known club, plus a neighborhood bar. Plus an apartment building that was probably worth two million dollars. Somehow he didn't look the part. He looked aggressive enough, but not smart enough. He looked street smart, but not financially smart, not sophisticated or subtle.

"Over the years," I said, "it sounds like you've spent a fortune on your sister's troubles."

"That's right," he said heavily. "That's it exactly. Which is the reason that, as far as I'm concerned, you can put Fred back in jail and throw away the key. I'm finished with him. I'm through. Period."

"You don't know where we can find him. You can't give me any idea where to look."

"Right. He just disappeared. Zip. That was it."

"Can you think of any friends that he had?"

"He doesn't have any friends. None."

"Do you mind if we search his room?"

"Hell, no." He rose and padded into the living room in his bare feet. A moment later he was back, dangling a key from his forefinger. "When you're finished," he said, "just put it in my mailbox. Okay?"

"Okay." I took the key, walked to the door, and handed him my card. "If you hear from him, or about him, give me a call. It's important. Very important."

"What's it about, anyhow? What's he done? You never told me."

"I know." I smiled, nodded goodbye, and opened the door.

Fourteen

"You realize, of course," Friedman said, "that there's practically no percentage chance of us finding him. Not unless he shows himself. We don't have any known haunts, no MO, no friends, nothing. What we've got here—" He tapped the printout sheet that lay on my desk between us. "What we've got here is an atypical criminal. And they're the worst kind to find." He picked up a copy of Tharp's picture and studied it. "He's a handsome devil," he observed. Then, smiling, he tapped the printout again. "I like that one comment, the one that says baby-faced crooks are the worst. Because he's right. Absolutely right. Have you ever noticed?"

I nodded. "Definitely."

"Are you considering telling the FBI?"

"About Tharp, you mean?"

He nodded.

"No. I thought I should talk to you first. What d'you think?"

"You know what I think," he answered. "I think we should keep it to ourselves for, say, twenty-four hours. After all, it's only Sunday, and the dedication ceremonies aren't until Wednesday. Why don't we give it until Monday noon before we call Richter? That way, if we haven't been able to find Tharp, Richter'll still have time to fall on his ass, too, before Wednesday."

"If we give Richter the reports, and he sees the dates, he'll know we've been jerking him around."

"What reports?" Friedman asked innocently. "After all, you were sworn to secrecy by the great man himself. If you put anything in writing, you're breaking your word to Donald Ryan."

"That's true."

In silence, we both stared at the picture and the printout. Friedman was frowning thoughtfully as he said, "The big unanswered question is why Ryan turned us on to Tharp. Where'd he get the name, for God's sake? What's his connection to Tharp? How'd he know he's in prison? How did he—"

My intercom sounded: two long buzzes. It was something important, probably concerning the Ryan case.

"Yes?"

"It's Culligan, Lieutenant."

"What've you got?"

"It was all done very simply. One, two, three, you might say. He gave a chambermaid forty dollars to put the letter under Ryan's pillow. Twenty dollars when he gave her the letter, twenty dollars when she did the job. It was done in the morning before Ryan arrived, when there really wasn't much security."

"Did the chambermaid identify Tharp from the picture?"

"She sure did. She said he told her that he was devoted to Ryan. She thought she was putting a fan letter under his pillow. She's not very bright."

"Did anyone else see Tharp on the hotel premises?"

"No. At least no one's told me, if they did."

"How many people have we got at the Fairmont?"

"Four, including me."

"All right. Stay in the lobby. Keep the desk and the elevators under surveillance."

"Yessir."

"And you'd better figure out some kind of a rotation with the teams at Byron Tharp's building and Trader John's."

"Yessir."

"By the way, don't show the FBI the pictures of Tharp. It's my ass, if they find out about him at this point. Understand?"

"Yessir," Culligan answered, knowingly laconic. "I understand."

"Keep me advised." I broke the connection, and told Friedman what Culligan had said.

"Tharp is smart," Friedman observed thoughtfully. "He's smart, and he's shifty." He paused, then said, "I hope you remember my prediction that, basically, extortion is what he's got on his mind. Because I think that's it. I don't think he's a mad-dog killer. I think he wants that million dollars."

"But if he doesn't get it, he'll sure as hell try to kill Ryan."

He shrugged. "Maybe yes, maybe no. Obviously he's following a plan. He's started slow, and now he's increasing the pressure. Maybe he even knows that Ryan's sick." Friedman paused again, looking thoughtfully away. "If he knew Ryan was sick, then all he'd have to do is fire a shot across Ryan's bow, so to speak, to sink him. He wouldn't have to score a direct hit. Ever think of that?"

"He'd die of a heart attack, you mean."

"Exactly."

"Once Ryan's dead, though, there's no hope of Tharp's getting his million dollars. Did *you* ever think of *that?*"

Friedman shrugged. "That's the risk every extortionist runs. His stock in trade is the fear of death or injury, not the actual fact of it."

"Are you going to be here for a while?" I asked.

"It looks like it." Friedman glanced at the clock. It was two o'clock on a Sunday afternoon. "Why?"

"Because I think I'll go see Juanita Tharp."

"Before you see Ryan?" Friedman spoke dubiously. But after a moment's thought, he nodded approval. "It might be a good idea. From the mouths of loonies, I've discovered, the truth often comes."

Fifteen

"Jeeze," Canelli said, pulling into the parking lot and staring at the white colonnade and brick facade of the Colonial-style administration building. "This is some layout. What's the name of it, anyhow?"

"Brentwood Sanitarium."

"Pretty fancy," he said. "And pretty expensive, I'll bet."

I didn't reply.

"Who's in here, anyhow?" He switched off the engine and set the parking brake. "Does this have something to do with the Ryan case?"

"Canelli, I've already told you that a lot of this is classified. I tell you what you need to know, but no more. Right?"

With his soft brown Italian eyes, he looked at me reproachfully. I'd hurt his feelings. Again.

"Just stay in the car," I ordered. "I won't be long. If Lieutenant Friedman wants me, come inside and get me. Clear?"

"Yessir," Canelli said, sighing heavily and settling down sulkily behind the steering wheel. "That's clear."

         *   *   *

"This way, please." Walking slightly ahead, the orderly guided me down an intersecting hallway that led past a large common room. I saw a handful of patients, each one struggling with his own particular demon. Some sat frozen, conversing with imaginary friends or enemies. Some repeated one movement or gesture over and over. Some simply wandered around the large, sunny room, searching for a way out. Looking bored but watchful, three attendants sat silently, waiting for their shifts to end.

The orderly turned a corner and stopped in front of a door, taking out his key. He rapped lightly on the door, listened, rapped again, then unlocked the door. "Stay out here for a minute," he said. "I'll just see if she's presentable." He opened the door, slipped inside and left the door slightly ajar. Standing alone in the corridor, I became aware of the background sounds: monotonous mutterings and mumblings mingled with small, stifled screams. The sounds, I realized, differed little from those at state-run institutions. Only the decor was different, and the noise level.

The door swung open. The attendant stepped out in the hallway, drew the door closed and said softly, "This isn't one of her better days, Lieutenant. Could you come back tomorrow, please?" He spoke in the flat, impersonal tone of institutional authority, as if he took obedience for granted. He was a young, delicately made man with his hair done in ringlets. He spoke with a lisp, faintly petulant.

"I'm sorry, but I've got to see her." I took a purposeful half-step toward the door. "It's important."

"Oh, all *right.*" He stepped aside. His eyes, improbably guileless and childlike, reproached me.

I pushed open the door and stepped into a small room. The bright rose-printed pattern of the matching bedspread and drapes dominated the room. A bureau, a small desk, a straight-backed chair and a small plastic-covered armchair completed the room's furnishings. As if to cancel the bedspread and drapes, the walls were painted an institutional green. There were no pictures on the wall, and none on either the desk or bureau. Light came in from a single window and a glass door leading to a vest-pocket patio.

Juanita Tharp sat in the armchair near the window. She was staring out at the low, fog-covered hills that receded into white mists gathering beyond Brentwood's manicured lawns and shrubbery, suggesting a Japanese landscape.

Moving quietly, I took the straight-backed chair and placed it before the window. She took no notice of me as I sat down to face her. She wore a plain cotton housecoat over a pink silk slip. Her open-toed sandals were glittering gold party slippers. Her toenails were painted red. But her matching fingernails had been bitten to the quick. Her gray-streaked brown hair fell in half-wild coils around her face and neck, even though her hair was clean and looked as if it had been freshly curled. Except for lipstick and eyebrow pencil, both drawn too boldly, she wore no makeup.

Yet even though she was disheveled, and her expression was utterly empty, I could see that she'd once been beautiful. Moviemakers and photographers talk of "good bones." In Juanita Tharp's face I could see what the moviemakers meant. The bones of her face made a beautifully sculptured whole: the classic American beauty, even in ravaged middle age.

But, stretched taut over the facial bones, her skin was dry as yellowed parchment, making a skull of the face. Beneath black-penciled eyebrows drawn in a wide, theatrical arc, her round mannequin's mouth was shapeless: a grotesque red-painted scar that looked as if it had been drawn for a stranger's face, not hers. Beneath the pink slip, her body was a gross, slack, sagging relic of something that once must have been exciting.

About to speak to her, I hesitated. Was the right word "Miss"? I compromised on the obvious, saying, "Ms. Tharp?"

Still no response.

I drew a deep breath, hitched my chair closer to hers and spoke in a louder, deeper voice: "Ms. Tharp. Juanita. It's Frank."

She blinked. Frowned. Turned her head, slowly seeking the sound of my voice.

"It's Frank," I repeated, leaning closer. "I've come to see you."

Uncertainly, her tongue-tip circled her lips. Then she pursed her mouth and squinted at me. Finally, with great effort, she said, "Frank?"

"Yes. Frank Hastings. I knew you in Los Angeles. Years ago. Remember?"

"Were you—" She frowned. "Were you at Warners? That Frank?"

I nodded. "Yes. Warners. I was with Warners for three years."

The black-penciled frown deepened. "Three years? All that time?"

"Well, almost three years. I should have said two years. Two and a half years, really."

"Oh. Yes." She nodded woodenly. "Yes. Two and a half years. I remember. I was at Twentieth for a while. And then Victor for a while. But just for a while. Just for a little while." She sighed and turned her head again toward the window. For a time she sat in an eerie, echoing silence. From somewhere behind me I heard the sound of a long, thin wail, then an answering wail. I remembered hearing, as a child awake in the night, dogs howling: first one dog, then another dog, and another.

Finally she began speaking. She spoke in a thin, halting voice, as if she were reading from a script and was uncertain of her lines.

"I was always pretty," she said. "I was always a pretty little thing. That's what Daddy used to say. He'd take me on his lap, and put his arm around me and tell me how pretty I was. And of course I always believed him. My daddy had

110

a certain smell. And I remember his hands. And his fingers, too. I remember his fingers very well, because I could look down and see them disappearing." As she spoke, she moved her bony, blue-veined hands slowly down her thighs until they touched the hem of her pink slip, stretched across her legs just above the knees.

"I always loved my daddy's hands," she said. "I always loved how they felt and how they made me feel. Even when I looked down and couldn't see them, I knew they were there. Because I could feel them." She spoke in a small, vague voice. It was a little girl's voice. Watching her, I saw the harsh, skull-like lines of her face soften. Her eyes were far away, blurred by distant memory. She was returning to her childhood.

"I could feel them," she repeated. "I can still feel them. First he touched me with his hand. Then his hand went inside. First his hand, and then the rest of him." As she spoke, I saw the fingers of her left hand disappear under the hem of the slip and begin stealing up the inside of her thigh. The flesh of her thigh was white, obscenely raddled. Now her right hand moved to the arm of the chair, gripping it hard.

"Daddy was southern," she said dreamily. "He came from Memphis. He never liked Byron. He used to take off his belt and beat Byron. I used to cry whenever I heard Byron screaming. And once I saw his blood on the floor. The drops were small. They were very small, but very bright. Very, very bright."

She broke off. Her breath was coming faster. Her dead eyes were coming dimly alive, as if a small spark of life were kindling deep in their depths. Now the hand was at her crotch. Her eyes were half closed. Her body was moving: rising, falling, beginning to copulate with itself—and with the incestuous memory of her father. Her lips drew back, exposing clenched teeth. Her little girl's voice began moaning softly. I sat silently, looking away as her moaning became more rhythmical, more intense, more focused. Until, finally, she had her orgasm. She removed her hand decorously, readjusted her slip and leaned back in her chair. Her sigh was a deep, shuddering sound that shook her whole body. Her eyes were closed. Watching her, I remembered the furtiveness I'd felt as a boy the first time I'd gone to a dirty bookstore and looked at the pictures.

I turned away until she began to speak again:

"My daddy's dead now. And my mommy's dead, too. She came in my bedroom one night when Daddy was there. She was screaming. She'd kill us, she said. And maybe she did, because now my daddy's dead. And my mother, she's dead, too. I always hated her after that night. So she died. I hated Byron, too, because he pulled my hair, and stole my toys, and made me cry."

She stopped speaking. Her eyes were open now, staring vacantly off across the manicured lawns to the foggy hills beyond. Her hands were quiet in her lap, fingers loosely intertwined. Then she began speaking again. Her voice had coarsened, no longer a little girl's voice but not yet a woman's:

"My mother died, but Byron didn't. I hated him, but he didn't die. So I went away. Far away, where no one would ever find me as long as I smiled at them, and let them touch me, and let them inside me, like Daddy. Because I was hiding, you see. I could always see them, but they could never see me. Not as long as I smiled and let them touch me. Because when you smile, you see, they never know you hate them. And they never know when you kill them, either. Not like Mother. She knew. When she was lying with her eyes closed, with white satin all around her and the organ music playing, I could hear her telling me that she knew. So I leaned over close, so no one could hear me, and I told her to be quiet and die again." She nodded over the memory. The death's head had returned to her face, her mask of insanity.

Suddenly she turned to face me. Searching my face with her empty eyes, she whispered, "I know why you're here."

I cleared my throat. "Do you?"

She nodded. Once more, pale fire kindled deep in her eyes."You've come from God. He sent you before, didn't He?"

"I—ah—"

"Didn't He," she suddenly hissed. "I know He did. I *know.* I can tell." Leaning forward, she spread her legs, saying, "Touch me, so I'll know. Touch me, and I'll tell you what you came to tell me, what Daddy told you to tell me when you came."

I realized that I was pressed back in my chair. Under my shirt, I was sweating. Irrationally, I was thinking that I should have sent Friedman to interrogate her. He understood the loonies that wandered constantly through the squad room. He could make sense of their ravings.

Friedman would know how to answer. But I could only shake my head, saying, "No, I can't touch you." I almost added, *It's against regulations.*

"Then you didn't come from God," she answered promptly. Indignantly flouncing, she turned away. Her body went slack. She'd lost interest in me.

"I came about Fred," I said. "Your son, Fred. I came to ask about him." I hesitated, then decided to say, "God sent me here to ask about Fred. He wants you to tell me where I can find him."

I saw her frown. "God? Sent you? For Fred?" She paused. Then: "Who's Fred?"

"Fred is your son, Juanita."

She shook her head. "No, Fred isn't my son. And he's not Daddy's, either. I know. I could have felt it, inside, if he'd been Fred. Babies squirm, inside. And so did Daddy. But not Fred."

"Juanita—Mrs. Tharp. I'd like you to think. I'd like you to remember that—"

"Think?" she suddenly shrieked. *"Think?* You come spying on me. You sit here signaling to them, and you want me to *think.* " She flung herself to her feet and ran to the farthest corner. Crouched down, cowering, hands thrown up over her

113

head for protection, she began to rave: "You came from *him*. You didn't come from God. You came from the Devil. I can smell smoke in your hair. I can hear flesh sizzling. You say Fred. But God knows better. And the Devil does, too. Because the Devil is Fred's father. The Devil, and no one else. He's sent you, just like he sends all the rest of them. But I can see through your clothes. You've got—"

The door came open. The orderly was in the room, gesturing angrily for me to leave as he approached her warily, hands outstretched, as if he were cornering a frightened animal.

I shrugged apologetically and left the room.

Sixteen

As I walked down the sanitarium's stately curved driveway toward my car, I saw the driver's door swing open. His face anxious, Canelli clambered out of the car—then saw me. Relieved, he waited for me beside the cruiser, saying, "Lieutenant Friedman just got off the radio. He wants you to call him right away. He says to use a phone."

"Let's go." I got in the cruiser and braced myself while Canelli jerked the car through a series of sharp, badly timed turns. Probably because Canelli had a long-standing disagreement with machinery, his driving was a series of skirmishes with the car, most of which he lost.

"There—" I pointed. "There's a booth."

"Oh. Right." He cut to the curb, muttering darkly when the driver of a white pickup truck leaned angrily on his horn.

I found a dime and dialed Friedman's private line.

"It sounds," he said, "like Frederick Tharp may have surfaced again. Susan Ryan just called. She's been attacked."

"Attacked?"

"Roughed up, I guess. I don't know whether it's any more serious than that. I told her we'd be right out. I decided to see if I could get you, since you've already talked to her."

"Where is she?"

"At home."

"How's she sound?"

"Terrible."

She took the photograph, glanced at it once, then threw it down on the coffee table. I could see her head and shoulders shake as she shuddered.

"That's him," she said. She reached for a dark-colored highball, gulped shakily and returned the glass to the table. Staring down at the half-empty glass, she said, "I'm glad they found you, Lieutenant. I—I know I'm going to have to tell you what happened if you're going to catch him. And I'm glad that I'll be talking to someone I know and like."

"Thank you."

She was sitting hunched forward in her chair, still staring down at the table. Her eyes were fixed. Her body was rigid. With her arms crossing her breasts, as if to protect herself, or warm herself, she was stroking each upper arm and shoulder with stiff fingers.

Finally, speaking in a low, cowed voice, she said, "Nothing like that's ever happened to me. I—I guess it's the penalty for living the kind of life I've always led. That's what I've been thinking about, sitting here and waiting for you. I've seen my whole life pass in front of me, as the saying goes. And—" She shook her head. "And it's not really much of a life. I mean, when you consider that my grandfather practically owned California, and my father practically owns the President, and when you consider that I spent most of my life reading about myself in the papers, then you'd think, wouldn't you, that when something like this happened to me, there'd be someone I could call besides the police." She raised her head, looking at me with a kind of timid entreaty. "I don't mean that to sound ungrateful, Lieutenant."

I nodded, saying quietly, "I know."

"What I mean is," she said, "that I don't really have any friends. Not anyone that I could call, and say, 'Come over, something terrible has happened to me.' And even if I knew where my husband is, which I don't, I probably wouldn't call him."

"What about your father?" I asked, probing.

Her smile was a bitter twisting of her mouth, painful to see. "I tried that once, when I knew I would be getting divorced. I went to Dad's office and sat down and started to tell him that Charles and I were going to split. But his super-private line rang. And that was that."

"Couldn't you tell your mother?" I asked, still probing. "Couldn't you tell her what happened today?"

"At the moment," she said sadly, "my mother happens to be drunk. The reason I know, I just came from a family dinner, so-called, at the old family mansion. Usually she paces herself to get through the afternoon. But today—" She shrugged.

"Is that when it happened? When you came home afterward?"

"That's right. Actually, it was a combination dinner and lunch, which is a family tradition going back to my grandfather's time. Every Sunday afternoon, we were required to assemble around my grandfather's table. It was a kind of state occasion, I guess you'd say. Grandfather talked and we listened. He told us what he expected of us during the coming week—and the years to follow, actually." She broke off, shaking her head at the memory. Then, drawing a deep, unsteady breath, she said, "So, anyhow, that was the occasion today. Except that it was a pretty pitiful imitation of my grandfather's dinners. My father was so pale and so sick that it was all he could do to keep his facade in place for the servants. And mother was drunk. Ladylike, as always, but still drunk. And James and I hardly said anything to each other—because we don't talk to each other much, not really. So, as soon as I could, I left. I excused myself and got in my car and came home. That was about five o'clock. For once, the sun was shining through the fog. When I got within a couple of doors of the house, I pressed the garage door

117

opener. This man was waiting for me. He was on the sidewalk, just beyond the house. He looked like anyone else, walking down the sidewalk. I looked at him—saw him—but I didn't pay any attention to him. I just waited for the garage door to go up, and I drove inside. As soon as I switched off the engine, he—he materialized beside the car. He had a— a gun. That's all I saw: that face, pressed against the window, with the gun just below it."

"So he has a gun," I said softly, speaking more to myself than to her. So far, Frederick Tharp had been nothing worse than a threatening voice on the phone and some words typed on white paper. Now he was flesh and blood: a man with a gun.

"Yes," she said, "he has a gun. And I—I'll never forget it, pointing straight at my face. The gun—the barrel—and his eyes, that's all I could see. It was as if they filled the whole world. His eyes, they were terrible. They were murderer's eyes. A madman's eyes. They were—" She broke off again, helplessly shaking her head. "They were terrible." Still shaking her head, she sat silently for a moment. Listening to her, I was remembering how she'd seemed when I'd first seen her: calm, assured, even a little haughty. Since then, since Friday, she'd changed. Violence and terror and a glimpse of utter evil had changed her. I'd seen it happen before, often. I could recognize the symptoms: that special shadow behind the eyes. Sometimes, eventually, the shadow disappeared. Sometimes it didn't.

"Did he say anything?" I asked.

She released a deep, tremulous exhalation. Then, painfully, she said, "He told me to get out of the car. And I— I did. I didn't have a choice. I got out of the car. Then he —he told me to go upstairs. And I—I did that, too." As she spoke, her eyes strayed to a small hallway that opened off the living room. Without doubt, they'd emerged into the hallway from the garage. In her mind, she was reliving the moment.

I watched her eyes as they moved from the hallway to the living room. "We came in here," she said. "He closed the hallway door behind us, very carefully. Then we came in here, in the living room. We—we stopped right there—" She pointed to a spot in front of the big fieldstone fireplace. "We stood right there, side by side, facing this way—" She gestured to the huge picture window that looked out over the city to the east. Glancing momentarily at the view, I saw a typical summertime scene, with fog rolling in over Twin Peaks and blowing down the slope to the flatlands of the Mission District, where it dissipated, letting the sun shine through.

"He began talking," she said. "He—he spoke very well, very articulately. It—it was as if he'd been invited, and he was being polite, telling me how much he liked the house, how impressed he was with the furniture, and the paintings, and the view. He talked for a long time. Or at least it seemed like a long time. And the longer he talked, the more   more normal it all seemed. And I thought that, maybe, after all, it would be all right. But then he said—" The sudden pain of memory made her stop for a moment.

"Then he said that he wanted to see the rest of the house. So I—I took him into the dining room, and then the kitchen. But I couldn't keep him there, in those rooms. Because he—" Once more, she shook her head. But, doggedly, she went on:

"Because he—he wanted to see the—the bedrooms. He—he made me go into my bedroom. And he told me to open the drapes. And then he told me to sit on the bed. I—I did. And then he stepped close to me. Very close. And he told me to—to open my mouth. I did. He raised his gun, and he put the barrel in my mouth. I could taste it—the metal and the oil. It—it seemed like forever, with that taste in my mouth. And all the while, he kept talking to me. And then—" She broke off. I saw her swallowing repeatedly. Her eyes were hollow and haunted, unfocused. "And then, he—he took the gun out of my mouth, and stepped back, and—and told me to get undressed." She spoke very softly, very precisely, as if an impersonal voice could make the scene she was remem-

bering less horrible. "And I—I did. I stood up and got
undressed. And then he told me to sit down again on the bed.
And then he—he put the gun in my mouth again. He held
the gun with one hand. It—it was in his left hand, I remember that. Because, with his right hand, he was unzipping his
pants and unfastening his belt. And then he—"

"Mrs. Robinson. That—that's all right. You don't have to
go on. I understand what you're telling me."

She shook her head slowly from side to side. "No, Lieutenant, I don't think you understand. I don't think you'll ever
understand."

"I—yes—I know what you mean. But I—I don't want to
put you through the—the embarrassment of telling me.
There are—procedures that we have, for this kind of thing.
We have people for you to talk to when you make your
formal statement."

"People?"

"Psychiatrists. And—and women. Social workers."

Suddenly she released a harsh, bitter laugh. "Social workers are for the poor, Lieutenant. You seem to forget that I'm
rich. And famous. And—" Abruptly she sobbed, a shattering
convulsion of her whole body. "Oh, Jesus," she moaned.
"Jesus Christ. It was so—so ugly. So terribly, unbelievably
ugly." She cried harshly, hopelessly, helplessly. Feeling like
a cheap voyeur, I sat motionless, watching her cry, head
bowed, hunched over her hands that were now clasped
across her stomach. She looked as if she were desperately
trying to hold herself together after receiving a mortal
wound.

Without conscious thought, I began speaking in a meaningless ramble intended to distract her from her desperate
sobbing. "It's terrible, what can happen. I see it every day,
every week, all year long. Someone goes through his whole
life without any trouble. Then, one day, some lunatic who
should never have been paroled, or some addict who needs
a fix, he comes up on you. And before you know what's
happened, you're lying on the ground, bleeding. You wake

up in the hospital. Or maybe—" I paused for emphasis. "Or maybe you don't wake up. Just last week, a seventy-five-year-old woman was opening her front door when some junkie came up behind her and hit her over the head and took her purse. She fell backward down some stairs, and she's been in a coma ever since. All her family can hope for is that she dies before they go bankrupt."

As I'd talked, the sobbing had stopped. She wiped at her eyes with the back of her hand, as a little girl might. Now, almost timidly, she peeked at me from lowered eyes. She sniffled, swallowed hard and finally said, "What you're doing —what you're trying to tell me—is that it could've been worse."

I shook my head. "No. That's not what I'm doing. If it happens to you, then that's the worst." I ventured a smile. "What I'm trying to do, I guess, is just—just keep talking, until you get it all cried out." I paused a moment, looking for a reaction. My reward was a small, sad smile.

"You're a very considerate man, Lieutenant. A very nice man. Somehow that—that isn't the image that a policeman has. Of being nice, I mean."

"I know. That's probably why I'll never make it to captain. In police work, nice only goes so far."

Now, almost without realizing it, we were smiling into each other's eyes. For a brief moment, I wondered whether her smile was an invitation: a declaration of desperation from a lost, lonely woman with too much money to have many friends.

I looked away as I cleared my throat before saying, "I'd like you to tell me what he said. Not the—the obscene things. But other things. For instance, you described him as speaking very well. Do you remember anything he said that could help me?"

"I—I'm not sure," she answered hesitantly. Then, frowning, she continued, "Except, as I said, it seemed at first as if he'd come on a social visit. As if he was a friend, or someone in the family. That's the way he acted. He was very urbane.

Very—very pleasant, in an eerie sort of way."

"Why do you say he acted like a relative?"

She looked puzzled. "I'm not sure that I know what you mean."

"When he phoned you, I recall your saying that he talked like there was some connection between the two of you. Do you remember?"

"Yes," she replied slowly. "And that was true today, too. He said things like, 'You've had it good all your life, but I've had it bad,' as if something I'd done, personally, had deprived him of things that were rightfully his."

"When you had dinner this afternoon with your family, did you tell your father about the phone call you received?"

"No, I didn't. I didn't have the chance. Actually, it was a very short dinner. Or at least the private part was very short. The French ambassador was in town with Senator Farber and a few others. They wanted to have their pictures taken with my father. So they were invited in for coffee, along with the photographers and a pool reporter. But, anyhow, I wouldn't have talked to Dad about the call. I'd been warned by Jack Ferguson. And when I saw my father, how sick he looked, I wouldn't've mentioned it to him even if Jack hadn't cautioned me."

"You didn't know, then, that your father had a scare last night."

"A scare? What kind of a scare?"

"Tharp put a note under his pillow. Or, rather, he had a chambermaid do it."

She was staring at me hard, straight in the eye. Then, speaking slowly and hesitantly, as if she dreaded the answer, she said, "Is that his name? Tharp?"

"Yes. Frederick Tharp."

"Then you—you know him." There was a note of accusation in her voice. If we knew him, she was thinking, we could have arrested him before he'd gotten to her.

"We've been looking for him all day," I said. "Ever since

last night, when your father gave us his name, we've been looking for him."

"When my father—" Her eyes widened. "My father *knows* him? He *knows him?*"

Holding her eye, I slowly, solemnly nodded. "That's right, Mrs. Robinson. Last night was the first time your father knew about the threats. When he found the note under his pillow, he demanded the whole story. As soon as he heard it, he sent for me. In private, he gave me Tharp's name. He didn't tell me how he'd gotten the name, and I didn't ask. But there was no doubt he knew Frederick Tharp was the letter-writer. As soon as he saw the initial 'F' for a signature, he knew."

"Why didn't you ask him how he knew—make him tell you?" But, even as she said it, she shook her head. Perhaps she was visualizing the scene, with me trying to browbeat her father.

"I'll try to talk to him again," I said. "I've got to find out how he knew. You can help me. If he knows what happened here, he'll cooperate. He'll *have* to."

She smiled bitterly. "It might surprise you to hear this, Lieutenant, but sometimes I have trouble getting through to my father. I have to go through channels like everyone else. Especially now that he's so sick."

"Yes," I answered, "that does surprise me." Without saying it, I tried to leave the impression that I didn't quite believe her. She didn't seem to notice the implication. Instead, she said, "God, it's all so—so grotesque. All his life my father has been at the center of power. He's used other people —manipulated them, bullied them, moved them like chessmen. And then he has a heart attack. One minute, he's the most important man in America. And the next minute, he's helpless. Powerless. And all because a single muscle quits working."

"Is he really that powerless, do you think?"

"You saw him. He's like a—a marionette. Jack Ferguson

and Katherine Bayliss pull the strings, and he responds."

"You don't much like either of them, I gather."

"No," she answered slowly, reflectively. "No, I guess I don't, really."

"What about Lloyd Eason? Do you like him?"

She nodded. "Lloyd's like a member of the family. He used to play with me when I was a child—push me on the swings and throw a ball for me."

I thought about what she said. "I can't visualize him playing ball. He seems—" I hesitated. "He seems like an ominous man."

She shrugged. "You see him differently than I do. I can see why. Lloyd's—" She frowned. "He's a mystery, in a way. Nobody really knows what he's thinking. I guess, when I was a child, he was like a—a big, wonderful dog who protected me. I just took him for granted, as you take your parents for granted."

I hesitated, then said, "Mrs. Robinson, I'd like to see your mother. Can you arrange it?"

"Yes," she answered. "As a matter of fact, I was just thinking that she might know something that could help you. After all, she wasn't always—" She winced, but went on: "She wasn't always an alcoholic. But you'll have to see her in the morning. Ten o'clock, say. That's her best time."

"Good. Thanks."

As I said it, she moved forward in her chair, unmistakably inviting me to leave. In response, I got to my feet.

"Thank you," I said.

Also rising, facing me, she said, "Thank *you*. I feel better." But as she said it, I saw her shudder.

"If I can help you," I said, "Let me know. There'll be guards posted, of course. Around the clock."

"That's fine. But I can't stay here. I'm going home. I'm going to go home and take a long, hot bath." As I listened to her, I realized that, ironically, in her distress she still thought of her parents' house as her real home. "When I get out of the bath, I'm going to tell the maid to burn my clothes. Then I'm going to get new clothes from my bureau at home —clothes that I probably haven't worn since college. And then I'll probably get drunk. Mother and I, we'll probably both get drunk tonight."

Seventeen

After I left Susan, I went to a phone booth and dialed Jack Ferguson's number, asking to be put through to Donald Ryan and explaining that Ryan had asked me to contact him personally and privately. Irritably, Ferguson replied that it was impossible. Mr. Ryan had had a "setback," and his doctors weren't allowing anyone to see him or talk to him. I tried Katherine Bayliss and got the same response. But she promised to tell the senator that I'd called as soon as she thought it was wise. Frustrated, I hung up the phone and decided to go home for Sunday night dinner with Ann. The hell with them all.

At ten o'clock the next morning, a stunningly beautiful woman with a melodic Scandinavian accent met me at the door of the Ryan mansion and escorted me to a second-floor sitting room where I was to meet Mrs. Ryan. I sat in a small armchair and looked around the room with its chintz-covered furniture, its glass-topped tables and its single floor-to-ceiling casement window that offered a view of the Golden Gate Bridge. The Ryan mansion occupied half a block of prime Pacific Heights real estate. Situated on the crest of the ridge that ran from Russian Hill to Presidio Heights, the mansion commanded a view from every room. Even the servants' quarters, over the huge garage, would have rooms with views.

I'd come to the mansion directly from home, so that I'd had time to linger over the newspaper and a second cup of coffee. On summer vacation, both Billy and Dan had slept in, so Ann had made scrambled eggs and bacon, and we'd eaten breakfast in a companionable Monday morning silence, passing parts of the paper back and forth across the breakfast table. Yesterday evening and again this morning both of us had avoided taking up the conversation we'd begun in bed on Saturday night when Katherine Bayliss had called. Yet I knew that Ann had been thinking about what we'd said—and hadn't said. For us, the time for decision was coming closer. Because if I moved out, back to my own apartment, we would lose something that we might never—

The door was opening. As I rose hastily to my feet, I realized that I couldn't remember ever having seen a picture of Belle Ryan. To me, she was as anonymous as her husband was familiar.

She was tall and expensively groomed, with the lacquered, frosted, shaped and painted look of the Elizabeth Arden women. Plainly, she was her daughter's mother, with the same boldly sculpted features, the same rangy, stylish body, the same high-fashion swing of hips and shoulders.

But as she came closer I saw the unmistakable damage that time and alcohol had done: the puffiness of the face, the thickening of the body, the uncertain movements and the uneasy eyes, avoiding mine as she gestured me to my chair. She was wearing a floor-length hostess gown of gleaming, rustling white silk with glittering gold trim, Grecian style. Her hair was carefully coiffed, softly shaped in a tinted golden halo. A thick chain around her neck complemented the Grecian motif. Her slippers, too, were gold.

She sat opposite me, across a small cocktail table. Immediately, she opened a crystal cigarette box and used a matching lighter to light a long, gold-tipped cigarette. She inhaled ravenously, as if the smoke were nourishment and she were famished. Her long, impeccably manicured fingers were shaking slightly.

Her voice was husky as she asked, "Are you with the FBI or the Secret Service?" She didn't look at me as she spoke.

"Neither, Mrs. Ryan. I'm with the San Francisco police. We're cooperating with the FBI." As I said it, I suddenly realized that I had no idea how much Belle Ryan knew about the threats to her husband. Until now, this moment, I'd assumed that she knew everything. But it was just an assumption, nothing more.

"I suppose," I said, "that Susan talked to you about what happened to her yesterday evening after she left here."

She nodded, drew more smoke deep into her lungs and said, "She told me this morning. She stayed here last night, you know." She spoke indistinctly, with a querulous note in her low voice. Her eyes were darting uncertainly around the room, unable to meet mine. Listening to her speak, watching her fugitive eyes, seeing her suck at her gold-tipped cigarette, I wondered whether Donald Ryan had assigned someone to dress and groom his wife and monitor her movements. It seemed possible, in fact probable. As an American institution, he couldn't leave anything as important as his wife's appearance to chance.

"Yes," I answered, "she told me that she was coming to stay with you." I hesitated, then decided to say, "I imagine that you're very glad to have her here."

"We saw Susan at Christmas time," she answered. "We're always in San Francisco, you know, for Christmas."

"Yes. I—I've read about your being here."

She nodded, but didn't reply. After one final lungful of smoke, she leaned forward and carefully ground out the gold-tipped cigarette in the crystal ashtray. Now she drew a deep breath and pushed herself back in her chair, crossing her long legs and gripping the arms of the chair with each hand. She was bracing herself for my questions. Momentar-

128

ily, she looked at me directly. Deep in her eyes, I thought I could see a small flicker of fear.

Or was it something else: some small, mute plea for help, or understanding, or compassion? Could she be a prisoner, an unwilling captive, held helpless within herself?

"Susan is terribly upset," she said. "Terribly upset." But she spoke without inflection, without apparent emotion.

Was she drunk? From what her daughter had said, I'd assumed that she didn't begin her daily drinking until noon. Yet tension could have caused her to change the routine. As I sat watching her, I was remembering the years I'd spent fighting the urge to drink—and losing. After a knee injury had ended my bobtailed football career with the Detroit Lions, and my high-styled wife had announced that she'd seen her lawyer, and my father-in-law had fired me from my make-work PR job, and my children's smiles had gone blank, I'd started drinking. Even after I'd crept back to San Francisco and retreated into the security of civil service, my last-ditch stand, I'd still continued to drink, waging a losing battle every night, locked inside a lonely apartment. For me, the moment of truth had come when my partner and I had disarmed a teenage robber. Without thinking, I'd put the suspect's gun on a window ledge. He'd picked up the gun and shot my partner in the stomach. That night, privately, my commanding officer had come to my apartment. He hadn't even bothered to close the door. He'd simply said that I could either continue as a cop, or continue drinking. But I couldn't do both. Then he'd turned and left the apartment, still without closing the door.

"Is Susan here now?" I asked, trying to start a normal-sounding conversation that might jar her out of her strange, empty-eyed lethargy.

"Yes," she answered, "she is. She's still asleep."

"I hope she'll be all right."

"Yes. I do, too."

I breathed deeply, sat forward in my chair and spoke in a firmer, more official voice. "Mrs. Ryan, I've come to ask

129

you some very important questions. Now, I'm sure Susan told you that your husband's life has been threatened, and that the same man who's been writing the threatening letters, Frederick Tharp, is also responsible for the attack on your daughter yesterday."

I paused, searching her face for a reaction. Except for a small, fretful frown that briefly disturbed the silken sheen of her expensive makeup, I saw nothing. She sat as before: motionless, posed drawing-room-perfect in her chair, staring fixedly at some faraway point beyond me. Frustrated, I drew another deep breath.

"When your husband finally learned about the letters, Saturday night," I said, "he gave me Frederick Tharp's name. I didn't press him, didn't insist that he tell me the connection between himself and Frederick Tharp. After all, he's a sick man. And, besides, all we had were vague threats, plus an effort to extort money from your husband. It wasn't trivial, but it wasn't especially serious, as these things go. Or, at least, it wasn't serious enough to warrant disturbing your husband unduly.

"But that all changed yesterday when Tharp broke into your daughter's home and threatened her with a gun, and attacked her. For that, if nothing else, we want Tharp, bad. But so far I haven't been able to get through to your husband, to find out how he was able to identify the suspect." Her blank face showed no reaction. Then I said quietly, "So that's why I'm here, Mrs. Ryan. I'm here because I've got to find Fred Tharp. I've got to find him before he does anything else. Like try to kill your husband." I let a slow, solemn beat pass before I said, "To find him, I've got to know more about him. And, especially, I've got to know what connection exists between him and your husband." As I said it, I took Tharp's picture from my pocket and extended it to her. Slowly, woodenly, she focused on the picture, holding it at arm's length. She frowned, then regretfully shook her head.

"I'm sorry," she said. "I don't know him." But still she continued to stare at the picture.

"He's twenty-six years old. He was born in Santa Barbara. He lived in Los Angeles for a while. His uncle is Byron Tharp, the owner of Trader John's. Fred Tharp has been in trouble with the law since he was a teenager. He was paroled from prison a month ago, about the time the letters began arriving. His mother is Juanita Tharp. She's insane. Totally insane."

"Juanita Tharp—" She said it dreamily, still staring down at the picture. But now her eyes had lost focus, as if she was searching her memory. Had the name rung a distant bell?

Or was she slipping off, wandering away through the dim mists of forgetfulness, thinking about the next drink?

"Do you know her, Mrs. Ryan? Do you know Juanita Tharp?"

"No," she answered. "No, I didn't know her."

Didn't, she'd said. Did she mean that somewhere, sometime, she'd known *of* Juanita Tharp?

"You know the name," I said. I realized that my voice was hushed, as if I were fearful of startling her out of her reverie.

She didn't answer. I sat silently for a moment, trying to solve the riddle of Belle Ryan's strange, almost eerie withdrawal. How could I get through to her? If she'd been an ordinary person I could shout at her, shake her up, threaten her. But raising my voice in the Ryan mansion was unthinkable. This was a hat-in-hand investigation. I was a mere policeman, a civil servant tiptoeing my way through the corridors of power, doing my best to—

"I used to hear about them," she was saying. "For years, I used to hear about them. At first I never believed what I heard. Because I was beautiful, you see. And rich, too. My father was a banker in New York. Daddy didn't really want me to marry Donald. Daddy was very intelligent. He always said that a financier had to know about people. Daddy called people his betting chips. He bet people, he used to say, like gamblers bet chips. And he usually won, too. Or, at least, most of the time he won. He always said that he only had to win fifty-one percent of the time, all other things being equal. That was one of Daddy's favorite expressions, 'All other things being equal.' " She nodded over the phrase and then repeated it once more, as if the act of repeating it gave her comfort. Her eyes were still empty, staring off at something far away: at some place of distant memory happier than the present.

"Daddy thought that Donald's father was a greedy, dangerous man. And Daddy was right, too. He said that Patrick Ryan wanted to run the country, but that he would ruin the country, because he ruined everything he touched, including his own son. They both knew President Roosevelt, my father and Donald's father. And I knew him, too. When I was seventeen years old, for my birthday, we went to the White House and I had tea with the President. We had our picture taken together, and the President gave me a necklace with a pendant inscribed to me. It was the best birthday of my life. I've never forgotten it. Daddy always used to say that the President never really liked Patrick Ryan. The President needed Patrick Ryan, Daddy said, but he never liked him.

"But—" She moved her beautifully coiffed head in a slow, resigned arc. "But I wanted to marry Donald. He was thirty-four years old, you know, when we got married. He was thirty-four, and he was already famous. He could've had any woman he wanted. He knew movie actresses, and English women with titles, and they all wanted him. I was only twenty-five, and I was still a virgin. But I got him." She paused, then said, "That was the trouble, I've often thought —that I was a virgin. Because I realized right from the start that I didn't excite him. I could tell. That first night, my wedding night, I knew that Daddy had been right. I'd made a mistake. But, of course, it was too late by then." She sighed, once more shaking her head. "It's so sad," she said, "how people change. When I was a little girl, I was always happy. And when I was planning my wedding, I was happy. President Truman called me the day before the wedding. Daddy was in his cabinet, you know. We talked for almost an hour, the President and I. But—" She sighed. "But that was the last time that I can remember being really happy." She paused again, as if she'd forgotten the thread of her story. I waited, hopeful that she'd continue. When she didn't, I decided to risk prodding her:

"There were other women in your husband's life," I said.

"Yes, there were other women. I always knew it, really. Even when I couldn't face it, I knew it. When we lived here in San Francisco, and I had my babies, I didn't mind. Donald's factories were down in Los Angeles, and he'd go down there once a week or so. He'd always stay for a day or two. Sometimes he'd stay for a week. And I knew that he had women down there. I hated knowing it, but I couldn't shut it out. At least—" She broke off, frowning. "At least, I couldn't shut it out without—" Once more she broke off, agitated by her own thoughts. I knew what she was thinking. She was remembering the time during her life when she began drinking. She was remembering the loneliness and the desperation and the endless pain of defeat. She was remembering the long, blurred nights and the stark, cruel days that always followed.

"And then," she said, "Donald went into movies and TV in Hollywood. He kept the aerospace business, of course. But that was in the early fifties, and my father-in-law told him to get into TV. So he did. He always did what his father told him.

"So then—" She sighed regretfully. Her moment of agitation had passed, and she'd once more succeeded in detaching herself from the story she was telling. "So then, because it was Hollywood and the newspapers loved to write about the movie stars, I began to read things in the paper about Donald. They were only hints, of course, in the gossip columns. But I knew, and everyone else did too. Of course, Donald didn't like it. He was furious. He ruined one of the columnists. Her name was Hilda Ware, and Donald arranged it so that Hilda Ware couldn't find a job."

"Hilda Ware . . ."

In the fifties, Hilda Ware had been world-famous.

133

"She was very bitter," Belle was saying. "She was ruined, and she was bitter. So every once in a while she'd call me or send me a note. They were always anonymous notes. But of course I always knew who sent them."

Anonymous notes . . .

"She'd tell you about your husband's lovers," I said. "Was that it?"

"Yes. That's where I first heard about Juanita Tharp, from one of those notes. There were other names, of course. But the reason I remember Juanita Tharp's name is because the note said that she had a baby. She went to Santa Barbara, and she had a baby. That's what the note said."

"You mean—" I realized that I could hardly bring myself to say it: "You mean that Juanita Tharp's baby was—the father was—" I couldn't finish it.

Calmly, almost serenely, she nodded, saying softly, "The father was Donald. Yes. At least, that's what the note said. Of course, I never showed the note to Donald. He would have been furious if I'd showed it to him. Simply furious."

Eighteen

I'd parked across the street from the massive verdigris gates that led into the Ryan mansion. All I could think about, crossing the street to my car, was that I had to get back to the Hall and find Friedman. Together, we must try to decide how to deal with the possibility that Frederick Tharp was Donald Ryan's bastard son.

Already, in the minutes that followed my interview with Belle Ryan, I'd become hopelessly confused just considering the possibilities. What if we found Frederick Tharp and arrested him for committing sodomy upon the person of his half-sister, and for attempted extortion on the person of Donald Ryan, his natural father? How would the media handle the story? How would Ryan's staff handle it?

No one could predict where it would go, or where it would end. But, at that moment, one person could decide how it would start. Me. Sitting in my cruiser and staring blankly off toward the orange spires of the Golden Gate Bridge rising above a billowing blanket of white ocean fog, I was the keeper of confidential information that, if made public, could ruin Ryan's career.

But the spot I was in could be dangerous. If I decided to

keep the secret, helping Ryan avoid a scandal, and if Tharp were arrested for trying to kill Ryan, then it would become obvious that I'd been guilty of suppressing evidence, concealing a motive for murder. If, on the other hand, I put the secret on record, and the media ran with it, my career could be finished.

Either way, I lost.

There was only one solution: buck the problem upstairs. I would tell Friedman, and Friedman and I would tell Chief Dwyer. It was the only way I could protect myself, by putting Dwyer between me and Ryan.

At the thought, I realized that I was sighing. By the book —by the civil service system of survival—everything was simple.

As I reached for my microphone, I saw a black Cadillac sedan turn into the street ahead of my car and come slowly toward me, on the opposite side of the street. As part of my security briefing, I'd been told that Ryan's staff would be using a fleet of four identical black limousines to shuttle all of them, in addition to his family and various dignitaries, between the Fairmont, the Ryan mansion, the airport and, later, the newly dedicated Donald A. Ryan Federal Building.

Now the Cadillac was swinging toward the center of the street, preparing to turn right into the Ryan driveway. As it drew even with me, I recognized the stolid face of the driver. It was Lloyd Eason.

I sounded my horn and waved urgently, beckoning for him to join me. He looked at me, nodded impassively and stopped in front of the huge gates. One of the two gates swung open and a man emerged, one of Ryan's staff. Eason got out of the Cadillac, spoke briefly to him and then crossed the street to my car. I swung the passenger door open. "I've been trying to get you," I said. "I left a message at the hotel."

"And I left a message for you," he said, "just about an hour ago at police headquarters." He turned his big body in the passenger's seat, half facing me. The movement stretched

136

the dark cloth of his jacket across the bulge of a shoulder holster beneath his left armpit.

"You carry a gun."

"Yes. I've carried one for years."

"What kind do you carry?"

"It's a Colt .45, the automatic."

"You couldn't do better."

He didn't reply, but only stared at me with his dark, still eyes. Waiting.

"How's the senator feeling?" I asked.

Eason raised his big shoulders, shrugging. "He should retire. He should've retired when he had the heart attack."

"I agree. Then all of this would be simplified. Doesn't he know that?"

"He has responsibilities."

"I know. But he can't discharge them."

"He tries."

I studied him silently for a moment. His expression didn't change. His eyes never left mine.

"Saturday night, Eason, when the senator called me, I gathered that only you and Katherine Bayliss knew that he sent for me. Is that right?"

"I believe so," he answered, speaking in a slow, even voice. "Did you find him? Frederick Tharp?"

I let another moment of silence pass before I said, "So he told you about Tharp—told you his name."

He nodded.

"When?"

"Yesterday—Sunday." Then, reproachfully, he added, "The senator was waiting for you to call yesterday."

"I wanted to see whether I could find Tharp before I called him. Then later when I tried to get through to the senator, I couldn't do it. Doctor's orders."

"Yes—" He nodded again. "The senator had a bad night." He paused, then asked, "*Did* you find him?"

"I think that I should talk to Senator Ryan about what I

found. I'm not trying to put you down. It's just that the senator wanted me to report to him directly. What he does after that is up to him."

Instead of replying, he reached into an inside pocket and produced a plain white envelope, which he silently handed to me. "Lieutenant Hastings" was written across it in big, decisive script. And in the lower left-hand corner: "Eyes Only." I ripped open the envelope and took out a single sheet of stationery imprinted simply *Senator Donald A. Ryan, The Senate Office Building, Washington, D.C. 20002.* The message was brief and to the point.

Lieutenant Hastings:

Regarding the matter we discussed on Saturday night, I would like you to communicate your findings to Lloyd Eason, who will relay them directly to me.

The signature, *D. A. Ryan,* was done with a flourish, matching the inscription on the envelope.

I reread the letter, refolded it and tapped it against the steering wheel.

"What this tells me," I said, "is that you're the senator's closest confidant. When the chips are down, it's you that he trusts."

He looked at me for a moment with his opaque eyes. Then, quietly, he said, "I've been with the senator for almost thirty years. His father hired me to look after him. That's what I do. I look after him. It's my job."

"You live with him, you told me. Wherever he is, you're with him."

"Yes."

"No days off?"

"Once in a while."

"You have no wife? No family?"

He blinked and seemed to wince. But his voice was still

steady and calm as he answered quietly, "No. No family. My wife died."

"How old are you, Mr. Eason?"

"Fifty-six, next month."

"So you were about twenty-six when you went to work for the Ryans."

"Yes." He paused, then frowned. "Why're you asking?"

"I just want to find out who I'm dealing with, that's all." I gestured with the folded letter. "This tells me to turn over what I've found to you. As it happens, I've discovered some things that, potentially, could be pretty important—pretty devastating, in fact, for the senator. I want to know that I'm not making a mistake telling you."

He pointed to the letter. "That should tell you that you aren't making a mistake."

"Except that I'm not sure how much the senator expected me to find out," I answered. "And, besides, I'm not sure how much I'm authorized to tell without orders from my superiors. I don't work for the senator, you know. I'm an officer of the law. Certain things I can reveal before an indictment has been rendered, but certain things I can't. I'd prejudice the D.A.'s case if I said too much."

He didn't reply, but only looked at me.

I decided to try to split the difference: tell him part of what I'd discovered and let the rest of it go unsaid, at least until I could talk with the senator privately.

"All right," I said, hopeful that I sounded resigned to telling the whole truth, "here it is. We discovered that Frederick Tharp is a habitual criminal. He's been in trouble since he was a teenager. He's been in prison until about a month ago, when he was paroled into the custody of his uncle, Byron Tharp. Byron Tharp lives in San Francisco and owns Trader John's, which is a well-known nightclub here. Fred lived with his uncle and worked at Trader John's. However, about a week ago he disappeared and hasn't been seen since —except for yesterday evening after Susan returned from her family dinner." I gestured to the mansion.

"Yesterday?" Eason said. "Susan saw him yesterday?"

I nodded. "He was waiting for her when she got home. He had a gun. He made her go into her house with him through the garage. He terrorized her and then forced her into giving him oral sex."

"He—Susan—" He couldn't finish it. He sat stiffened with rage, fists clenched on his knees, lips drawn back from gritted teeth. In the depths of his dark, obsidian eyes, I saw a small, murderous gleam.

"Where's Susan now?" He spoke in a tight voice, as if his silent rage were choking him. His eyes held mine, remorselessly.

"She's with her mother." Once more, I gestured to the bronze gates. His Cadillac, I noticed, was gone. Someone had driven it inside the compound.

"With her mother?" Surprised, he let his gaze follow mine.

"She didn't want to stay in her own house, not after what happened. It's understandable."

"But is she—is she all right?" He was still looking fixedly toward the Ryan mansion.

"She'll be all right, I think. These things take time. She had a hell of a shock." I watched him, waiting for him to speak. When he remained silent, still staring across the street with his smoldering eyes, I said quietly, "What can you tell me about a woman named Juanita Tharp?"

At first I thought he hadn't heard me. Then slowly he turned to face me fully. He was frowning. Was it a frown of puzzlement? Or was it something else? I couldn't decide.

"Juanita Tharp," I prompted. "She's Frederick Tharp's mother. She's about fifty years old, maybe more. She used to be an actress, I think."

He shook his head. "No," he answered, "I never heard of her."

"You're sure?"

Eason nodded. "I'm absolutely sure." Then suddenly he turned away, opening the door. "I've got to go," he said.

140

"I've got to see Susan. I've got to help."

"Don't forget," I said as he stepped out onto the sidewalk, "I want to talk to the senator. The sooner the better."

He didn't reply, didn't look back as he strode purposefully across the street; a big, burly man in an ill-fitting blue suit, walking with grim, menacing resolution.

Nineteen

"What we've got here," Friedman said, "is one very, very hot potato."

"I know—" Irritably, I finger-flicked a corner of the manila folder marked "Donald Ryan." The folder was one of three, each one bulging with meaningless directives and fruitless interrogation reports.

"Obviously," Friedman said, "we've got to cover our asses. If we sit on information that establishes a connection between Ryan and Tharp, we're asking for trouble. Like legal trouble for concealing evidence."

"But if the information gets out, and we're the cause, we could be in even more trouble."

"So, like I said, we cover our asses. Let's buck it up to Dwyer and then have lunch."

I studied him for a moment. Normally Friedman hated to call his superiors into a case. For as long as I'd known him, he'd been engaged in a guerrilla war with the "politicians," as he called them. Which, translated, meant anyone with authority over Friedman.

"That's pretty offhand," I said finally. "It doesn't sound like you."

He shrugged. "Whenever I'm trying to help someone who

142

doesn't want to be helped, I lose interest."

"You don't think Ryan wants to be helped?"

"Not if it means blurring his precious public image."

"I'm beginning to think," I said slowly, "that he doesn't have much to sell except his image. Which is why he has to be so careful."

Friedman snorted contemptuously. "Politicians," he grunted. It was his most damning epithet. He sat staring moodily at the papers on my desk, then said, "When you talked to Lloyd Eason, did he say much about himself—about his past?"

"I'm not sure what you mean."

"Just for the hell of it," Friedman said, "I decided to run Ferguson, Katherine Bayliss and Lloyd Eason through the FBI central computer." As he spoke, he opened the folder I'd been toying with and extracted a printout sheet. "And guess who killed his wife back in 1947?"

"Eason?" I asked.

"Right. Eason."

"What was the charge?"

"Originally, second-degree murder. He copped a plea and fell for involuntary manslaughter. At the time he was working for Patrick Ryan, Donald's father, right here in San Francisco. In fact, when I saw this—" He gestured to the printout sheet. "I even remembered the case vaguely. It was right after the war. Eason was a sergeant in the Marines, a war hero. He found his wife in bed with another man. There was a fight, and Eason killed both of them with his bare hands. The man, he really messed up. Beat him to a pulp and killed him with one of those Marine Corps chops to the windpipe that collapses the trachea. You know, like they show in the training films but no one really does."

I took the printout sheet and glanced at it. Aside from the usual officialese, there was nothing that described the crime.

"How do you know the details?" I asked. "Do you remember them from the papers?"

He pointed to the line marked "arresting officer." The

name was "Roger Sobel, Inspector First Grade." It was vaguely familiar.

"Sobel retired about fifteen years ago," Friedman said. "He's raising grapes down in Hollister. I called him this morning after I heard from the FBI."

"How'd Eason get the charge reduced?"

"According to Sobel, it was one of those unwritten law things. In fact, if it'd just been the other man that died, he probably never would've gone to trial. No question, there was a fight. But the wife died from a blow to the head. Eason claimed it happened during the fight when she climbed on his back and he threw her off and she struck her head on the corner of a table."

"Did he serve any time?"

"No. He got probation."

"He must've had a good lawyer."

"The best. Patrick Ryan picked up the whole tab according to Sobel. Also, that was right after the war, don't forget. Eason's war record helped—a lot. And his—"

My phone rang.

"This is Culligan, Lieutenant. I'm down at the Brentwood Sanitarium. Lieutenant Friedman told me to come out here and do some checking. Is he with you?"

"Yes." I gestured for Friedman to pick up my extension phone. "Go ahead. He's on."

"Well," Culligan said sourly, "I had a hell of a time getting any answers out here. I mean, it was like pulling teeth. But finally, after I threatened to subpoena their records, I found out that Juanita's brother Byron pays her bills, which average about two thousand a month."

"That's it?" I asked.

"That's it," he answered.

I glanced across the desk at Friedman, who said into the phone, "Why don't you get a court order to look at Byron Tharp's bank account, Culligan?"

"Do you know which bank?"

Friedman looked questioningly at me, and I took over the

conversation. "No, I don't, Culligan. He's in the phone book, and he owns Trader John's down on the waterfront. Find him and ask where he banks."

"What if he doesn't cooperate? Should I lean on him?"

"No, don't lean on him. Let me know if he doesn't cooperate."

"Right." Abruptly, he hung up. Culligan didn't believe in the amenities.

Immediately after Friedman and I both put down the receivers, my phone rang again.

"This is Byron Tharp, Lieutenant."

"Oh—" Surprised, I gestured for Friedman to pick up the extension again as I said, "What can I do for you, Mr. Tharp?"

"You can find my car," he snapped. "Fred stole it. The bastard."

"Are you sure he stole it?"

"Of course I'm sure. It was taken out of my garage. Right out of my garage. And he had the keys to the garage when he disappeared."

"That's not exactly proof that—"

"Jesus Christ," he interrupted furiously, "he was *seen* last night about midnight. One of the tenants saw him. That's what I'm trying to *tell* you. I *know* it was him."

"What kind of a car is it?" I reached for a pencil and paper.

"It's a metallic green Datsun 280 ZX. And it's brand-new. Christ," he grated, "If I ever get my hands on that—"

"Do you know your license number?"

"Of course I do. It's CVC 916."

"All right. I'll get this on the air right now." I paused, then said, "While I've got you, I'd like to ask you a favor."

"A favor?" he repeated truculently. "What kind of a favor?"

"I'm trying to tie the loose ends of this case together, and I'd like to have the name of your bank, if you don't mind."

A short silence followed. Then: "You want my bank?" He spoke carefully, cautiously.

"If you don't mind." As I spoke, I looked at Friedman who was shaking his head. He was betting Tharp wouldn't cooperate.

"Why do you want my bank? What's that got to do with anything?"

"It's just routine, Mr. Tharp." Hearing myself say it, I realized that the explanation sounded lame, unconvincing. I should have waited to ask the question until I'd thought of an angle.

"I don't know," Tharp was saying in my ear. "I'm not in the habit of giving out that information."

"It's up to you. It's just routine, like I said."

"Yeah. Well, let me think about it then. But, meanwhile, get my goddamn car back, will you?"

"Right. Where can I reach you?"

"Either here at home, or else at the club. I'm usually there from six o'clock until it closes. I just got up about an hour ago, which is why I didn't know the car was missing until now."

"I understand. We'll be in touch, Mr. Tharp. I'll have the car on the air in two minutes."

"Good. Thanks." He said it grudgingly, speaking in his normal voice, harsh and unfriendly.

"You're welcome," I answered shortly, frowning at the phone.

But Friedman was smiling as I ended the call. "All we've got to do," he said, "is contact the D.M.V. If he registered the Datsun and paid by check, or if he got any traffic tickets and paid by check, the clearing house numbers will be in the computer. We've got the license number. That's all we need."

"By God, you're right. I should've thought of that and saved a lot of talking."

"And then, after we've done that," Friedman said, "let's turn out the troops and find that Datsun—with Tharp inside, maybe."

Twenty

Over lunch, Friedman and I decided that we would sit on Belle Ryan's revelation until I'd made one last effort to contact Donald Ryan, putting the question of Frederick Tharp's parentage to him face to face. But even as we made our decision, I could foresee problems. Would I tell Ryan that his own wife was the source of the rumor? Would I try to stonewall it, fencing with one of the most powerful men in the country?

We'd finished lunch and were still arguing strategy as I pushed open the door marked "Reception Room, Inspectors' Division." Looking like a high-styled celebrity dressed for a diplomatic reception, Katherine Bayliss sat beside the receptionist's desk, pointedly apart from the ordinary victims of crime and violence waiting to make their statements, or lodge their complaints, or endure their interrogations.

I nodded to Katherine Bayliss, at the same time questioning the receptionist with a glance. Yes, the lady was waiting for me.

"Who," Friedman breathed, "is that sexy-looking creature?"

"That's Katherine Bayliss."

"Incredible," Friedman muttered. "Absolutely incredible. There's nothing more attractive than a woman over forty who's kept herself together."

"You want to sit in?"

I saw him steal another look at her, then shake his head regretfully. "No. But tell her she has an admirer, will you?" He turned down the private hallway to his own office. I greeted Katherine Bayliss, waited for the receptionist to press the button that unlatched the swinging divider that separated the desk from the reception room, and gestured for Katherine to precede me down the hallway to my office.

"I hope you didn't have to wait long," I said, surreptitiously taking my gun from my hip and slipping it into a desk drawer as I settled into my swivel chair.

"Not long," she said. "Ten minutes. No more." She put her purse on the floor beside her chair and crossed her legs. She wore a beige wool suit with a simple white blouse, high-heeled pumps and sheer stockings. Beneath level brows, her dark eyes were calm and steady as she sat silently for a moment, watching me. It was almost as if she were the interrogator waiting for me to begin my statement, coolly alert for some sign of telltale discomfort.

"What can I do for you, Mrs. Bayliss?"

"I've just talked to Lloyd Eason. He says that there've been new developments." She spoke in a slow, measured voice. Her eyes were steady. She sat relaxed in her chair, composed, in perfect control.

"What did he say?"

"He said that this—this person, Frederick Tharp, had written the letters and that he had attacked Susan." She allowed herself a small, controlled shudder of revulsion before she said, "Is that true?" She asked the question accusingly, as if I were somehow responsible for the attack.

I nodded. "Yes, it's true."

"Is Susan all right?"

"I think so. I haven't talked to her today. It happened yesterday afternoon."

"It's an encircling movement," she said. She spoke softly, abstractedly. Her eyes looked beyond me as she said, "He's using Susan in a campaign of terror."

I sat silently, studying her as she spoke. Something in her manner suggested that she was speaking of someone she knew, someone she'd expected to act as Tharp was acting.

I leaned across the desk, waited for her gaze to focus on mine, then quietly asked, "Who is Frederick Tharp, Mrs. Bayliss? What is he to Donald Ryan?"

"I understood from Lloyd," she said, "that you know who he is."

"I know about his criminal record. But I don't know his connection to Mr. Ryan—not yet. Do you?"

"I—" She looked away, saying, "I'm not sure what you mean." But something in her voice, some small faltering of her aloof self-control, suggested that she did know.

I decided to change my tack, relying on an interrogating officer's most effective tool: a long, uncomfortable silence, accompanied by a cold, steady stare. I waited until her eyes finally dropped before I said, "You told me you first met Senator Ryan in the fifties in Los Angeles where you were a TV actress. Were you in any movies, too?"

She nodded. "I had walk-on parts in three movies, all of them for Victor. Then I got smart and went to work for the boss."

"Mr. Ryan, you mean. He owned Victor."

Again she nodded calmly.

I decided to try for a quick score. "What about Juanita Tharp?" I spoke in a crisp, impersonal voice, all business.

"Juanita—" She looked at me with narrowed, wary eyes. I'd surprised her, shaken her. "Juanita Tharp?"

"She was a starlet, too, about that time. Also at Victor."

She smiled straight into my eyes. "Lieutenant, I'm sure you must know that, literally, there were hundreds of—" She broke off, suddenly frowning. "Juanita Tharp. Is she—?"

I nodded. "Right. Frederick's mother. She could've been working for Victor about the same time you did, about the

149

time Donald Ryan took over the company. And I understand—" Mentally, I drew a deep breath and took the first step into the unknown: "I understand that she knew Donald Ryan. Personally."

Once more, her eyes narrowed. Her face was closed and cautious as she said, "Are you suggesting that there's some connection that exists between this Tharp woman and—" As if the thought was too incredible to put into words, she let her voice die.

I decided to take the next step—maybe the biggest, riskiest step of my career. "I've been told," I said, "that Mr. Ryan and Juanita Tharp were lovers."

Almost theatrically, her eyes widened. "You must be crazy," she breathed, "to say something like that. Crazy."

"I'm just repeating what I heard this morning. You're the first person I've told. And the last, until I can speak directly to Mr. Ryan."

"You'd tell Don—" She shook her head in sharp, blind disbelief. "You'd tell him that? You'd tell Mr. Ryan *that?*"

I sighed. "Mrs. Bayliss, I got Frederick Tharp's name from Mr. Ryan himself on Saturday night when I came to the hotel. The senator's the one who started me looking for him. And, in the process of trying to find Tharp, I heard that his mother—" I decided to let the rest of it go unsaid.

She sat rigid for a moment, obviously making an effort to control herself. Finally, speaking very distinctly, very precisely, she said, "You should realize that someone like Senator Ryan is a target for everyone, Lieutenant. The crazier they are, the more likely they are to attack him. It happens constantly. Back in Washington, we've got a whole file drawer filled with nothing but crank mail."

"But Frederick Tharp is different," I said quietly. "You know he's different. And so does the senator. He's no crank. And I have to know the reason for that difference."

"But why? *Why?*"

"Because, in my business, we look for connections. That's

how we establish motives. And I think the connection between Donald Ryan and Frederick Tharp might constitute a motive for what Tharp's doing—and might do."

"And I think it's preposterous." She spoke coldly, viciously.

"Maybe," I answered quietly. "But police work is a guessing game, Mrs. Bayliss. We keep trying different scenarios until we get one that fits the facts."

Hands clasped white-knuckled on the arms of the chair, leaning toward me, she fought to control a furious tremor in her voice as she said, "I'd advise you to think about the consequences if you ever repeat this—this scenario of yours, Lieutenant. I'd advise you to think about them very, very carefully."

"Is that a threat?"

Suddenly she rose to her feet. She stood looking down at me while once more she struggled for self-control. Finally, cold-eyed, she spoke in a soft, sibilant voice: "Yes, Lieutenant, that is definitely a threat." She turned to the door and left the office.

I drew a long, weary breath and was about to dial Friedman's interoffice number when the phone rang.

"It's Culligan, Lieutenant."

"Yeah, Culligan—" I heaved another sigh. Whenever I fought with a woman, win or lose, I felt drained. Probably because, mostly, I lost.

"I'm down at Tharp's bank," he said. "And maybe I've got something."

"Already?" I asked, surprised. "Do you have a court order?"

"Whatever all this is about," he said, "the word must be out. The judge made a call. One call. I guess it was to the Chief's office. Anyhow, I had the order in a half hour. I couldn't believe it."

"So what've you got?"

"What I've got," he said, "is three thousand dollars deposited every month in Byron Tharp's account."

I felt a knot of excitement gather at the pit of my stomach. "And?"

"It comes from a Swiss bank," he answered. "The deposits go 'way, 'way back. They were two thousand a month five years ago. Then twenty-five hundred. For the last year they've been three thousand."

"He's making a profit," I said, half to myself. "Sure as hell, he's making a profit."

"What's that?"

"Nothing, Culligan. Have you got the name of the Swiss bank?"

"Naturally," he answered, offended at the question. As he spoke, my second outside line lit up.

"All right. Great. Come on down to the Hall, Culligan. And thanks. I've got another call."

It was Canelli. From the pitch of his voice, I knew that he had something too.

"They found the Tharp car, Lieutenant," he said.

"Where?"

"It's in a parking garage on Greenwich Street, right off upper Grant. It's one of those garages where you park for the week, or the month mostly."

"Are you on the scene?"

"No, sir. I'm right here in the squad room. I just got the word from Traffic, and I figured I should tell you right away."

"What's the name of the garage?"

"Russian Hill Carpark."

"Has Traffic got the car staked out?"

"Gee, Lieutenant, I don't know. I mean, I just got the call from Communications because of the alert you put on the car. So I'm at square one, you might say. Repeat, square one."

"All right. I'm going to put you in charge of this, Canelli. And I want you to understand this is important. *Very* important. Do you understand?"

"Yessir," he answered dutifully, "I do."

"What I want you to do first is make damn sure no uniforms show up around that car. I want it staked out by two teams of good plainclothesmen around the clock on my authority. I want them with their eyes open, and I want them out of sight. I don't want them parked across the street reading their newspapers. Tell them that I'm going to be checking the stakeout—which I will, believe me. Also, see if the people at the garage can identify Frederick Tharp from the picture. See if they talked to him. In other words, give it the full treatment. Do you understand?"

"Yessir, I understand."

"All right. Do it. Send one team out now. Don't wait until you get all the assignments made. Send out one team, set up the rotation, and then get out there yourself. And keep me advised. I'll be wearing my beeper. Clear?"

"Yessir," he said, "that's clear. That's very clear."

Twenty-one

"I think," Friedman said, "that we've definitely got to give the Chief a rundown. If Ryan's court jesters won't let you talk to the great man to either confirm or deny it, what choice have we got, if we want our asses covered?"

"Except that—" I hesitated. Then, to my surprise, I put into words the real reason for my reluctance to make Belle Ryan's rumor public: "Except that I feel sorry for Ryan," I admitted.

Friedman raised his eyebrows. "Sorry? That's like feeling sorry for Mount Rushmore."

"That's where you're wrong, though. If you'd talked to him, you'd realize that he's the victim of his own PR. He's a sick man, but he can't even admit it. He can't even lie down."

"Well," Friedman said, plainly skeptical, "it's your choice. Personally, though, I think you're asking for trouble if you don't tell Dwyer, and then the truth comes out later."

"That's assuming it is the truth. We don't know that yet."

Indifferently, Friedman shrugged. "Your choice, like I said."

"Let's get an appointment with Dwyer and see how it goes. Let's play it by ear."

"Right." He reached for his phone and dialed.

We were told to meet Dwyer in his conference room. When we entered, we found Dwyer sitting at the head of the big walnut conference table—and William Richter sitting at the other end. As I stepped forward, I heard Friedman's surreptitious disapproving snort. Suddenly he found himself facing his two prime antagonists.

"I was just going to call you in," Dwyer said, gesturing us to the table.

I took my seat and slipped a sheet of notes from my inside pocket. Across the table, Friedman remained silent, nodding first to Dwyer and then, barely, to Richter.

"We thought that it was about time we, ah, coordinated our thinking, so far as the Ryan case is concerned," Richter said, speaking in his precise, colorless voice.

"We were thinking the same thing," I said, addressing Dwyer. "That's why we called for an appointment. We wanted to bring you up to date."

"Oh. Good." Dwyer nodded cordially, at the same time touching the knot of his tie and adjusting his gleaming white cuffs. At age sixty-two, Dwyer was almost a stereotype of the successful Irish politician. His face glowed with ruddy good health. His carefully groomed white hair was thick and luxuriant. His eyes were a clear, genial blue. His voice was deep and rich. He always wore gray suits and ties, to complement his hair and eyes. His shirts were always white.

"What've you got?" Dwyer asked, still speaking to me.

After a glance at my notes, I outlined the developments of the last two days. But, because Richter was there, I didn't mention the possibility that Frederick Tharp might be Ryan's bastard son.

"Well," Richter said, exhaling quietly as he leaned back in his chair, "you've been busy, Lieutenant." His voice registered careful disapproval. His bureaucrat's stare was frosty. He was wondering how much more we'd discovered and weren't revealing.

"What about you?" I asked the FBI man. "What've you found out?" I tried to make the question blandly friendly.

"We've been working closely with Ferguson on the blackmail angle—the payment. Or rather the request for payment."

"Has there been a request?" I asked.

"No," Richter answered. "No specific instructions for payment. But just about two hours ago there was a phone call. Tharp—if it was Tharp—said to get the money ready in small bills and prepare to make the drop tomorrow, Tuesday."

"Who'd Tharp talk to?" I asked.

"He talked to Ferguson. Ferguson instructed his staff, finally, to put all anonymous calls through to him, no questions asked. And, of course, we had a man with him."

"Did you get a recording of Tharp's voice?" Friedman asked.

"Naturally," Richter sniffed.

"Well," Friedman said cheerfully, "maybe, between the two of us, we'll catch him before he can screw up the dedication. It sounds like it could all come down tomorrow. That's probably why he stole the car."

"That's the way I figure it," Dwyer said, nodding genial approval. Hands flat on the table, rings sparkling, he smiled at each of us in turn. "It looks like we're making progress, gentlemen. Good progress. The senator should be pleased. Very pleased."

None of us returned the smile.

Twenty-two

"I really think," Ann said, "that Billy could sleep past noon if I'd let him. And Dan, too, for that matter."

"As I remember, that's what summer vacations are for."

"Is that what you did?"

"Sure," I answered. "Didn't you?"

"You know," she said, "I honestly can't remember. I have a feeling that I did, but that I've forgotten. Which is what makes a generation gap, when you think of it. More coffee?"

"No, thanks. I had a cup while you were getting dressed."

She didn't reply, but instead got up from the table and stepped to the stove. She was wearing jeans and a checked gingham blouse, her favorite around-the-house outfit. Her tawny hair was pulled back in a ponytail and fell midway to her waist. As I'd done so often, I moved my eyes over her body, lingering on the particular tilt of her head, the small, squared-off shoulders, the subtle swelling of her breasts, the flare of her hips and buttocks. More than with any other mature woman I'd known, her body invited my touch. With Ann, as with no other woman, a casual touch, or a kiss, or the actual act of love were all of the same quality, differing only in the urgency of desire. And for her it was the same.

We'd never spoken about it in so many words. We'd never declared to each other, in so many words, that we were in love.

Yet the quality of the attraction we felt for each other had remained a constant, unchanged from the moment we'd first touched each other until now, this moment, when I was moved to get up and go to her and put both arms around her and draw her body intimately close to mine. If I should do it, she would respond. She would respond urgently, but gravely. Because, for Ann, the ceremony of love, before, during and after, was a serious celebration. She could sometimes be playfully bawdy, and sometimes she could tease me with sly, secret laughter. But her last word, and her final caress, were always serious. Always serious, and always—

In the hallway, the phone rang. As I moved quickly to pick up the receiver on the second ring, mindful of the sleeping boys, I checked the time. It was 8:15 A.M.

"Frank?" It was Friedman.

"Yes. What?" As I said it, I turned to look back into the kitchen. Ann was at the table, looking at me over the rim of her coffee cup.

"Juanita Tharp's dead."

"Jesus. How'd it happen?"

"I think someone broke into her room and killed her."

"Where are you?"

"At the Brentwood sanitarium."

"Any suspects? Any leads?"

"I don't know," he answered. "I'm not sure." Meaning that he couldn't talk.

"You want me to come out there?"

"It'd be a good idea. Nothing's been moved."

"All right. It should take me about half an hour. Maybe a little longer in the rush hour."

Except for Friedman and Bruce Taylor from the coroner's office, the small room was deserted. Twisted in an agony of violent death, the body lay on the bed. She was stretched on her back; her eyes stared at a point just beyond my left shoulder. In death her face was placid, no longer tormented by the demons that had disfigured her in life. Finally at peace, she'd reclaimed some of her lost beauty.

She was dressed in a plain pin-striped institutional-style cotton nightgown. As I stepped closer, holding my breath against the excremental smell of death, I saw a purplish bruise on her left temple.

Friedman waited for me to turn away, then said, "So far it's speculation, of course. But I think I have a pretty good idea how it happened." He spoke in a soft voice, unconsciously respectful in the presence of death. I waited for him to go on.

He pointed to the sliding glass door that led to the small private patio. The door was open about two feet. The patio was surrounded by a six-foot brick wall, unbroken by a door or gate. A straight-backed chair had been placed against the wall.

"On the other side of the wall," Friedman said, "there are three sacks of manure piled up high enough to let someone stand on them and get over the wall."

"Manure?"

He shrugged. "At least it's original." He almost smiled. But as his glance strayed toward the bed, he self-consciously cleared his throat, saying, "As I said, it's a pretty straightforward MO, at least on the face of it. There're five acres of grounds surrounded by an eight-foot cyclone fence. There's a big iron gate in front of the institution, as you know, for cars. That's closed at eight P.M. and can't be opened except with an electronic opener. There're two other smaller gates, one at the east side of the property and one at the west side. Both these gates are secured by a padlock and chain. Whoever did it simply brought along a pair of bolt cutters and cut through the chain."

"Are they drive-through gates?"

"The front gate is drive-through. The other two are pedestrian gates. He came through the pedestrian gate on the east side."

"Isn't there an alarm system?"

Friedman shook his head. "No, not for the east and west gates. There's a night watchman, but that's all."

"Where was he?"

"He was unconscious most of the time." Friedman turned toward a small bureau, and for the first time I saw a policeman's nightstick. It was encased in a plastic evidence bag. On the blunt end, I saw dried blood.

"Will he be all right?" I asked.

"He's got a bad concussion. A skull fracture, too. But he's conscious, and he'll probably be all right. He's at General."

"So how do you think the time frame went?"

"Putting it all together, I'd say that the suspect went through the east gate sometime between one A.M. and two. Obviously he was familiar with the terrain, and he was also very well prepared. He had bolt cutters and some kind of a pry bar, probably, for this—" He gestured to the sliding glass door. "Maybe he had a gun to disarm the watchman. It would make sense. He took a small path that led more or less directly from the east gate to the gardener's shed, where he got the manure sacks. I figure that, really, he was looking for something like a stepladder. When he didn't find it, he had to improvise.

"But—" He paused for breath. "But on the way, he came across the watchman. He used the watchman's own baton to knock him out. Then he hauled three sacks of manure about fifty yards to the patio wall here—" He gestured. "Each sack weighs ninety pounds. So you can see that he was pretty determined. Then he came over the wall, and pried open the patio door. He hit her on the head, possibly with something like a blackjack. He used a pillow, probably, to smother her. Then he put the chair to the patio wall, and climbed over and split. Nobody saw or heard anything. Except, of course, the watchman. And he won't be able to talk until this afternoon, if then."

"What about a car? Did anyone see him drive up to the gate?"

"Trees pretty much surround the perimeter of the fence," Friedman said, "so it would've been difficult to see a car in the dark, at least from inside the grounds, assuming anyone was looking at that hour. However, the area near the east gate is a popular lovers' lane, it turns out." As he spoke, he glanced at his watch. "Right about now, there should be a newscast out. Maybe someone saw something and will phone in. The victim was discovered at three A.M., when the watchman came to and started moaning. A night attendant found him and called the local police. They searched the grounds. When they saw the manure, they investigated and found the body. That was about four. As you know, we handle homicide investigations for Daly City. We were called about five A.M. Rafferty caught the call and gave it to Culligan, who was on the rotation. He called me at home. That, I regret to say, was about six. The local police conducted the preliminary investigation. Which is to say that they tried to preserve evidence as best they could. The reporters have already come and gone—one from the local paper, one from a San Francisco paper, and one from radio station KCBS, I think. And the radio reporter promised to broadcast a plea for information. So maybe we'll get lucky, like I said."

"How many men have we got here?"

"Culligan and Marsten and Holloway. They're questioning the staff. The photographers and the lab crew have already come and gone. The local police are working the grounds and the roads that go around the fence on the outside. There's quite a network out there, all dirt." As he spoke, he gestured to the small patio. "Why don't we go outside and let Bruce, here, get to work." He nodded to Taylor, standing patiently beside a small washbasin. He would make a preliminary examination and then co-sign an authorization for removal of the body to the morgue.

As we stepped out into the fresh air, I asked, "Will she go to our morgue or San Mateo's morgue for the post-mortem?"

161

"San Mateo agreed to a waiver. It took a little persuasion. The local D.A., I suspect, sniffs a chance for some pre-election publicity. But I put in a call to Dwyer, and apparently he pulled the right strings."

I was looking at the chair, placed beside the patio's six-foot brick wall. The chair was covered with fingerprint powder.

"Okay to stand on this?" I asked.

Friedman nodded.

When I stood on the chair, the top of the wall struck high on my chest. Experimentally, I stood on tiptoe and pressed down on the wall with both hands. If I jumped, I could raise myself high enough to swing a leg over. But just barely. I looked down to the ground outside the wall. The three plastic bags full of manure were still there, also covered with white powder. The topmost bag showed the imprint where the murderer must have stood.

"If you look to your left," Friedman said, "you'll see the gardener's shed. And just to the right is a path that the suspect probably took to get back to the gate."

Standing on the chair, I looked carefully at the surrounding area. The sanitarium was situated high on the slope of a low range of coastal hills that ran south from San Francisco. In recent years, the California real-estate boom had destroyed much of the pine forest that had originally covered the hills. But here, the pines had been left undisturbed, probably because the sanitarium had been built in a "green belt" where forests were protected by the state.

I looked again at the hard-packed ground beneath the patio wall. The lab crew had marked off the area with white tape. Soil sweeps would have been taken after the ground was systematically photographed. But I doubted whether either the sweepings or the pictures would help much.

I jumped down from the chair and turned to face Friedman. "How do you figure it?" I asked.

"How I figure it doesn't go much beyond the obvious. Whoever did it knew exactly what he was doing. He must've known exactly where to find her room by counting windows from the outside. Which is quite a trick, when you think about it. Also, he had to have been familiar with the inside of her room."

"Why do you say that?"

He pointed to the chair. "If he didn't know he could use that to get back the way he came, he would've trapped himself." He motioned to the top of the wall. "You're in good shape," he said, "considering your age. I'll bet you can't pull yourself over that wall without using the chair."

I nodded. "I know. I was just thinking the same thing. I was also thinking that this place doesn't really have much security, considering that it's a sanitarium. With a pair of bolt cutters and a little luck, anyone could get in."

"Right. I asked the administrator about that. He said that, first of all, they don't take violent patients. Basically, anyone who wants to go can go. There's a fence, of course, but it wouldn't stop anyone who wanted to leave. In fact, the barbed wire strands at the top are slanted outward, not inward. They figured the fence, and also the six-foot patio walls without gates, would be all the security they need."

"Do they keep a visitors' log?"

"Unhappily, no. They encourage visitors and want to make it as easy for them as possible. However, I've got Culligan and Marsten working on the staff. Maybe we'll luck out. The administrator, his name is Penziner, is sure she didn't have many visitors."

"I don't think we can say definitely that the murderer visited her."

He shrugged. "In this business, only a fool says anything is definite. But I think it's a lot better than fifty fifty that the murderer is familiar with the layout, inside and out. Also—" He pointed to the chair and the wall. "Also, we know that he must be fairly tall and fairly athletic. Otherwise, he wouldn't've made it back over the wall, even with the chair, let alone the manure sacks. Which, as it happens, aren't piled as high as the chair seat. Incidentally, speaking of manure, whoever handled those bags had to've gotten manure on him.

The pile of bags inside the shed was covered with manure, probably when one of the bags was cut open, or broke."

"All he'd have to do, though, is get rid of whatever he wore."

"You're in kind of a negative mood this morning," Friedman observed. "You know that?"

Ignoring the gibe, I said, "Any other theories?"

"Sure," Friedman answered airily. "It's obvious what happened. See, Donald Ryan has been secretly supporting Juanita all these years through Byron Tharp, courtesy of a Swiss bank. However, what with inflation and the high cost of maintaining two homes, and all, three thousand dollars a month got to be a problem. So Ryan hired a hit man to—"

The gaunt, stoop-shouldered figure of Culligan was stepping through the open doorway to the patio.

"Ah," Friedman said, regarding Culligan with a kind of owlish leer. "I can tell by his euphoric expression that he's made a major discovery."

To myself, I smiled. Culligan's long, gloomy, hollow-eyed face never changed. He always looked like an undertaker's assistant. Culligan had a nagging wife, a peptic ulcer and a twenty-six-year-old son who grew organic marijuana somewhere in Colorado. Long ago, Culligan had given up on the whole human race—the cops as well as the robbers.

"I've gotten through most of the staff," Culligan said morosely. "Or at least all the ones that have anything to do with visitors. And all of them seem to agree that during the past couple of months, say, she only had four or five visitors, all men. It was pretty easy to nail down three of the visitors. There was her brother once or twice, and her son a couple of times. And there was you, Lieutenant. And then, a few days ago, there was another man. Nobody seems to remember his name. But he was a big man, wearing a dark suit. About fifty, fifty-five. Someone said he looked like a KGB agent."

I exchanged a look with Friedman, then asked Culligan,

"When you say a few days ago, what d'you mean?"

"One or two," he answered. "Or, anyhow, it was just about the same day you came—or maybe the day after."

Again, Friedman and I looked at each other for a long, significant moment before Friedman said, "Okay, Culligan. Keep scratching. Try the nurses and orderlies. Get a description of that KGB type."

"Right." Culligan turned away and shambled off through the half-open glass door.

"I can tell you who he is," I said. "It's Lloyd Eason. Sure as hell."

"I figured." Friedman was staring off across the patio, deep in thought. "Christ, I was only kidding about Ryan's hit man. Or at least I thought I was kidding."

"You're still assuming that the murderer visited her beforehand, though," I objected. "But if someone was planning to murder her, he would've said he was visiting someone else, probably."

But as I said it I saw the hole in the argument. First the murderer must get the name of another patient. And secondly, an orderly would probably have escorted him to the strange patient, as I'd been escorted.

Friedman had another objection: "You're assuming that the murderer had already decided to murder her before the visit. Maybe he didn't decide to do it until after he visited her."

"What you're saying is that Eason visited her and reported to Ferguson, or Bayliss—or maybe even to Ryan. Then he came back and murdered her to shut her up."

"No," Friedman said, "that's what you're saying. Me, I figure I'll stay in this business until it's pension time."

"He could've done it," I said. "Honest to God, he could've done it. There's something scary about him. He's totally devoted to Ryan. Like a—a dog. If he thought she was a threat to Ryan, he'd do it, with or without orders." I realized that I was speaking very softly, awed at the thought behind the words.

"He's killed before," Friedman said. "We know that."

"Yes," I answered, "we know that."

For more than a minute, looking off in opposite directions, we didn't speak. Then Friedman said, "God, can you imagine the headlines if it ever went to trial? Can you imagine *Time,* and *Newsweek,* and the six o'clock news?"

Twenty-three

Driving downtown to the Hall, Friedman and I discussed
strategy. Assuming a fifty-fifty chance that Eason had murdered Juanita Tharp, how should we proceed? The first steps
were obvious: wait for the lab to report on physical evidence;
wait for more witnesses to come forward, ideally someone
who had seen the murderer at the pedestrian gate.

But waiting, Friedman pointed out, was a cop-out. Logically, our next step was to interrogate Eason, find out where
he'd been last night and whether witnesses could confirm his
story. If his answers gave grounds for suspicion, and if I
could convince a judge accordingly, I should ask for a warrant to search his person, his room and his car, looking for
physical evidence: bolt cutters with jaws that might match
the cut chain, a pry bar that might match the jimmy marks
on the gardener's shed and the sliding glass door—and traces
of manure that might match that found at the scene.

Friedman was still talking about the "horseshit connection" when I unlocked my office, and we walked inside.
Automatically, I began riffling through the small sheaf of
messages that had accumulated in my mailbox.

The first message read, "Contact Lloyd Eason at the Fairmont."

The FBI man stationed at the eleventh-floor elevators was expecting me, but I was surprised when we didn't stop at Eason's door. Instead the agent took me to 1101, Donald Ryan's suite.

Eason opened the door and let me inside. Dressed in gray flannel slacks, loafers and a soft white shirt open at the throat, Donald Ryan sat in an elegant wine-leather armchair. He was framed by large, richly draped casement windows that offered an eastward view of San Francisco Bay, with the sullen, boulderlike protrusion of Alcatraz at the left and the long gray line of the Bay Bridge to the right.

Sitting erect in the leather armchair, with his thick white hair dramatically combed back from his broad forehead, dark eyes alert, mouth firm, chin lifted in an attitude of command, Donald Ryan was the living, breathing embodiment of all the magazine and newspaper photographs, the same arresting figure from all the TV footage. Only the pallor of his skin hinted at the sick, saddened man I'd seen in this same room on Saturday night. His voice was deep and calm as he said:

"Sit down, Lieutenant." He gestured to a facing chair. "It's good of you to come so quickly."

"Thank you." As I obeyed, I glanced at Eason. He came to stand beside Ryan, awaiting permission to be seated. At a nod, Eason drew up a straight-backed chair and placed it to make a triangle with Ryan and myself. Eason sat with his feet flat on the floor, back straight, big-knuckled hands gripping the arms of the chair. He was looking at Ryan. His square, stolid face was expressionless.

Speaking slowly and deliberately in the same calm, controlled voice, Ryan looked me squarely in the eye as he said, "Lloyd just told me about Juanita Tharp's murder. I asked him to call you. Immediately."

"Good."

168

"The other night you proved to be a good listener, Lieutenant." As he said it, he smiled wryly, obviously recalling his Saturday-night monologue with mixed feelings. "However, as you know—and possibly knew at the time—there was a lot that I didn't tell you."

Looking at him steadily, I didn't respond. I watched him obviously gathering himself for the story he'd decided to tell.

"Some time ago," he began, "I spent a few years down in Hollywood making films. In retrospect, I did it because I was bored. Or, to give it a more positive cast, I was looking for new fields to conquer. In any case, again in retrospect, I think I was going through a kind of premature midlife crisis. I'd already made my mark in the aircraft industry, as you may know. I was married and had two children. But none of that was enough. It never is enough. Of course, I didn't realize that at the time.

"So, anyhow, I started to make movies. And, about that time, I began to play around—to have affairs; all of them, without exception, ill-advised. And the most ill-advised affair was with—" He hesitated. Then, firmly, he said, "It was with Juanita Tharp. It only lasted for a few weeks, actually—and I really have no excuse, except to say that, physically, she was one of the most exciting women I've ever known. She was beautiful. Absolutely breathtaking.

"However," he said, "she was also neurotic. I won't go into her past life—her psychotic mother, her absent father, all the foster homes, and all the stepfathers and guardians who tried to seduce her—and succeeded. Suffice it to say that almost immediately I realized that I'd made a big mistake. So I did what I'd done before—" As he said it, he turned to Eason, faintly smiling at the impassive bodyguard. "I made out a check to her, and gave the check to Lloyd, and asked him to deliver it. But—" Ryan shook his head regretfully. "But, with Juanita, it wasn't quite that simple, unhappily. That became apparent about a month later when I got a call from Byron Tharp." He looked at me. "Do you know Byron?"

169

"Yes, I do."

"Then you can probably imagine what he had to say."

"He wanted money. For his sister." I drew a deep breath. Then, holding his eye, I said quietly, "She was going to have a baby."

Smoothly, without visible emotion, Ryan nodded. He'd known I was going to say it. "Exactly. Byron was selling real estate then, down in Los Angeles. That was twenty-seven years ago. He's been collecting from me every month for twenty-seven years. He takes his cut and uses the rest to support his sister—and her child."

"Not your child. Her child."

Ryan looked at me steadily for a moment before he said, "I didn't want to contest his paternity, and Byron knew it. Even then, before I got into politics, I couldn't afford to do it, couldn't afford the publicity. For one thing, it would've meant a break with my father. He was a puritan, an unforgiving man." As he'd been talking, his voice had become steadily weaker and his speech slower, as if his voice were on a record that was running down. As I watched him, I wondered how much precious energy this interview was costing him and how much more energy he could afford to expend.

"Have you had any contact with your—with Frederick during the twenty-seven years?" I asked.

He shook his head. "No. None. It's been as if he didn't exist." As he said it, his eyes wandered away. What was he remembering—regretting?

"Then how did he know who you were?" I asked. "What decided him to come after you?"

"What must've happened," he said, "is that when Frederick got out of prison he somehow found out that I'd been supporting him—that supposedly I was his father. That discovery, added to the fact that his mother was institutionalized, must've decided him on this course of action—this attempt to punish me by extorting money from me."

"Maybe he found out from his uncle. Maybe Byron

refused to give him money and told him to go to you."

Ryan shook his head. "No. Frederick was Byron's golden goose. Or at least the secret of Frederick's parentage was Byron's leverage."

"Yes," I admitted, "that makes sense."

"In any case," Ryan said, "Frederick found out and, for whatever reason, he's decided to make me pay."

"And pay," I said, "and pay. You never end it with black-mailers. As long as they have a hold on you, they keep coming back for more."

Ryan's nod was a single wan inclination of his handsome head. He was tiring fast; my time was running out. "I know that," he said. "And, frankly, I don't know how this is going to end. Especially after the phone call I received this morning."

"Phone call?"

"Yes. Frederick called. Ferguson took it and told me about it. Apparently Frederick thinks I had his mother murdered. And he—he promised to kill me if he doesn't get the million dollars. Not just expose me, but kill me. He was raving, Ferguson said. Really raving."

"He's always said he was going to kill you, right from the first. It sounds like his raving might be staged, to put pressure on you."

"Perhaps." He spoke weakly, vaguely. Once more, his eyes were wandering away.

"Are you going to pay, Mr. Ryan?"

Instead of answering, he raised one hand in a kind of tremulous imitation of a papal parting benediction. Now, suddenly, his lips were pale. His eyes were half closed. Sweat glistened on his forehead.

"I'm sorry, Lieutenant. But I'm tired. Very tired. You'll have to talk to Lloyd."

With the words, Eason was on his feet, unconsciously putting his big, blocky body between me and his master. I rose too, nodded to Ryan and obediently followed Eason out into the corridor and then into his own room adjoining Ryan's suite. As he showed me to a chair, Eason shook his grizzled head. "He's sick," he muttered. "He's a sick man. He should retire now, before it's too late for him."

"You're right," I said. "You're absolutely right."

"It's his pride—the Ryan pride. All his life he's tried to be like his father and his grandfather."

"What about the extortion money?" I asked. "Are you going to pay?"

He looked at me for a moment, as if to make a final decision on my reliability. Then, plainly reluctant, he said, "Frederick Tharp called last night about ten o'clock. He said that the money was to be put in a blue suitcase, in bills no bigger than fifties. The FBI advised us to get the suitcase and bring it into the hotel through the lobby. They advised us to get twenty thousand dollars in old fifties, and they'd give us fake money for the rest to fill up the suitcase. Then they'll put a transmitter in the suitcase. It's about the size of a flashlight battery. They'll use that to trace him after he gets the money. And that's what we're going to do—try to catch him that way."

"Once he's caught, though, he'll disclose that his mother and Mr. Ryan—" I let it go unfinished.

"I know," Eason answered. "But there's no other way. Of course, Mr. Ryan will deny he's the father. He'll admit to helping her because he was sorry for her. That's all."

Looking him in the eye, I said, "If you're lucky, he'll resist arrest and get killed. With his mother dead, that would solve all your problems."

His gaze didn't flicker. "Yes," he answered steadily, "that would solve them. Except, of course, for the uncle, Byron Tharp. He knows too."

"That would only be hearsay, though. He doesn't have any real proof of parentage. All he has is his sister's word."

He nodded. "I know."

"Who besides you knows all this, Mr. Eason?"

He frowned. "I'm not sure what you mean."

"Jack Ferguson, for instance. And the senator's son, James. Do they know about Frederick—know that the senator's been supporting him and his mother?"

"No," he answered, "they don't."

"It's just you."

He studied me for a long, careful moment as his dark agate eyes slightly narrowed. Finally he said, "There were—arrangements to be made. Mrs. Bayliss made them—the financial arrangements."

"What it comes down to, then," I pressed, "is that you and Katherine Bayliss are the only people Senator Ryan trusts. Really trusts. Right?"

He didn't respond. He only looked at me. Waiting.

"Is that right?" I persisted.

"Several people work for the senator," he said finally. "They do different things. I'm in charge of security."

"And Katherine Bayliss does a little of everything."

Again he didn't respond.

"I gather that she's been with the senator for a long time."

He nodded, saying, "We came with the senator about the same time. In the fifties."

"She's a very attractive woman, Mrs. Bayliss."

"Yes."

"She's divorced."

"Yes. She married very young. Too young."

"Was she divorced, then, when she began working for the senator?"

He hesitated, then nodded. Possible meaning: the senator had been the cause of her divorce.

"What about you, Mr. Eason? Were you married when you went to work for the senator?"

This time, his eyes shifted uneasily as he answered, "I worked for the senator's father. Then I went with the senator. I told you that."

I studied him. Plainly, he was doing what I'd hoped he

would do: he was wondering how much I knew about him —about his marriage, and his wife's death. Finally I saw him draw a deep, slow breath. Meeting my gaze squarely, he said, "Do you know about the—the trouble I had, when I worked for the senator's father?"

"Trouble?" I asked, pretending innocence.

"I was in the Marines, during the war. I went through it all—Iwo Jima, Saipan, all of it. On my final leave, before I went overseas, I married a girl named Mildred Penrose. I— I shouldn't've done it, but I did. It was a mistake. A terrible mistake. And, besides that, I was wounded in the war. And I was—disturbed."

"In what way were you disturbed?"

"They called it periodic depression. And I—I couldn't always control my temper. I tried, but I couldn't. If it ever happened that I got into a fight, I couldn't always control myself."

"You'd try to kill the other guy?"

"Yes," he answered quietly, meeting my eyes steadily. "Yes, that's it."

"Were you hospitalized?"

"Yes. During the last year of the war, I was in the hospital for six months for my wound. Then, afterwards, I was an outpatient."

"A psychiatric outpatient?"

"I guess so. They called it an adjustment center. Mostly, I think, they just wanted to keep an eye on us for a year or two. At least that's the way it was with me. After about eighteen months, they phased me out."

"What was the trouble you mentioned?" I tried to make the question sound interested, but nothing more.

He sighed: a deep exhalation, infinitely regretful. "It was my wife. She was a tramp, a real tramp. All the time I was in the Marines, she was sleeping around. And afterwards, too. She never stopped. And so—" He began to shake his head, as if to deny the memory that still haunted him. "And so, one afternoon, I found her in bed with a man. He was a

bartender from a place around the corner. He was a big man
—big and tough. And he came for me. There was a fight. I
chopped him in the windpipe. He died in the ambulance.
And my wife, she died too. She—she tried to pull me off him.
I threw her across the room, and she hit her head on a table.
At least, that's what the investigators said."

"Were you found guilty?" I asked quietly.

"Yes," he answered, just as quietly. "I was found guilty.
I got a suspended sentence. Seven years."

Without knowing why, I said, "To me, you don't look like
a violent man."

"I'm not," he answered. "Not now. I'm fifty-six years old.
I'm a different person."

I nodded, sitting motionless for a moment, silently watching him. Once more, he remained implacable under my scru-
tiny. Finally I said, "How do you figure Juanita Tharp's
murder? Why do you think she was killed?"

Slowly, deliberately, he shook his head. "I don't know. I
thought her son might've done it."

"Frederick? Why?"

"For money," he answered. "Her money."

"But she didn't have any money."

"Didn't she?" he asked, still meeting my eyes. "I thought—"
He let it go unfinished.

"You thought she got money from the senator."

He nodded. "Yes."

I glanced at my watch, then moved forward in my chair
as if preparing to leave. I wanted him to think that I was
through with him, that he wasn't a suspect. "I've got to go,
Mr. Eason," I said. "Before I do, though, I have to ask you
where you were last night between midnight and three A.M."

For a moment he didn't reply, but only stared at me with
his inscrutable eyes. Then, without inflection, he asked,
"Why do you have to ask me that?"

"Because obviously the person who would most benefit
from Juanita Tharp's death is Senator Ryan. You understand?"

"Yes," he answered slowly, "I understand."

"Well?" I smiled as I said it.

"Well," he answered calmly, "I was here. Right here. I went to sleep about eleven."

"Alone?"

"That's right, Lieutenant," he said. "I sleep alone. Always."

I smiled again, thanked him and turned to the door. With my hand on the knob I turned back to face him, saying, "You visited Mrs. Tharp a few days ago in the sanitarium. How did she seem to you?"

"She seemed crazy," he answered. "I couldn't make any sense of what she said."

"Is this the first time you'd seen her in recent years?"

He shook his head. "No. The last few years, whenever the senator was in San Francisco and the newspapers carried the story, she tried to contact him. I'd talk to her. Sometimes I'd give her money."

"How much money?"

"Fifty, a hundred dollars. Whatever the senator gave me to give to her. Or else Mrs. Bayliss would give me the money."

"Was Mrs. Tharp always glad to get it?"

He nodded. "She was like a child in some ways. A little child."

"Did she drink?"

"I don't know. I don't think so. But she was always strange. Always."

"Did the senator tell you to visit her in Brentwood a few days ago?"

"No. Mrs. Bayliss did."

"Why?"

He shrugged. "She just reminded me that I should see her, like I always do when we come to San Francisco."

"And how did you find her? Did you notice anything different about her?"

"No. I told you. I couldn't make any sense of what she said."

"Did Mrs. Bayliss see her at Brentwood?"

"I don't know," he answered. "But I don't think so. You'd have to ask Mrs. Bayliss, though, to be sure."

"Thank you," I said, turning the knob. "I will."

Twenty-four

"I'm afraid I don't have much time, Lieutenant," Katherine Bayliss said. "This dedication, it's got us all running around in circles." She waved an apologetic hand, then gestured to a large sheet of paper that covered most of the Regency desk. "That's the seating diagram. Someone from White House protocol was supposed to be here to help. But the British prime minister is visiting the President on Sunday, as you know. So the White House can't spare him, apparently."

"I won't take much of your time, Mrs. Bayliss."

"Good." Sitting behind the desk, she pushed the diagram aside. She looked at me for a moment, then said, "I understand that they're getting the money together. Is that right?"

"I don't know. I'm leaving that to the FBI. I'm working the streets, trying to find Frederick Tharp before he goes for the money. At least, I was until now."

Her dark, gracefully arched eyebrows drew slightly together. "Until now? What d'you mean?"

"Juanita Tharp was murdered last night."

"Juanita—" Surprise—or shock—tore at her face like a spasm of pain. "Murdered," she said incredulously. "Does Don—does the senator know?"

"Yes. He called me. I've just talked to him and Lloyd Eason."

She sat motionless for a moment. The perfection of her features was frozen; her eyes were far away, empty of expression. "Jesus," she muttered. "Jesus Christ." She sat for another moment, staring at nothing. Then, with a visible effort, she recovered herself, finally focusing her dark, intense eyes on mine.

"Who did it?" she asked quietly.

"We don't know—yet. But the murderer took lots of chances and probably made mistakes. In a few hours, we should know something."

"In a few hours—" Once more, her gaze wandered away. But now her eyes were clear, calculating. "It's all coming down to just a few hours, isn't it."

"I'm not sure I know what you mean."

"I mean the death threats on the phone, and the extortion payment, and the dedication tomorrow—and now this. It's all—" She didn't finish it, but instead shook her head, as if to clear her thoughts.

"What I want—what I've got to have," I said, "is information about Juanita Tharp." I added, "When we talked in my office, you were a little less than candid about Juanita Tharp, it turns out."

Blandly ignoring the jab, she coolly asked, "What kind of information do you want?"

"Anything you can give me. For instance, how long have you known her? When was the last time you saw her?"

She frowned. "But I didn't know her. I never saw her."

With my eyes challenging hers, I delayed a bit before I said quietly, "That's not what Lloyd Eason says, Mrs. Bayliss. He says that it was you who arranged to pay her off."

"That's true. But I never saw her face to face."

"That's hard to believe. As I understand it, you acted for Senator Ryan from the mid-fifties until now, dealing with her."

As I said it, I saw her face close. The mannequin-like

perfection of her features had hardened into a stranger's face: all softness gone, all beauty frozen.

"Did Lloyd say that?"

"Yes, he did."

"Well, he's mistaken. I dealt with her brother, Byron."

"Ah—" I nodded. "Yes, that could be. But, still, you knew who Juanita Tharp was, I assume. You knew about her and the senator—about her baby."

"Yes," she answered, "I knew." She spoke very quietly, very cautiously. Her face was still closed. Still a harsh, stranger's mask.

"How did you actually pay Byron? In cash?"

"At first, yes. Later, though, I set up a Swiss bank account."

"When was the last time you saw Byron Tharp, Mrs. Bayliss?"

She shook her head. "I'm not sure. Ten, twelve years ago. Maybe more. I'm just not sure. However, about a year ago he called to say that she'd gone into an asylum. He wanted more money."

"Did you give him more?"

"Yes."

"Did you talk it over with the senator before you gave him more?"

"Of course. After all, it's the senator's money."

"Of course." I sat silently for a moment, then asked, "Who do you think killed her, Mrs. Bayliss?"

She, in turn, remained silent, carefully studying my face. Finally she said, "I have no idea. None at all."

"Her death could solve a lot of problems for you."

"Are you suggesting—" Her voice dropped to a low, ominous note that evoked all the power she could control—all the damage she could do to me and to anyone who threatened Donald Ryan.

"I'm not suggesting anything. I'm simply saying—"

"You're implying that we—the senator—had her killed."

"Mrs. Bayliss, that's not true."

180

"You're supposed to be helping, Lieutenant. You're supposed to be working for us, not against us."

"Mrs. Bayliss—" I drew a deep, tight breath. "At last count, we had fourteen men working on this case. Right now, right this minute, I've got four men, in three shifts, staking out the car that Frederick stole from his uncle. And, furthermore, we—"

"I think," she said, "that you should leave, Lieutenant. Go back to your—your cops-and-robbers games, whatever they are. I've got work to do. Important work." Across the desk, her eyes blazed. Her voice shook with suppressed fury.

"I've got work to do, too," I said. "I've got a murderer to find. And I'll find him, too. Believe me, I'll find him." I went to the door and left the room without looking back.

At the elevators, the FBI man told me that he'd gotten a message asking me to call Friedman at the Hall. I took the elevator down to the lobby and called him from a pay phone.

"What would you think," Friedman said, "if I told you that Frederick Tharp wasn't really Frederick Tharp?"

"What the hell're you talking about?" Ever since I'd left Katherine Bayliss, I'd been silently, impotently fuming. It was a relief to take my frustration out on Friedman.

"I mean," he answered, "that the original Frederick Tharp died two weeks after he was born. It was respiratory failure, apparently."

"Jesus—" Trying to comprehend it, I broke off. Then I said, "Are you sure? Positive?"

"I'm looking at the death certificate," he answered. "What happened, see, was that Santa Barbara sent us documents confirming what they'd said when we phoned them about Tharp. Except that, obviously, they don't match up. Interesting, eh?"

"Is there a birth certificate?"

"There certainly is." After a pause he added, "Under the circumstances, I figured that you might want to have a chat with Byron Tharp. So, to lighten your work load, I tracked him down. He's at Trader John's. He's expecting you."

"What'd you tell him?"

"Nothing, naturally. Except that there've been new developments."

"All right, I'm on my way. Anything else?"

"Not really. But I was thinking that as long as you're so close, why don't you stop by the Datsun stakeout? You know, inspire the troops. It's right on your way to Trader John's."

"Who's in charge of the stakeout now?"

"Canelli. I think he's inside the parking garage, ostensibly cleaning up."

"All right. I'll stop by."

"Incidentally, we tried to beep you."

I looked at the small pager clipped to my belt. The switch was in the "off" position. "My pager needs a new battery, I think."

"Hmmm." It was a skeptical-sounding response.

Twenty-five

Instead of driving into the parking garage, I decided to pull into a nearby loading zone. I would stay in my car for a few minutes, trying to pick out the two or three men, besides Canelli, who would make up the stakeout team. If I couldn't readily spot them, they were doing their job. If I saw them parked in plain sight, they would hear from me.

As I was using my microphone to clear my car with Communications, I saw a Ford Fairmont with two General Works men inside parked half a block away, opposite the garage. Both men were casually dressed, but otherwise they were obviously cops on stakeout: bored-looking, trying to be watchful without looking watchful. And, worse, their car was from the inspectors' motor pool and showed a telltale two-way antenna protruding from the trunk.

I had retrieved the microphone and was switching on the transmitter, when I glanced in my rear-view mirror and saw him: a slightly built man in his middle twenties, dressed in jeans, tennis shoes, a faded Levi's jacket and a gaucho-style wide-brimmed leather hat. His face was pale and drawn. Dark blond hair was visible beneath the leather hat. He was approaching the garage on my side of the street. As he came closer, I saw restless brown eyes moving uneasily beneath the hat brim, ceaselessly sweeping the street and the sidewalk.

From the picture hastily withdrawn from an inside pocket, I couldn't be sure the stranger was Frederick Tharp. But twelve years of police work told me that, whoever he was, he was on the other side of the law.

He was less than fifteen feet from the rear of my car, slowly sauntering toward me. The entrance to the garage was about twenty-five feet beyond my car on the same side of the street.

I must make my decision in seconds.

Normally I would let him pass, then use my walkie-talkie to alert the other members of the stakeout team. But I couldn't use the walkie-talkie; I had no idea what frequency Canelli had assigned.

Ten feet.

I propped my head in my right palm, pretending to stare idly down the street in the direction of the Ford, parked another twenty-five feet beyond the entrance to the garage, about fifty feet from my car. The two G.W. men were looking at each other, laughing together. One of them must have told a joke.

Without hope, I scanned the area for the fourth member of the stakeout team. The curbs on both sides of the street were lined with cars, all of them empty except for the Ford. A handful of passers-by were on the sidewalks, walking leisurely in both directions.

Five feet.

I unbuttoned my jacket, loosened my revolver in its spring holster, then put my hand on the door latch. I would wait for him to pass, then open the door. I would slip out of the car and fall into step behind him. Then, quickly, I would close the distance, jam my revolver into the small of his back. If he resisted, help would be close by.

And if the slightly built stranger wasn't Frederick Tharp, I would pretend that the operation was a drug bust. After a warning, we would release him—and hope he didn't call the ACLU.

He was drawing even with the rear of my car . . . Even with the door. Cautiously, I cracked my door. He was ahead of me now. Slowly, I swung the door open, at the same time glancing at the Ford. The two detectives were still talking, still laughing. I was out on the sidewalk now. Five, six feet separated us. As I closed the distance, he was drawing closer to the parking garage's driveway. Would he turn into the driveway? If he did, the odds were in my favor, not the ACLU's. I should wait, then, until he'd either passed the garage or else turned in.

And still the two G.W. detectives were chatting amiably.

With less than ten feet still separating the stranger from the driveway, a bright yellow Mazda sports car appeared from inside the garage. The driver was a girl, a cornsilk blonde. Waiting for traffic to clear, she stopped the Mazda in the driveway, blocking the sidewalk. The stranger was standing still, waiting for the girl to clear the sidewalk. Now he was turning to glance over his shoulder. With five feet between us, I stopped. Half turning, I pretended to glance pointedly toward the garage, as if I wanted to get my car and was impatient with the pretty girl behind the Mazda's wheel. I would—

Across the street, both doors of the Ford were swinging open. The two detectives were getting purposefully out of the car, unbuttoning their jackets. They'd recognized Tharp.

Simultaneously, Tharp and I lunged forward. With his left hand he grasped the Mazda's door handle on the driver's side. Momentarily his right hand disappeared from sight then reappeared holding a gun. The girl screamed. Once. Twice. Brakes squealed as a pickup truck stopped inches from the two detectives in the middle of the street. With my own gun in my right hand, legs pumping, I lowered my left shoulder, extended my left arm in a tackler's sweep. If I hit him hard enough I could jar the gun from his hand or spoil his aim.

But with my arm still inches away from him, I flung myself to the right, clear of the suspect.

Because the muzzle of his revolver hadn't swung toward me, or toward the two G.W. men. The muzzle was jammed cruelly into the girl's neck just below her ear. The suspect's hand was tangled in her hair, forcing her head back against the car's headrest.

"Back off," he was screaming, his mouth open wide, his eyes wild. "Back off, you bastards. *Now. Right now.*"

Slowly, impotently, I was straightening from my crouch. My revolver was pointed down at the sidewalk. I heard myself softly swearing. Standing with legs braced wide, revolvers steady on the suspect, the two G.W. men crouched behind a parked car.

"Drop it," they shouted. "Drop the gun." To my right, in the entrance to the garage, Canelli and Fowler appeared, both dressed in white coveralls, both with guns drawn. I gestured for them to hold their positions as I stepped back from the suspect, still with my revolver pointed down. As long as Tharp threatened the girl, we were helpless.

"Give it up, Tharp," I said, speaking slowly and quietly. "Don't get in any deeper."

Holding the Mazda's door open wide, he stood with his body pressed close to the girl still sitting motionless in the seat, staring straight ahead. Her face was colorless, her lips pale. Her eyes were wide, terrified. Tharp whispered something to her, then turned to me.

"You know me, then. You know who I am." He spoke in a thin, ragged voice. He was breathing harshly, unevenly. But his eyes glinted with a kind of manic clarity. He was calm. Dangerous, and calm.

"That's right, Tharp," I answered. "We're here for you. And we'll take you, too. Right now. Right here."

Mockingly, he shook his head. "No," he said softly. "You won't take me. Not as long as I've got her. You know you won't take me. You *know* it." For a moment his eyes held mine. In that instant I knew he was right. We wouldn't take him. Not here. Not now. Words wouldn't work with Fred Tharp. And threats wouldn't work, either. Because danger and violence were the focus of his life. He lived for the terror he inflicted on others.

"If you leave with her," I said, "it's kidnapping."

His only reaction was a slow, malicious smile. Did he know I was lying?

Suddenly he tugged viciously at the girl's hair, ordering her to get out of the car and stand between him and me for protection. As the girl stood up, I realized that she was a teenager. For a moment our eyes met. Mutely, she begged me for help, begged me to save her life. Helplessly, I nodded to her.

With his gun pressed to the back of her neck, Tharp shifted his grip, circling her waist with his free arm, at the same time whispering again into her ear. I saw her eyes widen. Then Tharp slid across to the passenger's seat, drawing her inside the car beside him, behind the wheel. With the gun threatening her, she would drive.

As the Mazda's door closed, I caught a furtive movement from the direction of the garage. Canelli was easing out of sight. In seconds he would be calling Communications. In minutes reinforcements would arrive.

As the Mazda's engine revved up, my hand tightened on my revolver. Now, in this instant, I had my chance. I could shoot out the Mazda's tires.

But in line behind the sports car I saw a cluster of pedestrians gawking. My shots would ricochet off the sidewalk, hitting them.

The sports car was moving forward. I saw the driver's window rise. Inside the car, a Levi's-clad arm reached out. With both windows up, he was locking the doors. The car moved out of the driveway, turning right with the traffic.

Thrusting my revolver into its holster, I was sprinting for my car. The G.W. men, too, were running for their car. On the sidewalk, big-eyed pedestrians stood rooted, still gawking. A small boy was crying. A man was swearing loudly, his arms above his head, as if he were calling for help from heaven.

As I fumbled with my key in the car door, I heard Canelli yell, "Want me with you, Lieutenant?"

"Yes. Come on." I jerked open the driver's door, unlocked the passenger's door and twisted the ignition key. The starter ground—and ground. The engine caught, faltered, died. Canelli was beside me. I twisted the starter again, floorboarded the accelerator, ordering, "Get on the radio. Get us a clear channel. Tell those others—those G.W. bastards." As the starter ground again, I looked ahead. The yellow Mazda was turning right on Columbus, two blocks away.

The engine caught again—faltered again—finally settled into a roar. Beside me Canelli was talking into his walkie-talkie, telling the other team to monitor our transmissions on tach four.

"Tell them to follow us," I said, swinging away from the curb. "And let's get some help, for Christ's sake." I jammed the flashing red light into its dashboard bracket and hit the siren switch. In the mirror I saw another red light flashing. Canelli was talking calmly into his microphone, calling out the suspect's route and giving our position. I cut sharply around a pickup truck and passed a white van. I was approaching the Columbus Street intersection on the wrong side of the street against the light. I glanced to the left, swung the cruiser to the right, narrowly missing an elderly couple standing motionless in the crosswalk. Canelli was pointing urgently ahead.

"He's turning left on Broadway, Lieutenant." And into the microphone he repeated the information, shouting over the wail of our siren. Ahead, coming toward us on Columbus, I saw a black-and-white car approaching, its red light flashing. As the distance between our two cars closed, I held up four fingers, signifying tach four, then gestured for the car to make a U-turn and follow us. The driver nodded, holding up four fingers.

Coming up on the Broadway intersection, I cut the siren,

saying, "He might be heading for the freeway approach. Let's get it blocked."

But ahead the yellow car had lengthened its lead, darting through a hole in the afternoon traffic that was streaming rush-hour-thick toward the approaches to the freeway and the Bay Bridge. The freeway entrance was four blocks away at the foot of Broadway.

"Get a helicopter up," I snapped. "My authority. Give him the number on the top of that black-and-white. *Quick.*"

Approaching the Kearny Street intersection on Broadway, I saw a huge truck nosing out into Broadway, heading south. Into the intersection the truck was slowing, stopping. I turned sharply to the right to clear the front of the truck. But a taxi was double-parked, cutting me off. I braked, turned sharply to the left. In the mirror I saw the G.W. detectives closing fast in the center lane. Tires screaming, engine roaring, my car was angled across the street, crossing the center line. Ahead, a red sedan was directly in my path. I braked, saw the sedan brake, swerve to its right. With inches to spare on either side, traveling on the wrong side of the street, I passed between the truck's tailgate and the careening sedan. Ahead, the Mazda had lengthened its lead; only one block separated it from the freeway entrance. Unless a responding black-and-white car coming from another direction could cut the Mazda off in the next block, we would never catch Tharp short of the freeway. Once in the heavy freeway traffic we could never gain on him, never catch him until he turned off, possibly in another county, in another jurisdiction.

"Where's the helicopter? Where's the goddamn helicopter?" Back on the right side of the center line, with a clear lane ahead, I floorboarded the accelerator. But two long blocks separated our car from the yellow sports car. We would never close the distance in time.

Suddenly a voice came over our loudspeaker, blaring above a whirring rush of background noise: "This is helicopter Zero Sierra Romeo, over the intersection of Third and Palou. Lieutenant Hastings, do you read me?"

"We read you," Canelli was saying. "We're approaching Montgomery and Broadway, on Broadway. A cruiser and a black-and-white car are following us, code three. We're in pursuit of a yellow sports car traveling east on Broadway, approaching Sansome and Broadway. Do you copy?"

"We copy," the metallic voice answered. "We're coming toward you over the freeway."

As he spoke, I saw the yellow car stop, wedged in traffic at Sansome and Broadway, the last intersection before the freeway entrance. This was our chance, our last good chance. But ahead the traffic light was turning yellow, then red. Traffic on Montgomery Street began criss-crossing the intersection, heedless of our sirens. With cars solid in front of us in both eastbound lanes and the westbound lanes impassable to my left, we were blocked. Helpless, I braked to a furious stop.

"God—*damn.*" I banged angrily on the steering wheel with my fist, then grabbed for the microphone.

"All units in the vicinity of Broadway and Sansome, detain a yellow Mazda sports car stopped at that intersection, headed east. Occupants, a man and a woman. The man is armed. Repeat, the man is armed. The woman is a hostage. All units hearing this transmission, acknowledge."

Three calls came in, all converging on the intersection. But as I watched, the traffic light at Sansome changed to green. The Mazda was moving into the intersection—onto the freeway ramp.

"They're on the freeway," I said bitterly. Then, as our traffic light changed, I handed the microphone to Canelli, ordering, "Get that 'copter over him. Right over him. Keep it there." Again opening the siren, I swung into the intersection on the wrong side of the street. On the freeway ramp, I saw the yellow car accelerating fast, weaving in and out through traffic, then swinging into the right-hand lane reserved for emergencies.

"If they get on the Bay Bridge," I said, "we've got them. We'll close the bridge at the toll plaza, if we have to do it."

"We're over the freeway at Portrero Hill," the helicopter officer was saying. "Where's the suspect?"

"He's coming up on the first turnoff," Canelli answered as I gunned our car into the Sansome Street intersection against the red light. In the mirror, I saw three flashing red lights. Another black-and-white car had joined the chase—too late.

On the ramp now, I swung into the emergency lane. Ahead, the Mazda was swinging into the left lane.

"He's going to the bridge," I said. "We've got him."

But instantly the yellow car veered to the right. Beside me, Canelli was calling out the suspect's position. With our engine at full throttle, we were gaining on the Mazda. But ahead the emergency lane ended at the bridge turnoff. The Mazda was now committed to the right-hand lane, making for the freeway spur that curved south down the peninsula that led toward Daly City, Burlingame and Redwood City. At the last moment Tharp had realized that he would be trapped on the bridge.

But he was back in rush-hour traffic, impacted. Ahead, traffic had slowed to twenty miles an hour, all lanes jammed with cars. As I braked, I heard Canelli speak to the helicopter pilots. "You should be able to see him now," he said. "He's about a half mile ahead of us, in the same lane."

Ahead, to the left, I saw the helicopter, low in the sky. I pointed and Canelli nodded, saying into the microphone, "You should turn to your left. You're too far east."

Obediently, the helicopter was turning south. A frustrating minute followed as we crawled forward at twenty miles an hour. Our siren was silent now, utterly useless. Finally we heard the radio crackle to life.

"We've got him," the pilot said. "We're right over him. He's just coming up on the Harrison Street off-ramp, going about twenty-five. He's—oh, oh."

"What?" Canelli said, anxiously looking up at the hovering helicopter."

"He's going off on Harrison."

"Stay with him," Canelli said, repeating the information

and ordering all available cars to converge on the Harrison exit.

"He's on the off-ramp," the helicopter man was saying. "He's approaching Harrison and Eighth, in light traffic. He's— he's pulling to the curb, on Harrison. The door's opening— the passenger door. He's getting out of the car. He's running up Eighth Street, toward Market."

Furious, I grabbed the microphone, shouting, "Let's get *cars* down there. He's wearing blue jeans and a Levi's jacket and a leather hat. He's armed and dangerous. This is code thirty-three. Repeat, code thirty-three."

Ahead of our car, the traffic was inching toward the Harrison Street off-ramp, still a half mile away. "Get Communications," I snapped to Canelli. "Find out what the hell's going on. Tell them I want some goddamn action on tach four— *now.*" Switching channels, he obeyed. Moments later a cold, remote voice came on the air:

"We've got another code thirty-three, Lieutenant. A man's on Market Street slashing people up with a machete. But there're three cars on the way to Eighth and Harrison."

As if the second code thirty-three were his fault, Canelli shrugged apologetically at me.

"Get back to the 'copter," I ordered impatiently, cutting sharply ahead of a white Mercedes and glancing into the mirror. Even with their sirens on, the three other cars had fallen farther behind, locked tightly in traffic.

"We're directly over an alley between Folsom and Harrison and Eighth and Ninth," the helicopter officer was saying. "There's a black-and-white on the scene now, just stopping." As he spoke, I heard an acknowledgment that Unit 782 was with us on tach four.

"Is the suspect still in sight?" Canelli asked.

"Negative," came the static-sizzled answer from the 'copter. "We've lost him." And, immediately, another voice came on the air. "Where is he, helicopter?" It was the man in Unit 782.

"He must be inside a building. He just disappeared about

halfway between Eighth and Ninth," the pilot answered. "It's Ringold Alley. That's where we lost contact. Ringold Alley."

We were coming up on the turnoff to Harrison. Ahead of us, responding to the siren I'd switched on again, cars were pulling to the right, stopping. Savagely I jerked the steering wheel to the left. Suddenly, miraculously, we were in the clear, *free.*

Ahead on Harrison I saw the yellow Mazda parked at an erratic angle to the curb. The blond girl was on the sidewalk, half supported by a uniformed man. The uniformed man waved me north on Eighth against the traffic. Canelli was on the radio, advising all units that we were leaving mobile tach four and going to walkie-talkie channel nine. Ahead, I saw an empty black-and-white unit blocking the entrance to Ringold Alley. I braked to a stop, took the keys, jumped out and opened the trunk, getting our shotgun.

"Here—" I handed the shotgun to Canelli and took the walkie-talkie. "Let's go." As I trotted down the alley, other cars drew to a stop around us. Suddenly the troops had arrived. Looking down the alley, I saw a uniformed man standing on the sidewalk waiting for us.

"He went in here," the patrolman yelled, pointing to an open door. "Send some men around to Folsom. *Quick.*"

I stopped in my tracks and gave the order on the walkie-talkie, carefully describing the suspect. Angrily, I realized that the situation was no longer a hot pursuit, but probably a search-and-discover operation with the suspect concealed. In the congested neighborhood just a few blocks from Market Street, we might have lost him.

I ordered Canelli to come with me, deploying everyone else around a block-square perimeter with double strength on Folsom. I stood staring at the dingy, paint-scabbed alleyway door standing wide open. Around the lock, the door had been splintered.

"What's inside?" I asked the patrolman from Unit 782 as I pinned my badge to my jacket.

193

"I don't know, sir. I thought I should wait out here for you. My partner's inside."

I glanced down a narrow, foul-smelling interior alleyway lined with garbage cans and buzzing with flies. The neighborhood was nondescript: rundown buildings that housed dingy apartments and marginal businesses, mostly sweatshops and cheap storage facilities. Ordering the patrolman to stay outside, I began slowly, cautiously advancing down the alleyway. An armed patrolman was somewhere ahead. He didn't have "the numbers": the walkie-talkie channel for this operation. He didn't know I was coming. I had no way to warn him, no way to protect myself if he mistook me for Tharp. Holding the walkie-talkie in my left hand and my revolver in my right hand, crouching slightly, I was approaching another open doorway, this one leading inside the building. This door, too, had been broken open. I turned, instinctively glancing back over my shoulder. Then I stepped through the door and into a small kitchen. It was a dark, dank room, littered and dirty. Another door led into a hallway, with an outside door at the far end. It was an old-fashioned long, narrow "railroad flat" with the kitchen at one end and three rooms opening in succession off the hallway to the left.

The first door was a bathroom, the second a disheveled bedroom. The third room, then, was the living room, facing Folsom Street. I realized that I was standing motionless, listening. From inside the living room, I'd heard something: some soft, furtive suggestion of a sound, nothing more. Then I heard it again, more distinctly.

Inside the living room, something was stirring.

I moved to the left wall and began inching toward the living-room door. Now I stood close to the door frame, my back pressed against the hallway wall. I held my breath—and heard someone else breathing. Instantly my stomach went hollow, my throat closed. My mouth was dry. How had it happened? With dozens of policemen in the area, with one patrolman ahead of me, I was alone, one on one with an armed suspect. I looked back down the hallway, automatically trying to find help. The hallway was empty, and the kitchen, too. I'd ordered Canelli and the uniformed man to stay outside.

Soundlessly, I moved one step away from the doorway, then another step. Undoubtedly the front door was covered. So I could retreat to the alley and call for—

I heard a hoarse, rattling cough, and saw a foot come through the doorway, then a leg and a hand, finally a full figure: a short, stumpy woman dressed in a bedraggled housecoat. Her face was broad and bloated, her eyes were small and vague: two dark, lusterless buttons, sunk deep in the flaccid flesh of her face.

"Jesus," she said, shaking her head wonderingly as she turned her ungainly body to face me. "Jesus, another one. I—" She hiccupped, coughed again, then belched. The odor of alcohol was heavy and rank in the squalid hallway. "I haven't had so much company in years, I don't think. Not in years."

Twenty-six

I spent a long, maddening hour parked at the corner of Harrison and Eighth, using my walkie-talkie to coordinate a fruitless search for Frederick Tharp. Even as I worked at it, though, I could reconstruct what had happened. Tharp had emerged from the front door of the flat and turned right on Folsom, walking slowly. He'd turned left on Eighth and walked to Market Street, disappearing in the sidewalk crowds. By now he was miles away, safe on a bus or a subway train. Good luck had guided him down Ringold Alley to a door that could be kicked in, but he'd done the rest coolly, efficiently, intelligently.

At the end of an hour, I turned the search over to Canelli and drove down Folsom Street to the Embarcadero and Trader John's. After checking in with Communications and talking briefly with Friedman, I switched to KCBS just in time to catch the local news. The Market Street Slasher, as he was already being labeled, had apparently hacked two innocent pedestrians to death and seriously wounded half a dozen others. He was now in San Francisco General under psychiatric observation. So far, his only explanation was that he'd only meant to kill his girl friend, who'd left him the night before. After he'd killed her, almost severing her head from her body, his mind had gone blank, he'd said. First reports stated that the suspect was Louis Fields, age twenty-four, released two months ago from Napa State Hospital. His last known employment was as a busboy. Previously he'd been an honors student at Calvary Bible College in Oklahoma. Fields hoped to be a preacher, the reporter said—and still thought he would eventually be able to preach. His girl friend, he stated, had turned his eyes from the sight of God's good truth, blinding him with urges of the flesh. Now that she was dead, he would be a better, purer, more focused person.

I sighed, switched off the radio and walked across the parking lot to Trader John's.

Byron Tharp's office was decorated like the rest of his nightclub in fake Polynesian. Tapa cloth covered the walls, hung with crossed spears, outsize tribal masks and elaborately carved paddles and totems. Cocomatting covered the floor. Tharp's desk was two tropical-looking tree stumps that supported an enormous slab of natural burl. Seated behind the desk, Tharp matched the decor, dressed in sandals, beachcomber khakis and a bright blue Hawaiian shirt. Around his neck he wore a lei made of plastic flowers.

"Have you found him?" he asked before I was seated. "Did you catch him?"

"No," I answered, sitting in a sunburst-style rattan chair that rose like a peacock behind my head. "We almost had him. But I'm afraid we lost him."

"What about my car? Did you get my car?"

I nodded. "Your car, we got."

"Christ—great." He slapped his desk with the flat of his hand. "*Great.* That's a fifteen-thousand-dollar car, you know." He paused as his heavy, uncompromising face registered an unpleasant afterthought. "It's all right, isn't it? Not damaged, or anything?"

"No, it's all right. We'll have to keep it for a while, until the lab's finished with it. But it's fine. No problem."

"That's great," he repeated heartily. Then, gesturing to a sea-chest-style cabinet behind his desk, he said, "How about a drink? To celebrate."

"No, thanks."

He shrugged. "Suit yourself."

I let a moment of silence pass while I looked at him. Unperturbed, he met my silent stare. If he possessed any guilty knowledge, or was uneasy about the real reason for my visit, he gave no sign. Finally, speaking in a normal, conversational voice, I said, "I'm sorry about your sister, Mr. Tharp. Her murder must've been a terrible shock."

His eyes narrowed momentarily—then opened wider, doubtless by design, to convey a brother's sorrow. "Well, yes, it was a shock. Violent death—you know—it's always a shock. But, frankly, if I'm honest with myself, I've got to admit that it's a relief, too. I mean, let's face it, all those years haven't been easy."

"It must've been a terrible strain. And a financial drain, too. The expenses of that sanitarium must've been appalling."

"Eighteen hundred a month," he said, nodding. "And that's not counting extras."

"Do you have any idea who killed her, Mr. Tharp? Any idea at all?"

He spread his hands, asking, "Wasn't it Fred? Isn't that what you think?"

"Is that what you think?" I countered. "Do you think he'd kill his own mother?"

Vehemently, he nodded. "Definitely. No question."

"But why? What motive would he have? There wasn't any inheritance."

"That little bastard, he doesn't need a motive. A few years ago, he beat her up when she wouldn't give him money for a radio he wanted. I figure he did it again. He got mad at her for something and hit her. Only this time, he hit her too hard."

"Do you really think that's what happened, Mr. Tharp?"

"Sure I do," he answered. "Don't you?"

"I'm not sure, not yet. I'm still trying to put the pieces together. That's the reason I'm here, to get information. By the way, when was the last time you saw your sister?"

"Oh—" He shrugged. "I don't know. Three, four weeks ago. I'm not really sure. I looked in on her every few weeks. Not that it did much good. She was never in touch, you know. Never."

"How often did Fred see her at Brentwood, do you know?"

He snorted. "Him. I think he went to see her once, after he got out of prison. And that was it."

"Did your sister leave a will?"

"Yes, she did." Defying me with his small, knowing eyes, he said, "She left everything to me. Which wasn't much, believe me. A few clothes, and that was it. That, plus burial expenses." Once more he snorted. "She was a lifelong problem. And if you're expecting me to say I'm sorry she's dead, forget it. I'm not. All she ever did was give me problems, her and Fred."

"Which Fred is that, Mr. Tharp? The first Fred, or the second Fred?"

He'd been looking down at his desk as I said it, absently fingering an ornamental letter-opener that lay on the polished wood. I saw his mouth tighten and his eyes harden. For a moment he didn't respond but sat motionless, still toying with the letter-opener. Then: "You know about that, then."

"That's right. We know about that."

He nodded slowly. "It was bound to come out," he said finally. "With all this happening, I knew it would come out."

"What happened twenty-six years ago in Santa Barbara? Who's Frederick Tharp? What's his real name?"

He raised his thick shoulders, shrugging. "It's Frederick Tharp. When she got him, she just gave him Frederick's name—her baby's name. She had the birth certificate. It wasn't legal, but it worked. It just showed him being a year older than he was, is all."

"And, all the time, Donald Ryan was paying you for the child's keep. Right?"

He shrugged again, for the first time raising his eyes to meet mine. "That's right. He paid. Of course he paid." Now he frowned, acting puzzled. "Why wouldn't he pay?"

"Because it's fraud," I answered. "Because you found another baby and substituted it for Ryan's child when that child died. All these years you've been collecting money from Ryan under false pretenses. He thought you were keeping his bastard son. But his son died. So you brought in a ringer. Didn't you?"

"What the hell're you—"

"It's a little ghoulish, Tharp. It's one thing to go to Ryan and demand that he do the right thing for your sister and their child. It's also understandable that you'd put a little in your pocket. Or maybe a lot in your pocket." I looked meaningfully around the office. "But then the baby died. You didn't tell Ryan. Maybe your sister was already pregnant again, so you didn't have to bother finding another baby. Was that it?"

"But—Christ—that's not what happened," he interrupted hotly. "You've—Christ—you've got it all wrong."

"Have I? Then you tell me how it was, Tharp. Tell me what really happened." I sank back in my chair, faking relaxation as I listened.

"Well—" He gestured sharply, pugnaciously defensive. "I'll admit that when Juanita told me that she was pregnant and who the father was, I saw dollar signs. Who wouldn't, for God's sake? But, Christ, somebody had to ask for money. Sure as hell, she never would've done it. Even then she couldn't take care of herself. She was beautiful. God knows, she was beautiful. But all it ever got her was trouble. Even when she was little, she—" Momentarily, his eyes lost focus. Then, speaking more softly, more reflectively, he said, "When the baby died, it tipped Juanita over the edge. Being pregnant and having Ryan turn his back on her, that was bad enough, not to mention postpartum psychosis, or whatever they call it. But at least she had her baby. She hated being pregnant. She hated what it did to her looks. Because all she had, you see, was her looks. But right after he was born, at least she had the baby. She used to play with it, I remember, like it was a doll or something. And it seemed to help her for a while. But then, the baby died. It was crib death, they said."

As he spoke, I stared at him hard, trying to decide how much of it was the truth and how much lies. Meeting mine, his eyes were still hard and defiant. Skillfully, stubbornly, he was bluffing it out. Finally I said, "Did Ryan know the baby died?"

"Sure he did. Or at least the Bayliss woman knew. See, I always dealt with her after the baby was born. She handled the money. And I figured, what the hell, if the baby died, all the more reason to get something for Juanita. You know— like a death benefit, something for pain and suffering."

"And for yourself. You wanted something for yourself, too. Didn't you?"

"Yeah. Sure. Why not something for myself? Christ, it's not like there wasn't enough to go around."

"You realize, of course, that I can check all this with Mrs. Bayliss."

Truculently, he waved a thick, brawler's hand. "Go ahead. Check. She'll tell you. She'll tell you everything just like I told it to you."

"Who was the father of the second child? Do you know?"

He shrugged. "Ryan, I guess."

"*Ryan,*" I repeated furiously. "You expect me to believe that? You're trying to say that he went back for seconds, for Christ's sake?"

"Seconds? What d'you mean, seconds?"

"Listen, Tharp," I grated, "I don't know how far you intend to push this, but I—"

"The baby *was* Ryan's," he interrupted hotly. "I'll bet on

it. I'd give odds. About a year later, see, after Juanita's baby died, I got a call from the Bayliss woman. She said she had a job for Juanita—a lifetime job, she said." He looked at me closely, then shook his head, wonderingly. "I thought you knew. Christ, I thought you knew. That baby—that second one—it was never Juanita's. It was someone else's."

Twenty-seven

"This is ridiculous," Friedman fumed, staring balefully across the Fairmont's lobby toward a bank of four elevators that served the hotel's first twelve floors. "This is the goddamndest, most bizarre, most illogical, most outrageous case I've ever worked. Right now—right this goddamn minute— we should be getting some answers, for God's sake. So here we sit, cooling our heels because of orders. It's like the goddamn war in Europe when we could've gone all the way to the Rhine but the politicians pulled the string. It's just the same. There's no difference. None at all."

"You're quite a historian."

"I'm no historian. But I was there. I know what I'm talking about."

"I thought you were a flyer."

"I *was* a flyer. But I could still—" One of the elevator doors slid open. Half a dozen tourists left the elevator, followed by Richter and Clarence Blake, the Secret Service man.

"Who's that with Richter?" Friedman snapped.

"His name is Blake. He's a Secret Service bigshot from Washington."

"Yeah?" Friedman's voice was sarcastic as he suddenly heaved himself to his feet. "Well, I think I'll introduce myself."

"Pete—Christ." Also on my feet, I put my hand on his arm. "All Chief Dwyer told us to do is wait for orders. How long has it been? A half hour? For all you know, he's getting warrants."

"He's getting crap," Friedman snarled. "He's sitting by the phone, waiting for *his* orders." But he wasn't resisting the pressure of my hand on his arm. Suddenly he turned disgustedly away, striding off in the opposite direction from Richter and Blake, who were walking purposefully across the crowded lobby toward the outside doors.

"Come on," Friedman barked.

"Where're we going?"

"To the bar, naturally. Where else?"

Even after two double bourbons, Friedman was still fuming. "We don't even know whether they're up there," he said. He glanced at his watch. "It's precisely eight-twenty P.M. Which is to say that we've been here for exactly forty-five minutes. We've got at least one possible suspect upstairs. And here we sit."

"Which suspect is that?"

"Eason," he answered. "I think it's very possible that Eason killed Juanita Tharp to prevent her from talking. He's got the motive, which is to protect the great god Ryan's reputation with blind, doglike devotion. He had the opportunity, probably. And he had the means. Which is to say that he's a proven killer. It's obvious. That's what a lot of people in this business overlook, you know. There're very damn few people who are capable of premeditated murder. Very damn few." He nodded over his empty glass, then signaled the bartender for another drink. Irritably, I sipped at my tonic water. I didn't like to sit in bars, and Friedman knew it.

"You haven't even talked to Eason," I said sourly. "How do you know he's the murderer?"

Friedman tapped his temple and winked. "I've got the instinct, you know—the hunter's instinct."

I snorted. "You've got a buzz on, is what you've got."

He turned his big body on the bar stool and leaned back to look me elaborately up and down. "Eason dunnit," he pronounced, raising a thick forefinger. "You *know* he dunnit. And here we sit, like a couple of snot-nosed rookies, trying to decide what to do about it."

"That's not really true. We're waiting for warrants."

"Do you really think," he said, "that Dwyer is going to approve warrants to search Lloyd Eason's room and whichever one of those Cadillacs he might've been driving? Which is to say that we've got to search them all. Do you think for one moment that Dwyer will risk having Donald Ryan find out that we're seriously investigating his faithful slave?"

"No," I answered, "I don't. But that doesn't prevent us from interrogating Eason. We don't have to lean on him. All we have to do is—"

"Interrogation, hell," he interrupted acidly. "All we have to do is take his clothes downtown and see if we can find any horseshit. We vacuum his room, and we vacuum the cars. It's—Christ—that goddamn horseshit is a once-in-a-lifetime piece of physical evidence. Usually the lab is trying to compare samples of different kinds of house-dust and getting all bogged down in how many particles of magnesium per million constitute proof. But here we've got horseshit, for Christ's sake." Despairingly, he shook his head over his drink, then smiled mischievously. "Can you imagine the defense attorney's pain, trying to explain how his client just happened to have traces of manure on his clothing, hanging around the Fairmont?"

I didn't reply, and we sat silently for a moment staring morosely down at our drinks. Then Friedman said, "I also think we should lean a little on the beautiful, mysterious Katherine Bayliss. After all—" He gulped down half his third bourbon and water. "After all, she's the one—maybe the only one, besides Ryan—who knows who Frederick

205

Tharp really is. And, more and more, it looks like his true identity could be the key to this whole thing. Who is he, anyhow?"

"Are you asking me?"

"You know," Friedman mused, "what we're getting on this case is a behind-the-scenes, under-the-counter civics lesson. These people—they do it with mirrors, you know that? Nothing is what it seems. It's all hype—all PR. None of these people are for real. They're in the make-believe business, just like in the movies. What you vote for isn't what you get, it's what you thought you got. It's nothing but—"

At my belt, my pager sounded. As I reached reflexively for the small black box to shut it off, I saw Friedman making the same involuntary gesture. Simultaneously, we'd both been paged.

"That's a first," Friedman observed.

"Finish your drink. I'll call in." Glad to get out of the bar, I walked out into the lobby, got a dime at the newsstand and called Communications.

"Just a second, Lieutenant. I'm going to patch you through to the field. Hold on." Thirty static-filled seconds elapsed before I heard Canelli's voice.

"What've you got, Canelli?"

"Well, Jesus, it looks like what we've got is Frederick Tharp."

"You've *what?*"

"That's right, Lieutenant. He's out at Stow Lake, in Golden Gate Park. Not too far from the boathouse here." But Canelli's voice sounded apologetic, not excited or pleased.

"The only problem," he continued, "is that he's dead. He's been shot."

Twenty-eight

"Do you know the way?" Friedman asked as I turned into the Seventh Avenue entrance to Golden Gate Park.

"I think so." I turned first to the left, then to the right, following a narrow, winding road through a night-time wilderness of pine and eucalyptus. Golden Gate Park was one of the largest urban parks in America: it had sixty acres of forest, a natural wonderland. During the daylight hours, the park's hiking trails and grassy meadows were lively and carefree, a vast and varied playground. But after dark the predators took over, some of them animal, most of them human.

Echoing my thoughts, Friedman said, "I have to admit, this place gives me the willies at night. You get off the main drive, and you feel like you're cut off from civilization."

"You *are* cut off from civilization."

"How many homicides have you worked on out here?" he asked.

"I don't know. A dozen, maybe." I turned into the main drive, relieved to be driving in the familiar, reassuring glare of sodium vapor streetlights.

"Did you hear about what happened here last month—about those Cambodian refugees?"

"No. What happened?"

"Well, you know there're dogs running wild out here. Dogs that people abandon. Right?"

I nodded. "Right."

"And you also know," he continued, "that Asians eat dogs. Right?"

I looked at him. "You're kidding."

"You think so?"

"No," I answered, turning my gaze back to the road. "No, I guess I don't think so." I turned left onto the narrow road that led to Stow Lake. Ahead, through the trees, I saw flashing red lights and the glare of portable floodlights. I sighed. Had it only been twenty minutes since I'd been sitting in the bar at the Fairmont, listening to Friedman's complaints about the bureaucracy? It seemed impossible.

Frederick Tharp was still dressed as I'd last seen him, in jeans and a Levi's jacket. Under a large flowering bush, I saw the leather hat. He lay face-down at the base of a huge pine tree. His right arm was doubled under him; his left hand was flung wide. His fingers were claw-crooked, dug desperately into the dirt as if he'd been trying to hold on to the world while it slipped away. His legs were widespread. A large bloodstain was centered on the Levi's jacket in back.

Working under the glare of floodlights, with the practiced flair of a movie director, Friedman was coordinating the efforts of our technicians, moving them in and out of the area surrounding the body, one group at a time: first the photographers, then the laboratory technicians, finally the coroner's team. All of it had to be done in sequence, with each step in the process certified by the officer in charge to preserve the chain of evidence.

I turned away from the body and moved to the drive that circled Stow Lake, gesturing for Canelli to follow me. It was a one-way drive, so narrow in places that branches touched both sides of the coroner's van.

"What's it look like, Canelli?" As I spoke, I surveyed the scene. Moonlight danced on the surface of the man-made waterway. During the day, if the weather was good, dozens of rented boats could always be seen moving from the boathouse through artificial bayous and backwaters until they finally emerged again at the far end of the lake, making for the boathouse. At night, though, both the boathouse and the waterways were deserted. The only illumination was a pair of dim lights that shone on the boathouse door and the front of the adjoining refreshment stand. A parking lot was located behind the boathouse. The narrow driveway beside which the body lay was a closed circle that began at the east end of the parking lot and ended at the west end.

"Well, Lieutenant," Canelli said, "we might have a break. Repeat, might."

Lately, I'd noticed, Canelli had been using the word "repeat" for emphasis whenever he was making a verbal report. The purpose, I imagined, was to give weight to his statements. But Canelli rambled when he talked, so the effect was often more puzzling than precise.

"What d'you mean, Canelli?"

"Well," he said earnestly, pointing toward the parking lot, "I've got an old wino, I guess he is, in my car over there. I've got a couple of uniformed men keeping an eye on him. Not that he's liable to go anywhere. I mean, he's really zonked out. Repeat, zonked."

"What'd he see?"

"Well, he heard shots, he said, which woke him up. He was sleeping on the ground, on the downhill side from the parking lot, there, in some bushes." Dolefully, Canelli shook his head. "You know, Lieutenant, it's sad to see, you know that? I mean, here's this old guy, sixty years old or so, probably begging all day just to get enough money to buy some muscatel, or something. And then, at night, he's got to sleep out under the—"

"Canelli. Please. Get to the point, will you?"

"Yeah. Sure. Sorry, Lieutenant. Well, anyhow—" He drew a deep breath. "He was sleeping down there, like I said, in this real ratty old sleeping bag, when all of a sudden he woke up, he says. Because, see, he heard shots. Several shots, he said."

"How many?"

"Well, Lieutenant, he's not sure how many. I mean, he thinks that at least one or two of them woke him up. Or maybe more, for all he knows. But, anyhow, he's sure that after he woke up, he heard three or four shots coming from there—" He pointed toward the glare of floodlights shining through the trees. "He was just about to—you know—investigate, when suddenly he heard a car, and the next thing he knew, there was this big old Cadillac barreling into the parking lot from the driveway."

A Cadillac . . .

"Is he sure it was a Cadillac?"

Decisively, Canelli nodded. "Definitely, he says. No doubt about it, according to him. Repeat, no doubt."

"How close was he to the car?"

"About ten feet," he answered. "No more. He was just right off the edge of the parking lot, like I said."

"What about the passengers?"

"One. A man, he says. A big man, he thinks, wearing a hat."

"What about the color of the car?"

Canelli shook his head. "No dice, Lieutenant. No color. It was pretty dark, don't forget."

"Just how drunk is he, Canelli? How do you rate his testimony? On a scale of one to ten, how do you rate it?"

"Well, gee, Lieutenant, that's kind of hard, you know. I mean, sure, he was drunk. But then, on the other hand, I've taken him through his story twice, and it seems to hold up. So I'd say—"

"Come on, Canelli. Give me a number."

"I'd say six and a half," he said. "Maybe seven." He looked at me anxiously, as if trying to decide whether he'd won a guessing game.

"Good. Stay with him. When we're through here, put him into protective custody. Treat him good, but put him in custody. If he objects, let me know. Don't hassle him. Kid gloves. Clear?"

"Yessir, Lieutenant, that's clear."

"Have you got any idea when the shots were fired?"

Canelli shook his head. "Afraid not, Lieutenant. I mean, I can make a guess. Because, see, this guy—his name is Claude—he said that when he first woke up, he wasn't sure if it was a dream. And then he saw the Cadillac leaving the scene, and he figured something was wrong. So then he walked up the driveway for a ways, but he didn't see the body. I mean, it was dark and everything. And even if it wasn't dark, with the body in the bushes and all, I don't see how—"

"What'd he do then, Canelli?"

"Well—" He drew a deep breath. "Well, Claude was still sort of uneasy and everything, and he figured that he didn't want to stick around here any more. Like he said, he wanted to go where there were lights and people. Which, for sure, you can understand. So he rolled up his sleeping bag and went down to the main drive. And after a little while he saw a black-and-white on patrol." Canelli pointed to one of the patrol cars, with a pair of officers standing by. "That's the unit there. Number 364. They saw Claude on the side of the road and did a routine check. They could tell something was bothering him. So they put him in the car and came back up here and examined the area."

"So they actually found the body."

"Yessir."

"And so far we don't have any independent confirmation of Claude's story."

"That's right, Lieutenant," he said, adding cheerfully,

"For all we know, he could've done it."

My involuntary response was an irritated click of teeth, followed by another anxious look from Canelli.

"What we need," I said, "is a time frame. Does he have any idea how much time elapsed between the time he heard the shots and the time the body was discovered?"

"Jeeze, I'm afraid not, Lieutenant. I mean—you know— he was pretty gassed. He's still pretty gassed."

"Does he have any idea how long he was standing on the main drive before he was picked up?"

"No. But Robinson and Walters, they checked him out on their second pass, so that was about twenty minutes, they said, right there."

Standing in the parking lot and letting my eyes wander across the parking lot and down through the dark trees to the intermittent headlights that marked the main drive, I mused, "It sounds like about an hour from the time the shots were first fired to the time the body was discovered."

Canelli nodded. "I was thinking the same thing, Lieutenant."

"What time was the body actually discovered?"

Frowning, he riffled through a notebook, finally pronouncing, "It was ten minutes after nine. Repeat, ten minutes after—"

"Lieutenant. Lieutenant Hastings." Someone was hailing me from the murder scene.

"What is it?" I shouted in return.

"Lieutenant Friedman is ready to move the body."

"All right, I'm coming." And to Canelli I said, "Remember, keep Claude on ice."

"Yessir."

"And keep scratching around here. It's a big park. Somebody else must've heard those shots. We need witnesses and a time frame. Clear?"

"Yessir, that's clear."

I turned away and strode toward the floodlight glare. Friedman had used white cloth tape to mark off the area, and now only Friedman and an assistant coroner stood inside the tapes beside the body.

"Come in, Frank." Friedman gestured.

I stepped over the tape and stood between Friedman and the coroner's man.

"This is Paul Garvey," Friedman said. "Frank Hastings."

While Garvey and I nodded silent greetings, Friedman stepped over the body, bent double, took hold of the victim's jacket and his jeans, braced himself and heaved the body over on its back.

A revolver was clutched in the victim's right hand. The gun had been completely concealed beneath the body. It looked like the same gun that I'd seen pressed to the blond girl's head earlier in the day.

Above the body, Friedman and I exchanged a quick, meaningful look. Theoretically, it would have been possible for the revolver to fire when the body had been rolled over. We'd been lucky.

Friedman and I stepped aside while the photographer snapped half a dozen pictures. While we waited, I briefed him quickly on Canelli's witness.

"All right, Paul," Friedman said, "he's all yours. Any chance you can still do an autopsy tonight? It could be important."

"Well—" Doubtfully, the coroner frowned. "It's quarter to eleven already. I don't know whether we could make it."

"It really could be important," Friedman urged, holding the other man's eyes. "When you read the papers, you'll see what I mean."

Garvey's glance was skeptical, but finally he shrugged. "All right, I'll see what I can do."

"I'll call you first thing tomorrow," Friedman said earnestly. "And I won't forget it. I'll owe you one, guaranteed."

Reluctantly, Garvey smiled. "I won't let you forget." He turned away, and gestured to the two ambulance stewards waiting with their stretcher. But Friedman signaled for them to wait, then called for a pair of surgical gloves. Wearing the

213

gloves, he took the revolver from Tharp's hand and stepped back from the body, beside me. Handling the gun gingerly, he first sniffed the barrel, then swung the cylinder out and ejected the six cartridges into his hand. Four of the cartridges were intact; two had been fired. Friedman carefully dropped the revolver into one plastic evidence bag and the cartridges into another bag, then gave the gloves and the two bags to a waiting lab man. Friedman pointed to the body.

"It looks like he's been shot twice, at least."

"I know."

"So there were probably four shots fired, maybe more."

"Which would tie in with the witness's statement." As I spoke, the two ambulance stewards put the stretcher on the ground beside the body, leaned forward, took firm hold of the body at the shoulders and knees, braced themselves and heaved. The body settled gelatinously on the flat canvas: a formless mass of inert solids and liquids, incongruously dressed in jeans and a jacket, with hands and boots and a lolling head attached. Whatever he'd been, whoever he was, Frederick Tharp was nothing more than dead meat now, on his way to the morgue.

"Has Canelli got that witness sewed up?" Friedman asked.

"Yes. I told him to put the guy in protective custody, at least until he sobers up."

"Any other witnesses?"

"Not yet. Canelli's looking."

"Does Canelli really think it was a Cadillac leaving the scene?"

I nodded.

"Well, then," Friedman said, "it seems that our next stop should be the Fairmont."

"What about Dwyer? I think we should tell him about this—"I gestured to the murder scene. "And then ask for orders."

"I don't agree." Friedman spoke in a flat, uncompromising voice. "Don't forget, we've already been waiting for orders. We've been waiting for hours. And maybe if we hadn't been waiting, we'd have one less corpse to worry about. So I say we go down to the Fairmont and start knocking on a few doors." He glanced at his watch. "It's now almost eleven. By the time we get there, Ryan and company should be getting ready for bed. In my experience, that's a good time to catch people off balance, when they're in bed."

"Who're you planning to wake up?"

"Eason, naturally. Do we have a time estimate?"

"I figure the shots were fired about eight P.M. Maybe a little later."

"Then, for openers, let's find out where Eason was between, say, six o'clock and nine o'clock. And if he can't give us a good answer, corroborated, I say we take him downtown."

"Just like that."

He nodded. "Just like that. I'm getting sick of this crap, waiting in hotel lobbies with my hat in my hand."

"You're also sick of your nice big office, it seems to me. And maybe your nice big pension, too."

"The office, yes. The pension, no. Come on." He led the way across the parking lot toward our car.

Twenty-nine

When we got off the elevator at the eleventh floor, we were met by four FBI agents instead of the usual two. Looking at their faces, I realized that something had happened. Of the four men, I knew only Parsons, their spokesman. When he learned that we'd come to see Eason, Parsons slowly shook his head.

"Mr. Eason isn't here, I'm afraid," he said solemnly. "But Mr. Richter and Mr. Draper are in Mr. Ferguson's suite. I've got orders to bring you there."

"How about Chief Dwyer?" Friedman said. "Is he there too?"

Still speaking solemnly, his face expressionless, Parsons nodded. "Yes, Mr. Dwyer's there, too."

"Anyone else?" I asked.

"I don't know," he answered, already turning away down the corridor. "I just came on duty, after—" He let it go unfinished.

Exchanging a quick look, Friedman and I followed the impeccably dressed agent down the hallway to the third door, where he stopped and pressed the bell-button. Almost immediately, James Ryan opened the door. He was dressed in a sports shirt and corduroy slacks. With his hair disheveled, blue-jowled and bleary-eyed, James Ryan looked strangely out of place in his elegant surroundings.

"Oh—Lieutenant." Anxiously, he looked back over his shoulder for instructions. As he turned, I caught the strong odor of alcohol.

Fastidiously dressed in his trademark gray suit, white shirt and understated gray-on-gray silk tie, white hair dramatically swept back from a broad forehead, Chief Dwyer sat in a silk brocade armchair, the perfect complement to his air of complacent self-importance. A pained look crossed his face as he saw Friedman and me. Covertly, Dwyer's glance fled to Richter standing in front of a marble fireplace, one elbow resting gracefully on the mantle. Reluctantly, Richter bent his head in subtle assent.

"Come in," Dwyer said. "Quickly, please."

I nodded to Ferguson, sitting behind a small writing desk. Ferguson was robed in a blue dressing gown, wearing house slippers. His dark eyes were alert and calculating. His face revealed nothing as he coolly returned my greeting.

Friedman and I sat side by side on a sofa facing both Dwyer and Richter. Ferguson was seated obliquely to our left. Returning from the door, James Ryan took a straight-backed chair set against the wall. Somehow it seemed expected that the senator's son should take the least comfortable chair, putting him subtly outside the privileged circle. Something in his sullen eyes and petulant mannerisms suggested that he resented his exclusion but was unable to change his status. In the same room with Ferguson, James Ryan would always be subordinate.

At the fireplace Richter cleared his throat. Looking directly at me, he said, "There's been some, ah, movement."

As Richter continued, I wondered how he could have heard about Tharp's murder so quickly.

"The fact is—" Richter glanced at Ferguson, as if for support. "The fact is that this whole situation seems to have come down to some kind of a split. And at the moment we're not sure which direction things are moving."

"I don't think we understand," Friedman said. "We've just come from the field."

"Yes. Well, initially, Eason and Katherine Bayliss were going to get together a dummy packet of money with our help. Then they—and we—were going to wait for instructions from Tharp for the drop. Eason was going to make the delivery. We were going to wire him and the money. Then we were going to take it from there.

"However," Richter said heavily, once more glancing at the impassive figure of Ferguson sitting motionless, eyes still revealing nothing. "However," Richter continued, "it's becoming pretty obvious that they, ah, had other ideas."

"By 'they' whom do you mean?" Friedman asked quietly.

"I mean Eason and Mrs. Bayliss," Richter said. "And, I gather, Senator Ryan. Or at least they would've had to have his approval to get the money and then to, ah, do what they did."

"What'd they do?" Friedman asked.

"What they did," Richter said, "was to slip away and apparently make the payment on their own. Or at least so it seems. Because both Eason and Mrs. Bayliss have disappeared."

"Did they leave together?"

"We're not sure. From what we can discover so far, Eason has been gone since about seven-thirty while Mrs. Bayliss was reportedly last seen an hour or so ago."

"Didn't you have them under surveillance?" I asked.

"Of course not," Richter snapped. "After all, they're not the enemy. And they're not the target, either."

"What does the senator say?" I asked.

"Well, that's the—" This time, Richter's frustrated glance fled first to Ferguson, then to James Ryan. Finally he said, "That's the problem. The senator left strict orders that we were to communicate with him through Mrs. Bayliss. *Only* Mrs. Bayliss. So far we've honored his request. In fact, he's in bed right now. His doctor gave him something to sleep,

I think. After all, tomorrow's the dedication."

"What kind of cars were they driving?" Friedman asked.

"We aren't sure," Richter answered, "but we assume that Eason took one of the pool Cadillacs. He had the keys to one, anyhow. And that one's missing."

"Are all the other Cadillacs accounted for between seven-thirty and now?" Friedman asked.

Richter nodded. "Only one went out during that time." He turned to James Ryan, saying, "Mr. Ryan checked one out, I believe."

"I drove out to the airport to meet the Vice-President," Ryan said, adding resentfully, "but he's been delayed until tomorrow morning, it turns out."

"You mean you weren't told that his trip was delayed until you'd actually gotten to the airport?" Friedman asked.

Petulantly, James Ryan nodded. "That's right. Some god-damn clerk forgot to make the call, apparently. I was furious."

"Did you make the trip alone?" I asked.

"Yes." Ryan shifted uneasily in his chair, avoiding my eyes.

Suddenly Ferguson's telephone rang on the desk. Quickly Ferguson lifted the receiver, listened for a moment, then spoke quietly into the phone: "No, I've got some people here, senator." He listened for another moment, frowning, his eyes fixed on the desktop. Then: "There's James, and Mr. Richter of the FBI, and Police Chief Dwyer. And then there's the two detectives, Friedman and Hastings. As a matter of fact, we were wondering whether we should—" He broke off, listening again. Slowly, his eyes lifted from the desk to focus on me. I could see concern in his eyes, and surprise. Finally he said, "Well, certainly I will, if that's what you want. Yes. Sure. I understand. Fine. I'll tell him. And then will you get back to me, or should I—" Still with his puzzled eyes fixed on mine, he said, "All right. Yes. Fine. I'll tell him." Slowly, reflectively, Ferguson replaced the phone in its cradle while his gaze shifted from me to Dwyer, then to Richter.

"He wants to see Lieutenant Hastings," Ferguson said. "Right now."

I got to my feet and moved to the door, aware that everyone in the room was watching me. I opened the door, then turned to look at Friedman. He was struggling to keep glee from showing too plainly on his face.

Thirty

Using a walkie-talkie, Richter ordered the FBI men stationed in the corridor to let me pass down the hallway to Ryan's suite. I pressed the buzzer, listened, pressed it again. Had I heard Ryan's voice, or had I imagined it? With a reassuring glance over my shoulder at the watchful FBI agents, I tried the door. It swung slowly open. I stepped inside.

"Senator Ryan?"

"In here, Lieutenant. In the bedroom."

Except for a small lamp, the large sitting room was in darkness. The bedroom door was ajar, throwing a narrow band of light across the room. I pushed the bedroom door open to find Ryan sitting up in his bed. Even in the shaded glow from a bedside lamp, I could see that his face was ashen. Pain pulled at the corners of his wide, expressive mouth. His eyes were sunken, smudged by illness and fear. He was propped up in bed with his head resting on the pillows behind him. On the wide white counterpane, his hands were motionless. Tonight Donald Ryan was making no pretense at animation or vitality. He'd run out of larger-than-life poses. He was tired, and he was sick, and he was alone: the king in his

221

royal bedchamber, facing the terrible truth of his own mortality.

"Take a chair, Lieutenant. Bring it close to the bed so we can talk." He waited for me to obey. Then, moistening his dry lips with an uncertain tongue, he said, "Here we are again, Lieutenant, you and me." He smiled: a wry, sad twisting of stiffened lips. "I guess you must know by now," he said, "that I find myself in a strange position where you're concerned. Circumstances have forced me into a situation where I have to trust someone—one person, no more. And you seem to be that person. Do you understand?"

"Yessir, I understand."

"I realize," he said, "that my confidences before the fact and after the fact tonight might well make professional problems for you—conflicts of interest and duty. But—" He lifted a blue-veined hand, then let it fall helplessly back on the counterpane. "But I don't have a choice. I have to trust someone. I need someone beyond my immediate circle, an officer of the law. You."

"Yes. I know. I'm—I'm flattered, sir, that you trust me."

"Well," he said, "I'm glad you feel that way, Lieutenant. In honesty, though, I must tell you that I'd rather we weren't having this little talk." Once more he smiled, this time more successfully.

"Yes—" I answered his smile. "I understand."

For a moment he lay motionless, head heavy against the pillow, eyes closed, mouth slack, hands as still as a dead man's laid out in his coffin. In the silence, I heard the sound of a siren from the street far below. Did the sound have anything to do with me? At my belt, my electronic pager was switched off. I was on my own time—alone with Donald Ryan, a fading, frightened American institution.

Finally he opened his eyes and said, "Tell me what you know, Lieutenant. Tell me what you know and what you suspect."

Friedman and I hadn't had a chance to decide how much I should tell him without checking with Dwyer first, privately. So, walking down the corridor with my FBI escort, I'd had to consider all the possibilities. I'd decided to tell Ryan all of the facts but none of the speculation.

"Do you know who killed Juanita?" he asked. His voice was neutral, his eyes blank. He was inert, totally unresponsive. Was he using all his energy to keep himself together? Or instead was he making a performer's effort to keep his misgivings from showing?

"We have a suspect," I said. "But frankly, I don't think I should go into detail until I've talked to my superior officers."

He nodded, moving a hand in indifferent acknowledgment of my point, as if he wasn't really curious about the suspect's identity. Was he acting again? Did he realize that his bodyguard was the prime suspect? Looking at him closely, I couldn't decide. So I tried to probe deeper. "I've interrogated several people since Richter first called me. I've talked to Byron Tharp, the victim's brother. And I've talked to—" I hesitated, taking a deep breath. The hard part was next: "And I've talked to your wife and your daughter, trying to find Frederick Tharp. That was before I knew his identity." I paused for a reaction. This time I saw him wince, as if he'd felt a small pain but nothing more. Instead, he allowed his eyes to slowly, deliberately close. To myself, I smiled. In all the interrogations I'd conducted over the years, I couldn't remember anyone simply closing his eyes to avoid revealing telltale emotion. Senator Ryan had scored a first.

"Also," I said, "we were in touch with the city hall in Santa Barbara. We understand that Juanita Tharp had a baby, Frederick Tharp, twenty-six years ago. Our information indicates that she—" I breathed deeply before plunging off the precipice: "She believed that you were the baby's father. We know that her brother asked you for money to support the mother and child. The brother says that, in fact, he's been getting money from you all these years. He says the payments were approved by Mrs. Bayliss and routed through a Swiss bank. Of course, that's speculation on his part.

"What's not speculation, though, is the fact that the baby, Frederick Tharp, died two weeks after he was born." Again I broke off, watching his face for some sign of emotion. Again I was disappointed. With eyes closed, mouth compressed, his motionless, colorless face could have been a death mask.

"Then about a year later," I went on, "Mrs. Tharp was given another baby to raise, according to Byron Tharp. We don't have a birth certificate for that baby. But we do know that he was raised as Frederick Tharp. And we also know that Mrs. Tharp and the baby were supported by the same bank account in Switzerland."

This time, I decided to wait until he reacted. The seconds dragged by while the face on the pillow remained as before: eyes closed, motionless, silent. Then I saw his lips move.

"The birth certificate is in Bermuda," he said. "The name is—" For a final moment he hesitated, then plunged off his own private precipice.

"The name is Potter," he whispered. "Donald Potter." As he spoke, still with his eyes closed, the pale skin of his face seemed to tighten across the skull beneath. At his temple a vein throbbed.

"Potter?" I asked. "Whose name is that?"

"It's Katherine's maiden name," he breathed.

Donald Potter—his name and hers, given to their bastard child.

I realized that my stomach had suddenly gone hollow. Because, incredibly, I had discovered a secret that could make me the master of Donald Ryan. I held power over one of the most powerful men in the world.

"Katherine Bayliss's child," I said. "And yours."

His head moved, silently nodding. Then, as if to formally acknowledge the parentage, he whispered, "Yes. Her child. And mine."

"Mr. Ryan—" I waited until he finally opened his eyes. Unknowingly, he was preparing himself to receive the final blow. "Mr. Ryan," I repeated, "I've just come from Golden Gate Park. I—" My throat closed. Suddenly, inexplicably, I was afraid. Was it because the statement I was about to make could cause a heart attack—could kill him? Until that moment, the risk hadn't seemed real.

But I'd given myself no choice. I had to finish it.

"I have to tell you, sir, that your son is dead. He was shot about eight o'clock this evening."

His eyes were expressionless; his face revealed nothing. For a long moment we sat motionless, staring silently at each other. Until, finally, I saw his eyes fill with tears.

"I made so many mistakes," he said. "All my life, I've made mistakes—terrible, heartbreaking mistakes. But there was never anyone to tell me. Even now they don't tell me. My father told me. But he was an arrogant man. He wasn't interested in knowing right from wrong, only what was expedient. And I didn't care either. Not until I got sick. And then —now—it's too late." Slowly, sadly, he shook his head. "Too late," he repeated.

"I hate to do this to you, sir," I said. "I hate to put you through this. It's a—a risk, considering your health. I realize that it's a risk."

He blinked against his tears and raised a trembling hand to wipe at his eyes. Then, unexpectedly, his mouth twisted into an exhausted smile. "No," he said, "it's not a risk. There comes a time, Lieutenant, when lies are the only risk. And that's where we are now. This is the time for truth."

"Then I'd like to talk to Lloyd Eason and Katherine Bayliss," I said, catching his eye as I spoke. "I'd like to get the truth from them. And I'd like to talk to them now. Right now. Tonight."

Once more he slowly shook his head. "It's impossible, Lieutenant. They aren't here. That's why I sent for you. They're both gone, and I'm worried. I want you to help me find them."

"Then you'd better tell me all you know, Senator. You'd better tell me everything."

"Yes—" He allowed his eyes to close. I saw him nod, as if he'd made some silent agreement with himself. At last he opened his eyes. His voice was steadier as he said, "Lloyd and Katherine are the only ones I really trust, as you know. Katherine and I—" He smiled. "We go way back. We understand each other. It was a mistake for her to give the baby away. I didn't want her to do it. I wanted her to raise it as her own. But in those days she was just as intoxicated by power as I was. She knew where I was going, and she wanted to go along—all the way. And she knew that with the baby, it would have been impossible. So we decided to give the baby to Juanita to raise. I didn't realize how neurotic Juanita was, of course."

"Did Katherine keep in touch with the boy?"

He shook his head. "No. Not really. She never saw him, except over the schoolyard fence, that sort of thing. And of course she told me about him."

"You must have both suffered when he started to go bad."

"Katherine suffered," he said. "I didn't. I don't think I've ever suffered for someone else's troubles. Not until now."

"Now?"

"Tonight," he answered. "Now. I'm suffering now. Finally."

For a moment I didn't answer. Then, quietly, I asked, "Did Eason know about Frederick—or Donald?"

"He knew about Juanita and her child—Frederick. But he didn't know that Frederick died. Initially, before Frederick was born, Lloyd dealt with Byron Tharp, when Tharp was being difficult. But after that Katherine handled everything. Which is why it made sense, we thought, to give the baby to Juanita. Katherine knew she could handle Juanita, you see."

"What was Katherine's reaction when she learned that Frederick—or Donald—was threatening you?"

"She was disturbed, naturally. As I was. However—" He drew a slow, regretful breath. "However, we both realized that a danger to me might exist if the threats were real. We realized that I had to protect myself."

"How did Frederick—Donald—discover that you were his father?"

"I have no idea, Lieutenant. Perhaps from his mother's ravings."

"Let's get back to tonight, Senator. You say you want me to help you. How?"

"This afternoon," he said, "we heard from Frederick again." He waved a hand. "That's how I think of him, as Frederick."

"You say 'we.' Who actually took the call?"

"Katherine took it from Ferguson. Those are the new orders, you see. Any communications from Frederick go to Ferguson, and then to Katherine, and finally to me."

I nodded. "I see. What did he say?"

"He was beside himself. We'd killed his mother, he said, and then we'd tried to kill him. I gather that the police chased him but couldn't catch him."

"That's right," I answered ruefully.

"He said that we were to deliver the money tonight. Either that or he'd kill me tomorrow at the ceremony. He said that even if he failed and was captured, I'd be the loser because the story of his parentage would come out. He knew it, and I knew it too. He had me in a vise."

"So Eason handled the payoff," I said. "Is that it?"

"Yes," he answered. "Ostensibly, he was going to work with the FBI. But actually, of course, he couldn't."

"So he left with the money. He was going to Golden Gate Park to meet Tharp."

He didn't answer. But his eyes answered for him, revealing the terrible, mortal dread he must feel, facing the truth.

"Lloyd Eason killed him, Mr. Ryan," I said, speaking quietly, regretfully. "And he probably killed Juanita, too. He thought he was protecting you, saving your reputation."

"And maybe he was," he whispered. "Maybe he was. We'll never know, will we?"

"Did Eason have the money when he left? The whole million dollars?"

He nodded. "Yes. It was collected secretly over the last two days. The FBI thought we were only collecting twenty thousand. But Katherine got the rest. It wasn't too difficult, actually. A million dollars isn't as much as it was just a few years ago."

"Have you heard from Eason since he left the hotel?"

"I haven't heard from him," he answered. "But about nine o'clock he called Katherine. He wanted her to meet him. He told her something had gone wrong and he needed help."

"Where was she to meet him?"

"Somewhere on the Embarcadero. Pier 3." He paused, then said, "Katherine was upset. She was as upset as I'd ever seen her. She was trying to control it. She's a very controlled person, you know. A very cold, unfeeling person, some think. But—" He sighed deeply. "But I know better."

"Did she know that her—that Frederick, or Donald, had been killed?"

"If she knew," Ryan answered, "she didn't tell me."

I glanced at my watch. The time was eleven-fifteen. She'd been gone for more than two hours.

"I'll see what I can do, Senator. I'll see what I can find out, and I'll try to help you. But I must tell you, sir—" I rose to my feet. "I must tell you that I've got my duty, where the law's concerned. There's a limit to how much I can help you."

I saw a slow, sad smile tug at his pale lips. "I envy you your duty, Lieutenant. I envy you its clarity and its simplicity. I used to think, all these years, that I was acting out of a sense of duty. But it seems that I was wrong."

"I don't think you were wrong, Senator. I think we owe you a lot. All of us." But, even as I said it, I knew I didn't mean it. I was doing what they all did: I was telling him what he wanted to hear, to make myself feel more important for having told him.

He didn't reply but only nodded. He didn't believe it either. Not any more.

Thirty-one

"I hope we aren't making a mistake," Friedman said, peering out into the darkness at the criss-crossed thicket of wooden pilings that supported the pier. "It's all very well to try and protect the senator's anonymity, but we don't want to get into something we can't handle without more troops."

I'd driven the last hundred yards without lights, easing the car along the Embarcadero's uneven cobblestones and across countless spur tracks, past the huge, boxlike shapes of the waterfront's loading sheds. This section of the Embarcadero was derelict, part of the industrial flotsam left when San Francisco's waterfront began to change from a working port to a tourist attraction. The trend had started at Fisherman's Wharf and was gradually spreading south as trendy shops and business enterprises took over the old piers. But the renaissance had stopped far short of Pier 3, a massive rectangle jutting out so far into the bay that its farthest end was partially obscured by the thick fog that rose from the calm water.

I stopped short of the pier, pulled into the shadow of an abandoned loading shed and switched off the engine.

"Do you want to call for some backup?" I asked.

Still staring out into the darkness, Friedman said, "Let's give it a few minutes."

"You want to get out, or what?"

"You decide," he answered. "After all, you're the field man."

"Let's give it a while."

"Suits me." He settled down in his seat.

"I still think," I said, stubbornly returning to the running argument we'd had, driving from the Fairmont to the Embarcadero, "that you made a mistake not telling Dwyer about Tharp. When he finds out, Dwyer's going to make you pay."

"I'll just tell him that I couldn't get him alone," Friedman answered. "Which is the precise truth. Christ, he's so infatuated, hanging out with Richter and Ferguson and, by proxy, with Donald Ryan, that he wouldn't've cared if there'd been a general slaughter. Nothing would've gotten him out of that hotel room. I tried. Believe me, I tried."

"Still—" Doubtfully, I shook my head, staring silently out into the fog-smudged night, registering my disagreement.

"What I'm wondering about," Friedman said, "is why Katherine Bayliss took a cab when she left the Fairmont."

"She didn't want to take one of the Cadillacs," I said. "It's obvious."

"But cabs can be traced."

"Maybe she doesn't have anything to hide."

"I think," Friedman said, "that both Eason and Bayliss have something to hide. For years they've had something to hide."

"Not any more, they don't. It's all come out."

"Yes and no," he answered wryly. "To me, it's plain that Ryan's real purpose in telling you the whole story was his hope that you'd keep the lid on. For the good of the country and all that crap."

I snorted.

"You laugh," he said. "But it's true. And what's more, it's working. You know damn well that if ordinary mortals were involved in this thing, we'd have Eason in custody right now. After the Juanita Tharp murder, we'd've gone to work on him. We'd have an indictment right now. Which, incidentally, would've prevented another murder.

I shrugged. "That's hindsight. You're always telling me that you can't look back in this business."

Ignoring the remark, Friedman continued his musing: "Assuming that he went to the park to murder Frederick," he said, "I wonder why he took the million dollars along. I mean—Christ—nobody in his right mind carries his wallet in Golden Gate Park after dark, never mind a million dollars."

"If he didn't take the million," I answered, "Ryan or Katherine Bayliss would've suspected something was wrong."

"That's true," Friedman admitted.

"I wonder why he called Katherine?" I said.

"Maybe Tharp wounded him," Friedman said. "Maybe he needs help. Don't forget, Tharp was shooting, too."

"You could be right. Listen—" I gestured toward the pier. "Let's take a look around. Okay?"

Friedman sighed. "I was afraid you were going to say that."

"You don't want to?"

"No, not really." He sighed again, and opened the door. "But I'll do it." He took a flashlight from under the dashboard and slipped out of the car, softly closing the door behind him. Side by side, we walked across the deserted street, our footing uncertain on the wet, uneven cobblestones. On the bay in front of us, a large vessel was moving slowly through the foggy night, its running lights disembodied against the dark, moonless sky. Overhead, green and red lights alternated, blinking. A big jet was letting down for its landing at San Francisco International ten miles to the south.

We were on the sidewalk now, with two storage sheds still between us and Pier 3. During the years of my childhood when the port of San Francisco had been operating at capacity, this part of the waterfront had been a beehive of activity day and night. Trucks rumbled down the Embarcadero to unload in the cavernous storage sheds. Switch engines were as busy as toy trains, pushing boxcars into these same sheds where their cargoes would be unloaded, then reloaded on the waiting ships.

As we were passing the second of the two sheds, I felt Friedman's nudge against my arm. "Look," he whispered, pointing to the shed. "One of the doors is open."

He was right. Four huge doors, each one large enough to admit a truck, gave access to the sagging, abandoned shed. One of the doors was ajar.

"Let's take a look." As I said it, I unbuttoned my jacket and loosened my revolver in its holster. Beside me, Friedman was doing the same. Ahead of us at the curb two cars were parked, one a small Japanese sedan, the other a pickup truck. I lowered my head until I could see the dim light from an isolated street lamp shining through the windshield of both cars. Either the occupants were lying flat on the seats, hidden, or the cars were both empty.

Standing side by side in front of the massive door, Friedman and I glanced at each other and nodded. Friedman moved to his right. I pushed the partially open door slowly inward on its creaking hinges as I moved with it to my left, so that I wouldn't be silhouetted against the night sky.

When the door was fully open, Friedman clicked on his flashlight. A Cadillac was parked just inside the doorway. Standing cautiously to the right of the doorway, Friedman played the flashlight beam over the car. I saw a shattered side window on the driver's side.

Behind the steering wheel I saw a head resting motionless against the top of the seat, face raised.

"Bingo," Friedman breathed.

With my revolver in my hand, I was moving slowly to my left, toward the driver's side of the car. On the far side, flashlight in one hand, revolver in the other, Friedman was also advancing. Moments later, we stood on opposite sides of the car, both of us peering inside as Friedman played the light on Lloyd Eason's dead face.

I holstered my revolver, took out my handkerchief and opened the door on the driver's side. As the door swung open the interior light came on. Also using a handkerchief, Friedman was opening the door on the other side, now pressing his handkerchief to his nostrils against the odor. Gritting my teeth, I touched Eason's neck just below the left ear. The flesh was cold.

"He's been dead for a while," I said. Gingerly, I reached in and opened his dark blue jacket across the chest. Two six-inch circles of blood stained his white shirt, one stain centered on his chest, the other lower, at the belt line. Powder burns surrounded both wounds. I looked at the driver's window. The glass was crazed by countless tiny cracks radiating from two bullet holes, one about four inches down from the top of the window, the other directly opposite Eason's shoulder where I saw a third wound. The blood that had come from the two abdominal wounds glistened in the pale light, not yet coagulated. But the blood from the shoulder wound was drying on the blue fabric of his jacket. Looking carefully at the opposite side of the car, I saw a small hole where one bullet had doubtless buried itself in the headliner above the front passenger's door. On the seat I saw a Colt .45 automatic lying beside Eason's hand.

With the flashlight Friedman was examining the floor of the car, back and front. "There's nothing here," he said.

"The money, you mean?"

"Right. The money." He took the keys from the ignition and stepped to the rear of the car. Carefully, using my handkerchief, I picked up the .45 and sniffed at the barrel. Even through the excremental stench, I could smell cordite. As I replaced the revolver exactly as I'd found it, Friedman slammed down the trunk lid and replaced the keys in the ignition.

"Nothing." He pointed to the automatic. "Has it been fired?"

"Yes."

"What'd the wounds look like?"

"It looks like two shots to the torso, producing death. They were probably fired from inside the car. Two more shots were fired through the window. One is in his shoulder and the other is still inside the car. The shoulder wound is older than the other two."

"Hmm." He looked carefully at the dead man's chest wounds, then drew back. "Let's close it up," he said, "and get some goddamn air."

As I slammed the driver's door, a few fragments of shattered glass fell on my shoe. I moved toward the shed's open door, following Friedman.

"This," he said, "is developing into a busy night." He snapped off the light, then stood thoughtfully tapping the flashlight against his open palm. We were standing side by side, both of us staring back into the pitch-black cavern of the shed. Except for the nighttime sounds of the city in the distance, the Embarcadero was silent. Looking up, I saw pale starlight showing through gaps in the shed's roof.

"What d'you think happened?" I asked.

"I think that Eason met Tharp at Stow Lake about eight P.M.," he said. "I think he probably intended to kill Tharp. I think there was a shootout. Tharp was killed and Eason was wounded in the shoulder. He probably drove to a phone and called Katherine Bayliss."

Still staring into the darkness of the shed, I nodded. "It had to've happened like that. But what happened next?"

"Obviously," Friedman said, "someone killed him and took the money."

"Katherine Bayliss." I realized that I was whispering, awed at the thought.

"Who else knew he was here?" Friedman's voice, too, was hushed.

"But why? It couldn't've been for the money."

"No," he agreed, "it probably wasn't for the money. Not even for a million dollars."

234

"Then why?"

"He killed her child," he answered softly. "He didn't know that he'd done it. He thought he was killing Juanita's child to protect Ryan. Don't forget, he didn't know that Katherine was Frederick Tharp's mother."

"But Tharp was Ryan's son," I said. "Either way, Eason knew he was killing Ryan's son."

"His bastard son," Friedman corrected. "There's a difference."

"Not to Katherine, there wasn't a difference."

"No," he said, "not to Katherine."

Thirty-two

As we walked slowly across the Fairmont lobby, the clock above the registration desk read exactly midnight. From the night clerk, we'd already learned that Katherine Bayliss had returned to the hotel less than an hour ago. We'd stayed at the Embarcadero only long enough to see the area secured, leaving Culligan on the scene to handle the details.

"I've got to admit," Friedman said, "that I'm a little shook up. I mean, here we are, about to—" He tossed his head. "About to what? What're we going to do? How're we going to do it? Do we arrest her for murder? Is that what we do?" As he'd been talking, we'd slowed our steps until we'd come to a stop beside the locked-up newsstand.

"We can't do it now," I said. "Even if she was just—just anyone, we can't do it now. We've got to get her paraffin-tested. And we've got to wait for the lab reports and the ballistics, too. Besides, she's not going anywhere. Not until tomorrow, anyhow, after the dedication."

"You're assuming," Friedman said, "that we aren't going to get a confession out of her. You could be wrong."

"Yes," I said, "I could be wrong. But don't count on it."

*　　*　　*

On the eleventh floor, the corridor was deserted.

"The dogs have been called off," Friedman said, sotto voce. Behind us, the elevator doors slid closed.

"Well," I said, also speaking softly, "Tharp's dead, after all."

"Do you know which room is hers?"

"Down here—" I turned to the left, then to the right at the first intersecting corridor. I realized that my steps were lagging. I didn't want to do it—didn't want to accuse Katherine Bayliss of murder. "Maybe we're making a mistake, doing this," I said. "Maybe we should call Dwyer."

"Calling Dwyer would be the mistake," Friedman answered. "This is the best time to interrogate her, while she's still shook up. You know as well as I do it's the first rule."

"What if she didn't do it?"

"We're still within our rights. Besides, we've got to tell someone on the Ryan staff about Eason, don't we? And Bayliss is the logical person to tell."

"You're right," I admitted, stopping in front of Katherine Bayliss's door and pressing the buzzer.

After several minutes and three more attempts at the buzzer, she still hadn't answered. Cautiously, I tried the door. It was locked.

"What now?" I whispered.

"We've got to try the senator."

"The *senator?*" I hissed.

"Certainly," he answered. "He sent you out, didn't he? So naturally he wants a report, doesn't he? What better excuse could you have? You're checking in."

"At midnight? Without preparing him? Without going through one of his staff? Pete, he's a sick man."

Irresolutely, we'd walked a few feet down the hall. Finally Friedman turned to face me. Speaking in a low, firm voice, looking me squarely in the eye, he said, "Any other way, we're taking a chance. When all this—this political fallout has settled, it comes down to the simple fact that we're either doing our job, or we're not doing our job. Don't forget,

237

there's some money missing—a lot of money. That's how all this started, with the money. And we've got to find it. That's our job. And if we don't do our jobs now—right now—then we're liable to charges." He paused to let his words sink in. Then, still deadly serious, he said, "Don't fall into the same hole Dwyer's in, Frank. Just think about the law. That's what it's all about for us. The law."

"But Ryan—Christ—he's—" Helplessly, I let it go unfinished.

"It doesn't matter," Friedman said, speaking very slowly, very seriously. "That's what I'm trying to tell you. It's the job that matters. The law."

Momentarily I looked away from him, glancing up and down the silent corridor. How had it happened that this particular choice had been forced on us, in this particular place, so far from the grifters and hoodlums and whores that filled up our days—and our nights?

I looked at him one last time, muttered a heartfelt obscenity, then led the way to Ryan's suite at the end of the hall. I took a deep breath and pushed the button beside the door. Moments later, the door swung slowly open. Wrapped in a brocade dressing gown, Katherine Bayliss stood before us. The gown was gathered close at the waist, accenting the soft, exciting curve of her breasts. The "V" of the neckline revealed a froth of lacy nightdress. Beneath the hem of the gown, she wore silken slippers. Her hair was loose. She stood motionless. Her eyes were unfocused, staring at me but not seeing me. Her arms were rigid at her sides, fists tightly clenched. She held her head high, as if to silently, disdainfully deny fate itself. It was a regal posture. She looked like a noblewoman about to climb the gallows.

"We'd like to talk to you, Mrs. Bayliss." I took a short step forward. "Can we come in?"

She didn't reply, didn't step back before me. Her eyes were blank, still so strangely unseeing. We were standing close together. I could smell her perfume. I could feel myself responding to the closeness of her, man to woman.

"Can we—" Hesitantly, I nodded to the darkened sitting room behind her, and the narrow shaft of light coming from inside the partially opened bedroom door beyond. "Can we go inside, please, Mrs. Bayliss?"

Without signifying that she'd heard, she finally turned away and moved like a sleepwalker toward a nearby armchair. She sat in the chair, gathering the rich folds of the dressing gown across a lace-covered thigh. Friedman and I sat side by side on the sofa facing her. I switched on a table lamp, tilting the shade slightly toward her, away from us. Then I settled back. I'd decided not to start it. If Friedman was so sure we were right, then I wanted to hear how he would begin.

I heard him clear his throat, then heard him say, "There've been two killings tonight, Mrs. Bayliss. Two murders. That's why we're here. You know that."

She didn't respond, didn't look at him. She sat rigidly in the high-backed chair, one hand on either chair-arm, head held high. Once more she reminded me of royalty: a queen on her throne.

But still her eyes were utterly empty. She hadn't spoken to us. Except to move obediently into the living room, she'd given no sign that she'd heard us.

"Mrs. Bayliss—" Friedman leaned toward her, sharpening his voice. "Do you understand what I'm saying? Frederick Tharp was killed tonight about eight o'clock. Later, Lloyd Eason was killed after he left to meet you at the Embarcadero. We've come for you—come to question you about Eason's death. You know that's why we're here."

Finally, almost imperceptibly, she nodded. I saw her lips part, heard her say, "Yes, I know. I know that's why you've come."

"Then—" Friedman hesitated. "Then will you tell us about it?"

Once more she nodded: a slow, disembodied inclination of her handsome head. She could have been in a hypnotist's trance.

For a long, empty moment the silence continued. Until, finally, her lips parted again. Her voice was almost inaudible as she began speaking:

"I was like all the rest of them, then. I wanted to be in the movies. But it didn't start out like that for me. Not at first. I'd already been married. I was only nineteen years old when I got married and we moved to Los Angeles. I was twenty when I had my first child. I carried it almost full term, but it was stillborn. I could feel it die inside me. I felt it die and told my doctor, and they cut it out of me. I never saw the baby. I didn't want to see it, and they didn't want me to see it." She paused, drew a deep, unsteady breath. She sat as before, rigidly. Her eyes were still empty, still fixed on some memory from long ago.

"By that time," she said, "we hated each other, my husband and I. So I left him and went looking for a job. I didn't want to be in the movies. Not at first. I knew it was a skin game. I'd always known that. But I had what they wanted. They knew it, and so did I. Men wanted me. But I didn't want them. I hated them for what they'd done to me. I hated them to touch me. But the more I hated them, the more control I had over them. Because hatred—pure hatred, controlled—is the secret of everything. I knew that. Even then, I knew that. Or at least I felt it. So I decided to see how far I could go—how high I could climb. And that's what I did. And it was so easy. Until I met Donald one night at a party, it was all so easy. Anything I wanted from a man, I could get. Because they were all so stupid. And so weak, rutting and posturing and preening, playing their pitiful sex games.

"But the moment I met Donald, I knew everything was different. I'd heard of him, of course. And when I saw him, that first night, I remember feeling a kind of exhilaration. I suppose—" She broke off, frowning slightly. It was the first sign of emotion I'd seen since she began her story. "I suppose that he was to have been my ultimate conquest, the final proof that I could do whatever I thought I wanted to do.

"But, of course, that's not the way it happened. We left the party together, and we've been together ever since. We're part of each other."

"And the boy, too," I said. "Frederick—or Donald. He was part of you, too." I spoke very softly, unwilling to disturb her reverie.

"Yes," she answered. "Yes, he was part of me."

"And Eason killed him," Friedman whispered. "Tonight, in the park. Eason killed your son."

I saw a momentary flash of pain tear at her face before she nodded, trancelike again. Once more, her face was without expression, as empty as her eyes. She was drifting away.

"Eason didn't know the boy was your son," I prompted. "Did he?"

No response.

"Mrs. Bayliss—" Reluctantly, I knew, Friedman dropped his voice to a hard, uncompromising note: "Mrs. Bayliss, we know what happened tonight. We know that Eason called you. We know that you met him."

"And when Eason told you that he'd killed your son," I said, "you killed him. You used Eason's own gun."

"You might not've even been aware that you were holding the gun," Friedman prompted. "You might not've intended to do it—to kill him. But you did it. You killed him because he'd killed Fre—Donald. That's what happened, isn't it?"

Still she gave no sign that she'd heard. I leaned forward, asking, "Where's the money, Mrs. Bayliss? Do you have the money?"

I saw her look toward the half-open door. "The money is there," she said. "In the bedroom."

Hearing her say it, I felt myself relax. If Friedman and I had lost track of a million dollars, Dwyer would have lifted our scalps. As if to echo my thoughts, I heard Friedman sigh.

I decided to try another approach. Speaking softly, soothingly, as if I might be consoling a close friend, I said, "You brought the money back, Mrs. Bayliss. That'll go in your favor with the D.A. And you killed the man who killed your son. You didn't know whether your son was alive or dead until Eason told you and admitted that he'd killed him. All you knew was that Eason needed help. That's all he told you on the phone. So when you learned that he'd killed your son, you acted in anger, on impulse. That's mitigating circumstances. You could go free. You'll have to stand trial. But you could go free."

"It's like the unwritten law," Friedman offered, also speaking in a low, intimate voice, trying to get through to her.

It worked. I saw her eyes quicken as she looked wonderingly at me, saying, "All those years, and now he's dead."

"Yes," Friedman said. "We know. And we're sorry, Mrs. Bayliss. We're very sorry."

"But—" The frown returned as she turned to look at Friedman, puzzled. "But you couldn't know. How could you?"

"I—I don't understand," Friedman said. But, even as he said it, he looked quickly at me before his eyes darted toward the bedroom. Watching him, she nodded. "You see, you're surprised. You didn't know."

Involuntarily, both Friedman and I rose to our feet as she said, "It was all for nothing." Her eyes lost focus as she looked gently toward the bedroom. Once more she'd retreated from reality, deep in delayed shock. "All for nothing," she repeated. "All that killing, for nothing. Because he's dead, you see. He died at eleven-eighteen, after I told him about Lloyd. I remembered the time, you see. Because it'll be important. For history."

Thirty-three

Three hours later, at three-thirty Wednesday morning, I was sitting alone in Ann's kitchen drinking a glass of milk and considering whether or not to eat the generous slice of cherry pie she'd left for me. Earlier, about four o'clock Tuesday afternoon, I'd called her to say that I couldn't make it home for dinner. I'd promised to be home by midnight, though—if possible. When I'd said "if possible," I'd heard her sigh. She knew what that phrase meant. And so did I.

Four o'clock Tuesday . . .

The whole world, it seemed, had tipped on its axis since four o'clock. By pure chance, I'd found Frederick Tharp—and lost him. By nightfall Tharp was dead, doubtless killed by a bullet from Eason's gun. Carrying a bullet in his shoulder, Eason had called Katherine Bayliss for help. She'd met him at the Embarcadero and killed him with his own gun. Carrying the suitcase filled with money, she'd left the loading shed and walked along the dark, deserted Embarcadero until she got to Market Street. She'd hailed a cab and returned to the Fairmont. She'd told Ryan that their son was dead—and Eason, too. Then she'd watched Ryan die.

She hadn't admitted to Friedman and me that she'd killed

Eason, but she hadn't denied it, either. By tomorrow—Thursday—we would have the evidence complete: the fingerprints, the dust and soil samples, the ballistics tests, the paraffin tests on Eason and Katherine Bayliss. We would have the tests of Eason's clothes and his car, looking for traces of manure. We'd have the certified Yellow Cab records and the Fairmont's phone records. When we forwarded the evidence to the D.A., our job would be finished. If he asked for an indictment and Katherine Bayliss was still in San Francisco, we would arrest her. If she was in Washington, we would begin extradition proceedings.

If.

If she incriminated herself. If she admitted the murder, she would be indicted.

But by now she had a team of the best lawyers money could buy. They would advise her to simply keep quiet while they worked out a convincing scenario. Following the cardinal rule, they would use the truth whenever possible, improvising only when absolutely essential. In the shootout with Tharp, the lawyers would contend, Eason had been wounded. He'd called Bayliss for help. But when she arrived at the loading shed, she'd found Eason dead. An unnamed third party—the dead Tharp's accomplice, possibly—had followed Eason and killed him with his own gun. Unfortunately Katherine had handled the gun, accounting for her fingerprints on the gun and the burnt powder on her hands.

But why, the D.A. might ask, would the mysterious accomplice kill Eason and then leave the money behind for Katherine to find? Obviously, the lawyers would reply, Katherine had scared the murderer off.

All she had to do was remain quiet, as she'd done tonight. The lawyers and the politicians would do the rest. Already Friedman and I had been ordered to keep our suspicions strictly to ourselves. The D.A., too, was keeping his suspicions secret. In the hush surrounding the death of Donald Ryan, suspicions of murder seemed obscene.

When we'd learned that Donald Ryan was dead, Friedman and I had turned to the bedroom to see the body for ourselves and to secure the suitcase full of money. Then, out of long habit, I'd put in a call to the coroner. It had been our first mistake. We should have called in additional witnesses, protecting ourselves against charges of publicity-seeking—and worse. Yet instinctively we'd wanted to get the death of Donald Ryan on the public record. We didn't want the responsibility of keeping the news a secret even for a minute. Without admitting it to each other, Friedman and I had been awed to think that chance had put us in the path of history.

With Katherine, we'd returned to the suite's living room. It was then that we made our second mistake. Instead of continuing to question Katherine while we waited for the coroner, trying to force a confession from her, we'd called Dwyer, in Ferguson's suite. The result had been a madhouse, with Dwyer and Richter working at cross-purposes, giving contradictory orders. Instantly, it seemed, reporters materialized, snapping at our heels. Whatever chance we had of getting a confession had been squandered.

Finally drawing him aside, Friedman and I told Dwyer that Frederick Tharp was Donald Ryan's illegitimate son by Katherine Bayliss and that Katherine Bayliss had probably killed Eason, avenging her son's death. Dwyer had literally paled at the news. When we told him that in her own room Katherine Bayliss was being given a paraffin test, he'd had to sit down. For Friedman it had been the only redeeming moment of a long, hard day.

Jack Ferguson had been the first civilian to enter Ryan's suite. He'd looked once at Ryan's body, then returned to the living room where he'd begun making phone calls. Neither his voice nor his manner gave any clue to his feelings. But when Ferguson learned that a detective had escorted Katherine to her room and that she might be arrested, he turned on me in a cold fury, demanding an explanation. I could only tell him that he would have to talk to Dwyer and Richter, or the D.A. For an instant I thought Ferguson would hit me. But in the next instant he'd regained his self-control, turning again to the phone, his most potent weapon. A lawyer was called and told to stay with Katherine. Then a publicist was summoned and instructed to put out the news of Ryan's death. Listening to Ferguson, I realized that a publicity release had already been prepared and needed only an update. James Ryan was summoned and instructed to call his mother and sister. Then he'd been told to hold himself in readiness for further orders.

To keep the chain of evidence intact and to see that the body remained undisturbed until the coroner took over, I stayed in the suite, sitting on the velvet sofa. Across the room, Ferguson was still making one staccato phone call after another, many of them to Washington—and one to the White House. As he talked, I could hear excitement building in his voice as he began to formulate a plan. Instead of a tribute to Donald Ryan, he began to tell the people he called, tomorrow's dedication ceremony would become a eulogy, a living memorial. Of course, the President would want to come, along with the Vice-President. It would be a built-in opportunity for high-level drama and world-wide publicity, Ferguson suggested, all in good taste. And, naturally, the media would cooperate. Already, the plans were developing nicely. Yes, the family would rally around, thoroughbreds all, even in their sorrow. (And, yes, Belle could be "managed.")

Slowly, the suite began to fill with people. The coroner and Ryan's two doctors took over the bedroom, along with the lab crew. In the living room, Richter and Dwyer still bickered viciously over their jurisdictions and their prerogatives. In the hallway, talking to the reporters, the two men jockeyed for the best camera angles. Friedman suggested strongly that Dwyer and Richter move their "command post" to the FBI room down the hall. Then we told Ferguson that Ryan's suite must be cleared in preparation for the removal of the body. Grudgingly, Ferguson helped us clear the suite. When last seen, Ferguson was walking down the corridor talking simultaneously with three men. Two of the men, I later discovered, were Ryan's lawyers, acting for Katherine Bayliss. With Dwyer's permission, the lawyers had already talked to Bayliss, a clear breach of established procedure since she hadn't yet been booked. Dwyer, it seemed, would do anything to keep Katherine out of jail. I wondered whether the D.A. would take the same view.

Friedman and I were the last to leave the suite, following Ryan's body on its gurney to the freight elevator. We sealed the door to Ryan's suite and ordered a guard posted. We verified that Bayliss's room would be secured, along with Eason's. Dwyer had just finished talking to the small group of network newsmen, eagerly answering questions and posing for the cameras. Friedman and I drew Dwyer aside and asked him whether we should take Katherine Bayliss into custody. No, he answered, he'd handle it. Friedman and I were relieved of further duties.

So, exhausted, we'd gone downstairs and said goodnight in front of the Fairmont. Without saying it in so many words, we'd agreed that we'd go along with Dwyer, whatever he decided to do about Katherine. We wouldn't talk to the media. Breaking our promise, we wouldn't even talk to Dan Kanter. We'd let Dwyer do what he wanted, without comment—or help. We would cover our asses.

As I finished the milk, I heard a key turn in the front door. The time was almost four A.M. Dan had been out on the town.

"Hi, Frank. Still up, eh?" With a loud sigh, he sat across the table. "Working?"

"I'm afraid so. What about you? Playing?"

Ruefully, he grinned. "Playing—yeah. I guess you might call it playing. Nancy and me, we went to a movie."

"A late movie."

"Yeah, well, you know. We listened to some music afterwards. And then we, ah, talked."

"Talked, eh?" Having decided against the cherry pie, I poured myself a second glass of milk.

He grinned again, then shook his head, sighing heavily. "I guess I'll never be able to figure women out, you know? Honest to God, it's—" Once more, he shook his head. "It's impossible to figure them out. Completely."

"You're not the first man to have said that," I answered. "And I'm sure you won't be the last."

"I guess it was the same when you were young, eh?"

"Dan, it never changes. It's always the same. In fact, in some ways, it can get worse, the older you get."

I saw his glance sharpen speculatively, then saw his eyes slide subtly away as both of us realized that I could be talking about his mother. What was he thinking as he looked at me across the breakfast table? Was he imagining Ann and me in bed, making love?

For a moment we sat silently, looking in different directions. Then I heard him clear his throat.

"I—ah—guess my father, he's making things pretty tough for you and my mom." He was frowning down at the table as he said it, concentrating on an invisible design he was tracing with his forefinger.

"Yes," I answered, "I guess you're right."

"Yeah. Well—" He retraced the design. "Well, Dad can be pretty—you know—rigid, sometimes. He doesn't think so, but he is."

I decided not to reply. I simply sat sipping the milk—and hoping.

"What I'm saying," he said, "is that I think it's—you know—it's kind of neat, that you and Mom—you know—get along, and everything. I think it's really okay. And so does Billy. He's even got a scrapbook about you, and everything."

"He—" I blinked. "He does?"

"Yeah. Really."

Suddenly I realized that I couldn't think of anything to say. Across the table, I heard Dan clear his throat. "I guess that if you and Mom, if you ever got married, then that would—" Once more, he cleared his throat. "I guess that'd solve a lot of problems."

"Yes," I answered slowly. "Yes, I guess it would." Now I was tracing my own design on the table. We sat through a long, taut silence, both of us aware that something more must be said.

"You want some milk?" I asked finally, pushing the carton across the table.

"No. We had pizza, Nancy and me." As he said it, he ventured a direct look at me.

"Oh. Well, in that case—" I pushed my chair back. "In that case, if you'll excuse me, I think I'll go down the hall, and wake up your mother and tell her about this little talk we've been having."

We grinned at each other, and shook hands across the table.

About the Author

COLLIN WILCOX was born in Detroit and educated at Antioch College. Since 1950 he has lived in San Francisco, where he operated a small business before becoming a full-time mystery/suspense novelist. Mr. Wilcox writes that "the most important things in my life are my two sons, my Victorian house, my typewriter, my airplane, my books and my ten-speed bike."